David Brennan won the Frank O'Connor Mentorship Bursary Award in 2016 and in 2017 he was longlisted for the Colm Tobin Award. He was one of the winners of the Irish Novel Fair in 2018 with his debut novel, Upperdown, which was published by époque press in June 2019. David lives and writes in China.

SPIT is David's second novel.

SPIT

DAVID BRENNAN

époque press

Published by époque press in 2025.

Typeset in EB Garamond Regular & Italic,
Adobe Ming Std and Acier BAT Text Noir, Gris & Solid.

Original cover art by Sinéad Brennan.
Typesetting & cover design by Ten Storeys®

Printed and bound in Great Britain by
Clays Ltd, Elcograf S.p.A.

British Library Cataloguing-in-Publication Data.
A catalogue record for this book is available from the British Library.

ISBN 978-1-0687162-1-8 (paperback edition)
ISBN 978-1-0687162-2-5 (electronic edition)

This product complies with the requirements of the General Product Safety Regulation (EU Regulation 2023/988) EU GPSR Authorised Representative, LOGOS EUROPE, 9 rue Nicolas Poussin, 17000, LA ROCHELLE, France.

'Send your other soul beyond the mountains, beyond time.
I'll wait for you to tell me what you've seen.'

Czeslaw Milosz, 1962

SPIT

For Xiao Xue

小雪

I once inhabited the body of a dead dog for two weeks. I just wanted a rest, I didn't want to see anybody or listen to anybody, you know the way you'd get sometimes, especially round here, with everybody knowing everybody else's business, with those eyes always looking, probing for cracks and weaknesses so that they can burrow in and lay a few eggs.

Maggots, who can escape them?

Poor mutt hung in a small hollow, roofed over by clutters of hazel, through which a tiny stream trickles when there's rain. More of a drain really, but there's always rain, of that we can be sure. Nobody ever sets foot in there much, except the likes of me, though as far as I can tell there's only one of me round these parts.

I came upon him – or was it a her – one evening, end of summer, the ditches still fat with the greens. Shuttled in there by a breeze I was. First thing I noticed was the commotion of bluebottles, shimmering in a haze, an ungodly murmuration. Sniffing the air, I caught the ever so faint whiff of death. A few minutes later I came upon her – yes it was a her – hanging by blue bailing chord from the branch of a hazel tree, tongue protruding, rolling down past her ears, blackened. A sheepdog with an injection of mutt.

In all my years in Spit I'd never seen anything like it. Sure, I'd seen quickly killed and half buried cows, calves, donkeys, even dead babies buried in ditches near the backs of graveyards. I'd come across suicides, swinging jobs as Radio Molloy called them, lads hanging in the groves and hollows, in barns and from the rafters of houses built by their grandfathers. More often than not, I was first on the scene and last to leave. It would be nice to report that they are still there, their spirits now free, and so on. But far as I can tell I've never met any of the dead after they are dead, except what's left over: decaying lumps of matter.

Yes, I sighed, looking up through the hazel at the sky then back at the dog. The evening spreading itself over the rolling hills had little business with the scene I stood looking at and what I stood looking at had little business with the evening, and yet there they were staring each other in the face.

I'm not much of a one for feelings.

What is, is.

But at that moment I felt an awful sorrow for the poor dog and an awful anger for who, or what, had done it to her.

So up and into the dog I decided to go, partly out of sympathy for her, but also, I must be honest, from a desire that I too might rot away and be eaten by the maggots that would in a few days swarm over his putrefying flesh.

I lay there, hiding I suppose, from the world till the flesh dripped from her bones, and them bones fell unto the grass and moss beneath.

When that was done, I played with her bones for a while.

I would have liked to keep one, mostly likely the inner ear bone, smallest bone in the body. I don't know why, perhaps I just wanted something to remember her by.

But that's not my lot.

I'm bound by rules and stipulations different to yours. The best I could do was tap out a few messages on those bones in the hope she could hear. You know, just a few words like:

I was with you until the end. You were not alone as you rotted. They remember you and miss you. We all have to meet our end sooner or later. At least you fed a few maggots. Don't take it so seriously. Give them another hundred years and they'll all, every man, woman, dog, child, cat and rat, and every other beast in the parish of Spit, be the same as you. The truth is...The truth is a far-away land. I'd nothing much to do, so those tapings on the bone killed away the time. I wanted to promise revenge, but that was beyond me, I'd no way of knowing who'd done it. I'd have to have been granted access to the information, and who would determine that is another story. Tell you the truth, and I'd give any this advice, I've stopped thinking about those sort of things:

Those mysteries.

Those questions.

They do nothing but give you ulcers and bad breath, and restlessness, and heartburn, epilepsy even, if you are that way inclined.

We have three epileptics in the Parish of Spit. Three is a high number, I've looked into it. Three times the national average. For the population of Spit is about the same as the number of caterpillars you'd find in a half-acre of cabbage heads. One of them, Patsy Heffernan reports of visions, says he's peered into god's kingdom, purple and a most vicious blood red. Most think he's raving. But I'm pretty sure he sees what he sees as I see what

I see. And don't get me started on the things I've seen.

Anyway, I should go back to the dog.

Yes, there I lay, hiding I suppose, from the world, till the flesh dripped from its bones, and them bones fell unto the grass and the moss beneath. With them I then tapped out melodies until one evening a sudden darkening of the sky, a rustling over the rushes and a quick thick shower signalled my leaving. I was scattered then on to my next assignment.

Nobody ever discovered the poor dog. Her bones and bits of her fur are still above in that creek. Oh, wait, that's not quite true. Anyway, it's the kind of place that a man mightn't have set foot in for centuries. Such places, though few, still exist in Spit. People walk right past them all the time but they never set foot in them. I'd know. When I'm not on business it's in these little crevices I like to lull and kick the days away.

Since then, I've not given the dog much though but I've been around long enough to know that everything is connected, that all the events I witness are like pieces in a puzzle which sooner or later fall into place.

Could take a week, could take a decade. Doesn't matter a damn to me. I've nothing but time.

Each event is preceded by a different event and followed by another.

Well, in my world not always. More on that later.

Now that I think of it, the location should have told me something. That little hazel covered hole marked the boundary of the only piece of land that touched both the Quinn's and Delahunty's, the two biggest farmers in the parish of Spit. There's bad blood between the Quinns and the Delahuntys, constant and ever present, like the little stream that trickles down the boundary of their land.

*

The Delahuntys rise early. The mother Maureen is first out of the bed before the cock even senses a streak of light in the sky. From the bottom of the frozen-churn winter to the birdy singsongs of summer she lights the candle under the scared heart, mutters a few Hail Mary's, then lugs her large frame – limp in the right leg since she slipped on the frost a few years ago – into the kitchen, rustles up the porridge, puts to the boil a few eggs, cuts the brown bread, plasters thick lumps of butter on it, finishes it off with a swipe of marmalade or jam. On special days there'd be the odd rasher or sausage, but the Delahuntys consider such things extravagances, and besides Eamon Delahunty – the father – has a delicate stomach, grease does it no good. He'll start to grumble about it on the long winter evenings when there's not much else to do but complain about something.

Eamon, having a nose of a shape so odd and of such mass, that when meeting him for the first time, one finds oneself staring at it wondering at its mathematical beauty, but at the same time asking oneself if it is the ugliest of all possible noses. Without doubt it's the largest nose in the parish and I'd even go so far as to wager it's one of the largest noses the length and breadth of the country. His grandfather's wasn't far off but by my calculations Eamon's shades it. You could in no way say that they are a good-looking family, and yet there she is, walking among them. Rosalyn Delahunty how are you?

He, the father – always first at the table – sighs and moans as he slurps the hot tea and butters a good skelp of soda bread. Michael, the fellow with the squint in his eye, soon joins him. Tell you the truth, I think this is the first time I've been inside their house since that time I was here all those years ago.

If I'm in your house, or if you have cause to meet me, then you can safely say there's no good coming, or the no-good coming has already well arrived. It is well known the great works of art are primarily tragic. And yes, if I am anything it is an artist I am. Grant you, it's a strange form of artistry, but there's no denying I have the eye and the feel for it. Most of all I'm drawn to the flow of words, the music in them, and there's no doubting the people round these parts have a musical tongue. I've often sat for hours listening to two men talk about nothing and been fascinated. You'd be mistaken for thinking I don't love them. I do. All of them. They're all I have now, and all I've had for a long time past. You see, I was something once, a man of importance, and the memory of it comes and goes like a mist I can't catch up with. Wolves once roamed this land, great Elk too. And hounds the size of heifers. But all that was way before my time.

Once, there were two sons. The one no longer with us used to sit on the seat by the window next to his father. Yes, I sense it now, in the air, under the soles of their footsteps, an uneasy thickness like a secret that does not dare to show its face.

I'm a yoke that gets fat on secrets.

I hoover them up.

My mouth an abyss, head like a tape worm, I suck and I suck and I suck.

Was it James, the name escapes me, the first son; he who ended up swinging from the pine grove that borders Nesbit's land. It's best not to mention his name. These things are better left unspoken. I was with him the three days he was missing, though you understand the length of a day has not as much meaning for me as it might for you.

Yes, I swung back and forth alongside him singing old tunes to keep us both off our minds.

Well now, here she is, the youngest of the brood.

Squint looks up.

Her raven hair falls in tussles over her white t-shirt.

Of where have I known her?

The smell of the oatmeal, the brewing tea, sends pangs of memory rippling through my throat. Before I was what I am now I was something else altogether.

I was once something great. Of this, I'm sure.

I was loved once too.

What keeps me going is that I will again be loved.

The sound of slurping. Old Eamon head bent over the bowl of gruel.

She throws her eyes back at Squint. Like a fish on a taut line, he quivers to her every movement.

There there, I speak out to myself – though I have no voice – what on earth have we here?

Oh, I'm drawn to disaster. Like I said, if you see me, you know there's something bad in the post. I'm an artist of misery, a master of tragedy. Yes, a good one too. I know my job. And my job knows me. Inside out and outside in as they say. Púca in the form of a black horse? Not really, I myself prefer the goat. Less conspicuous round these parts.

The sight of her has set my mind to reminiscing. A terrible uneasiness pours through me. Something I did. Yes. Whatever it was lies inside me like the dense black bog. If I have a body it is bog. Arms and legs of peat, and eyes of dirty bog water, eyebrows of bog cotton, hair of heather, tongue of bog lizard, and blood of bog inside my veins. This place where the two worlds collide, the land that is not quiet land and the water that is not quiet water, the border where the people and the not-quite–people, the gods, and the not-quite-gods pass from one realm into the other. A real fucked up stew of a place. The wee folk. The little people. The other crowd. Whatever.

Around the table, in silence broken only by the sounds of eating, they sit. She was born soon after the suicide. The locals claimed it was a miracle; for her mother was at that time forty-two. I know a little about miracles. I was in the bed beside them on the night of the conception. Perhaps I was there to ensure its success. As I've said, I've little choice in these matters. There'd be better beds to be in of a cold winter's night in Spit. And though the love making of the people of Spit, might, on the face of it, appear rudimentary, they have – over centuries – moulded their own perversions. What surprised me most was the life left in Eamon, the old goat. Then again, it's not for nothing a man like him succeeds.

When she, dark Rosalyn came, in ways, she took away the pain of the loss of their son. Eamon would have survived anyway, would've put the head down and just driven himself into the ground until there was nothing left of him. But he doted on the little girl, a snowdrop she was, coming up out of the harsh winter of his heart. Yet now, now he can barely bear to throw his eyes at her. The torment. The way she walks. The get up on her. The length of the skirt when she was going into school. The faces of a hundred hidden desires she displays, all of which he knows, as all men know them. Somehow, he knows that given air and fuel she might bring down the whole world. In the bottom of his sensitive stomach he feels it, yet he has no words to articulate. It is for now, a knot, a twisted dark little worm rolling around in the bottom of his gut.

The light of the morning creaks through the window. Slurps the tea, does Eamon, shovels the bread into his gob. Before him the day and its endless tasks. Bare a word to break the thick silence and the slurping and gulping. The mother, Michael – the fellow with the squint – the dead silent brother, all of them a world unto their own thoughts. Yet she, she hums and smiles and spreads herself like the light. Is there bog in her blood? Yes child, you are blessed, I can't help but blurt out.

There's a wise saying, so wise that it slips right by people and they pay it no mind: *There's no good without its bad.* All that joy she brought. There has to be a reckoning. His own mother's words and they have never proved wrong. Eamon knows there is but one solution, put the head down and work. She was rarely wrong that woman. She'd break the necks of fifteen turkeys under the handle of a yard brush in thirty minutes and have them plucked in a few hours, all the while getting the dinner ready and the children rightly engaged.

The father's chair scraps the concrete floor. A simple people not given to airs. Simple chairs and a plain tablecloth of green. From their mouths words fall in obtuse utterances separated by long silence. Fluency is for the birds outside. The crows make better conversation. Old Eamon Delahunty hardly speaks more than two sentences a week. Grunts and commands. More badger than bird. Squint is little different. I watch him now, poor boy, he cannot keep from peaking, lifting the one good eye and the other bad one, scouring her contours, drinking in her sweetness. Sweet dark Rosalyn. If thine eye offends thee. Brother and sister and sister and brother. There are laws of nature and there are man's laws. And all sorts of laws in between.

No words or nod of thanks, father stands up leaving the cutlery on the table.

The sons follow.

Yes, the dead one too.

Yes, from now on we will christen this Michael, Squint, it's an old habit of mine. He won't be half the man his father is, and he, Squint, knows it. The best of them left himself at the end of the dog collar above in Nesbit's grove.

Around the kitchen Rosalyn dances picking up the dishes like they are golden things and she's the very queen of Sheba. With the craft of a butterfly, she moves, her mother telling her to calm down, telling her she's like a crazed cat. But she pays no more heed to her mother's words than if she were a bird in the air and someone was shouting at her to stop her flying round. She whistles, she sings, the dishes clatter and clutter, her mother angry one minute, laughing the next, looks at her at times and wonders where in hell she came out of. But wherever she did come out of she's glad she came, for the place before she came was unbearable. She remembers, how furious in the hour of love but gentle in the months of growth. With her there was no morning sickness and her birth was almost easy.

Rosalyn Delahunty – Rosie as everybody calls her – is a thing of beauty. I lie there on the ceiling looking down on her, the memory of her the end of a rainbow, a fistful of mist, the flash of a trout's back, gone and going like the hare in the long grass. Skin white as lime, hair black as the Friesian bull's eyes pacing the yard out the back, her neck a miracle of sinew, bones and muscle, her tongue a livery pink, her mouth a rogue country on the warpath. She's been built to echo down centuries. Mark my word, I say to myself, it will be a long time before Spit forgets the name of Rosie Delahunty.

Mother, I've something to tell you.

I hope it's something worth hearing.

Mother. Your always so dour. Give me a little smile. Life isn't all about work and Mass.

Nothing wrong with Mass. The more you get the better,

they're like money in the bank. Missus Delahunty groans as she bends to sweep under the table.

Is your back at you again?

When you're my age everything is at you. The whole world is at you, and soon enough you'll find that out. Now what is it you want to say? Spit it out and quick about it.

You know the festival that's coming up.

Silly business. People ought to spend their money on better.

Well, you know the competition?

The what?

They have a competition for the most beautiful Rose. There are women coming from all over the country and abroad too, Scotland, England, New York.

Jesus Mary and Joseph don't tell me you're involved.

I'm to be Spit's Rose.

Mother of God, she says, laying the brush against the table and blessing herself. When in god's name did this happen and why didn't you tell me sooner, you're barely twenty. You'll call up that Hanley fellow and cancel it immediately.

Mother, I'm doing it, she says, her voice changing, her eyes freezing over like stone.

Sit down and we'll talk about it.

There's no need for talking.

The mother blesses herself again.

Who's going to tell your father?

You are.

He'll have a fit.

He'll get over it.

In truth, I could give the day looking at her, humming and singing her little melodies, brushing her light feet in little mimes and jigs but just as I'm getting comfortable, a darkness breaks across the bright morning, the wind gusts over the heather up on the hill, bringing in a fat shower from the west and next thing I know I'm in Paddy Corcoran's wife's house. She's after taking a turn for the worse. Nobody much believes in us anymore, except Paddy Corcoran's wife. Paddy's long dead. She once gave seven years in bed. A gnawing on the heart. Believed herself the victim of a *piseog*. She'll be ninety-seven next March and she still leaves little plates of milk on the windowsill for the *good people*.

*

The best way to think of it might be that I'm kind of like a mist. I drift about from place to place, end up in creeks and crevices, lonely bogs and bustling meadows, in all kinds of crooks and crannies, and more often than not I spend my days stranded on the sides of windswept mountains. I don't know why I'm there half the time. It's a patient game. Doesn't suit everybody. Gets awful lonely. Anyway, here I am again blown to the corner of the most run down shed on Delahunty's farmyard. It's late. Must be closing in on midnight. There's little to do but wait. That's how it goes. Something will happen. And then I'll have to make something of that something and connect it to something else. At times it feels like I'm a blindman trying to make a jigsaw. That's the way things work in my department. I answer to none, don't have any co-workers so to speak. I figure stuff out as I go along. A lot of what I do seems without order or reason, but I have to believe there's something – a power, a force, an entity – directing me, but what it is I can't say precisely. The word god doesn't really fit. The devil neither. Something in between maybe? A hybrid deity. Something with seventeen heads and an odd number of feet. A being that slobbers on the chaos and pain of the world, stuffing its face till it passes out each night.

The rain hammers on the galvanized roof overhead, such a commotion you never heard. An upset cow lows somewhere close by. The house is dark except for the outside lights which throw their beams on the yard. Silhouette of tractors, sheds, trailers, silage pit, and the slurry house. The sweet sickly smell of cow shit thickens the air. It's rare I get to visit the Delahuntys and yet here I am twice in as many weeks. General rule of thumb here is I don't be coming round for the happy times, and though everything is humming along normal and safe, wherever I be you know there's something not right.

I sense the yard light coming on, then hear footsteps. The front door slides open and out he comes, which one I can't tell, only that it's a man, and he's headed right for me, big long strides like the men round here are apt to take.

Soon he's upon me.

Shaking the rain from his hair he flicks the switch; a low bulb hung from the high ceiling, covered in a crude plastic dome lights up the empty calf shed, but no sooner has it breathed its first than he shuts it off again.

In the darkness, back and forth he paces, muttering words, no sense of which my ear can make. Out in the shed, in the middle of the night, something queer afoot.

The reason for my being here, as always, is to witness.

If I am anything at all it is a thing that bears witness. The minutes pass. He walks with too much excitement for a man this hour of the night.

Whoopsie daisy. Company. I hear footsteps. Light ones. Delicate. I throw my eyes upwards, thinking how stupid I am to forget that this is almost always the instigator of all my missions: the pleasures of the flesh, the chambers of the heart, the pit of love, the reason why many a good lad and lass end up face down in the earth. I often envy them you know, because I'm not like that at all, I have no inclinations at all in this area, neither man nor woman nor beast. Oh, the stories I could tell you.

But who could it be? The nearest neighbours are the Quinns and there's bad blood between them for generations. No. Couldn't be a Quinn. On a night like this, the rain bucketing down. No, nobody would come by foot. Bit closer to home perhaps. Too close to home. Maybe. Wouldn't be a first. Won't be the last. He hears them now too – the footsteps gathering in intensity as they come closer. He slips behind two large round bales of straw. All eyes on the door waiting, but the footsteps cease, then recede in what I estimate to be in a direction past the house. Out from behind the bales of straw he takes to pacing again, back and forth, then, after a minute or two, he carefully unclasps the door and emerges into the rain, me behind him.

The light of the moon is nowhere to be seen, the darkness deep, and yet long strides he makes. He's away quickly up the field with surprising stealth and agility. Ahead of us in the distance we can see a small light tossing as if it were the light from a ship being tormented by a raging sea.

Up at the top of the hill he pauses, panting and catching his breath. The rain comes in waves, easing off for a time, then once you get to thinking it's done, back it comes with vengeance. In the distance, at the bottom of the south side of the hill, sits Nesbit's place, the only light in the vast night.

Well well well, I say, quare goings on indeed. Squint moves. I trial along behind him, down the slippery muddy well-worn cow path.

Rumours abound about her origins, how could she, one so beautiful be born into a family very much on the ugly side. Some say there's an aunt on the mother's side the same, died childless in her fifties. It was said she never married because she was too beautiful and that men gave up before they tried.

Squint crouched at the window, drenched to the bone, will catch his death, breathing heavy, birds eye view of what's going on. Behind us Nesbit's chained dog barks weakly.

She's wearing a long overcoat that looks much too big for her, a man's overcoat, her father's perhaps – holy Eamon they call him behind his back on account of his mass going, but there's not much holy about him if you know him – reaches down below her knees. Her toned calves are bare and glisten with the rain.

Within seconds they are stuck in each other. I've little choice but to look. It's that or my cloven hoofs. Yes, sometimes, or rather most often, I take the form of a goat. They attract little attention, as there's a pack of them that has the run of the land from Nesbit's hill, down Delahunty's, cross Patsy Ryan's land and all the way to the old quarry by Larry Heffernan's place. Twenty or thirty at times. Twenty plus generations of them I've seen so I've gotten well used to their stink. I've had nothing but time. Goats don't change much. Don't chat much either. Always chewing. Restless kind. Not fussy at all. Sleep out in the rain. Sleep out in the cold.

Well, back to the show in front of me. In front of the kitchen table, down on her knees, doing the thing with her mouth. Squint moans.

She stops, says something, I'm no lip reader, then fills her mouth again. There's a few minutes of this carry on then she stands up and turns her back to him. The overcoat is still buttoned up but now she hikes it over her hips revealing her nakedness. She angles herself to receive.

Again, she speaks, looking back at him, the words, because we've no inclination as to what they are, assume greater importance.

Would you agree Squint, I say, but he's too busy to reply, moaning now he is, his right hand moving frantically.

Inside, young Nesbit is upon her in seconds.

He goes at her hard and fast as she arches herself over the table. A cup shakes violently precariously close to the edge of the table. I'll put money it won't last. The cup that is.

She bites into her hand.

The whole shebang is over before it begins, thank God for small graces.

The cup lies shattered on the ground.

I read once below in Philly Ryan's house that if you were to wait for all eternity there would be a chance the cup might reassemble itself, that there are no laws that prohibit it from not getting back together. I've thought about this for a long long time and still can't get my head round it.

They embrace, kissing and hugging gently. Eyes closed, she stands there trembling, a thing like a smile painted on her face.

She speaks again, arranging the long coat back into a respectable angle, with her eyes closed.

At times like this I'm glad I don't have a body. It just seems altogether too complicated and messy. If I had to choose, I'd pick the goat – the form I most often take – as it's just a lot less stressful, and all you have to do is eat all the time. No eating for me though. No drinking either. Six hundred years or so since anything wet my throat.

She leaves first.

Squint waits standing against the wall gathering his breath.

The rain raps long sermons off Nesbit's roof.

Nothing good will come of this, I'm thinking. Suppose it's to be expected, things have been quietish now for a while.

DANNY MULCAHY

Your parents they fuck you up don't they. That Larkin fellow was never far off the mark. Sometimes I can't bear to look at them. This doesn't upset me much because sometimes I can't bear to look at myself. It's not so much how did they ever end up together, it's more, how do they manage to stay together. Then again, at times, their union seems fated, their fucked-up dynamic strangely balanced. In important matters they consult each other in subtle indirect ways, taking extreme care so as neither will ever have to admit this.

He, the old-man, throws things out there, and she, the mother, approves or disapproves. If she disapproves, she gets an eating, through which she will sit, taking everything he can throw at her without a word back, as if she knows that in the end victory will be hers and no matter how much he riles against it; it – her opinion – is the most important of all opinions to him. And actually, when you think about it deeply, as I have the misfortune to do to everything, except matters pertaining to my

17

own well-being, he never really makes a decision by himself, and that she is, in the end, the end all and the be all.

My brother Tony, named after out grandfather, shoves another spud in his mouth. Don't forget your brothers, and your sisters, and your cousins Mr. Larkin, and I suppose you can throw the neighbours in there as well. It's simply unfair to assign all the blame on the parents.

Tony is the tit and I'm the bollox, or I'm the tit and Tony's the bollox. You get the idea. We're close but so far away.

Apparently, Hanley's got the Darky Kellys in to play, says Tony.

The Darky's. That's great. They have some great songs, says mother, making that noise while she eats.

Shure yer man can't sing at all, Mahone, says the old man.

It's Malone, says Tony, laughing, Malone.

The lad with the teeth. Mumbling is all he does. Listen to John McCormac, now there's a man who could sing.

Well, he can write a song can't he, says mother.

If that's singing, I'm an Arab. Anyway, Hanley is going to bring this festival to an end, and no harm either. Mark my words, ideas about himself that lad Hanley – big ideas, wearing that suit everyday like he's a big shot, he's nothing only a pawner of insurances, a money lender, anything he puts his hand to turns to dust. He's the opposite of that fellow Methuselah.

Who, I ask, without really meaning to.

Methuselah, says father, reading the paper as he eats, a habit which drives the mother mad.

Methuselah was the oldest man who ever lived according to the bible. According to the good book he lived to be nine-hundred and sixty-nine, I say.

Well, Radio Molloy was in good form last night, says Tony

trying to change the subject, something he does whenever I say anything.

I shove another spud in my mouth.

Fathers jaw tightens.

Tony waits for a reply.

Tell you the truth I envy Tony, not his lack of education, not his absolute belief in his own wisdom, but rather simply, that he can talk to my father like he, my father, is just another person.

I think he meant to say Midas, I say.

Yes, Midas, that's the man, the fellow who turned everything to gold, says father, refolding the paper.

There is, always has been, and always will be, something between us. What it is, I cannot say with certainty.

Mother slurps on her cabbage. For a moment, I question how a mere sound produced from the mastication of the mouth can make you hate your own mother. Maybe it's me that's fucked up after all.

Father coughs, refolds the newspaper, shirtsleeves rolled up, the muscles on his forearms rippling. Get me another sausage there, missus will you, he says, not looking up.

You've already had two, she says.

He looks up from the paper. In the light of the morning sun the scar on his chin is suddenly very visible. We don't know the origins of this scar, we don't ask, but it looks like somebody stubbed the broken end of a bottle out on his face.

Here we go, I think. If Tony notices what's coming he shows no signs of it.

So what if I have? Is there a law against three, the old man says, his voice tensing.

Well, make it yourself then, she replies.

His face reddens, eyes begin to bulge. Another day he might

19

laugh it off. But whatever way the day is lying it's lying heavy on him. It's fair to say there are more days like this than the good ones.

All I wanted was another fucking sausage. No need to be like that.

Mother gets up and starts banging the dishes in the sink. The old man sparks up a fag. Tony wolfs down the last of his food, stands up, and says he has to go and help the Hurleys – neighbouring farmers – with dosing the cattle. All he wants to be is a farmer, but he can never be a farmer because we don't have any land. Around here we're unusual in that respect.

I'm sitting here, face reddening, like a fucking eejit caught between the crossfire sucking up the rest of a lump of bacon as fast as I fucking can and wanting to get the fuck out of there and back to college as quick as I can get some loot.

Most of the time I'm an enigma to myself. I flitter between images. One minute I see myself as delicate tubercular prone to poetry and depression, the next minute I might imagine myself as some kind of hard man. There's no denying I'm well-read, educated, but on the other hand I am, and always have been, drawn to thuggery, criminality, and more generally, doing things I shouldn't be doing. However, I must point out that I lack the gumption, the balls, to be a real criminal, to be a real anything really, to be an either / or.

Covering the banging of the dishes, him sucking on his smoke, the sighs and groans, a deep thick blanket of silence. Halfway down the fag his anger has burnt off and he accepts he's wrong, or knows from experience there are wars he can't win. Clearing his throat with a sharp quick cough, he says, well, it's a wonder he didn't try and get that *Bone-no* fucking eejit. Might as well break the whole parish while he's at it.

It's Bono, I say, then immediately regret it. It's not recommended to correct a man like my father often, let alone twice in one day.

But he doesn't acknowledge my comment, continues sucking on his fag. Mother looks out the window at the birds feeding at the bird house. She'll do that for hours at a time. Often, he'll just sit there reading the paper back to front smoking while she looks out the window. It's not uncommon for him to read it all twice. Frequently they'll talk about the birds, the conversation will be one they've had hundreds of times. You don't have to travel very far to find mysteries in this world.

Sometimes I play with their bones. Sometimes I'll follow a notion and end up on their grave for the night. Sometimes I hop into the beds of the lonely and I weep along with them in the dead hours of the night. I'm not sure if they feel me at all but at least there's someone there with them. Into the beds of the dying too, not a bother on me. At times, I can slip into their dreams, at times into their minds. I hide out in the hills and hollows, linger by the back of graveyards, into the confessional box for a bit of gossip when the mood is on me, dangling off the ceiling, caught between the breath of the priest and the confessor.

I can see them, feel them, taste them, be them even, but I can never alter the nature of their fates. This is my curse. And who or what does, is beyond me.

I once gave the night lying beside Neddy O'Sullivan. Dead drunk, he fell into a drain on the way home from the pub and drowned in a bit of water that you'd think wouldn't drown a fly, but it drowned Neddy O' Sullivan alright. Nothing much I could have done but I felt the poor man needed some kind of company there.

Púca, Spook, Jack O Lantern, Will O' Wisps, Changelings, Dullahan, Aos Si, Bean-sidhe, fairy, fairy darts, spells and piseogs, the wee folk, the good people, the little people...and so on. Truth is, I can't direct you, as I don't know myself what it is I am myself. You can imagine the stress of this.

If Spit have a spirit, I am it.

If Spit has a guardian angel, I am it.

If Spit have a spook, I am it.

If an old brown owl hoots in the dark of night, I'm but a feathers breath away. If the window you are sure you closed is open, then the draft that's blowing in like it's seen something it shouldn't have, that's me too. If you wake up screaming in the middle of the night haunted by some nightmare then I'm likely to be sitting on your chest looking into your eyes. Yes, I do be there in the darkness, I do be there in the shadows, I do be there in the hungry hours, and most of all I do be there when they think there's nobody there.

And it's only when there's nobody there do I have some control over the matter around me. I can pick things up, tap out melodies on the bones of dead dogs, but the thing I do most, and the thing that keeps me going is my ability to scribble down my thoughts, not just my thoughts you see, but precise details of all the local happenings. Indeed, this activity has become so precious to me that I ascribe it a higher meaning – i.e. somebody somewhere reads them. They'd want to be quick because as soon as I've downed them, they're gone.

On the grass, on frozen potholes on frosty January mornings, on the feathers of dead crows, I scribble them. I pulse them out on dew laden cobwebs delicate as a child's tooth, etch them on the sides of freshly ploughed potato furrows. Of late, I'll write to vent my frustrations, like the one I've fingered just now on the dried bark of an old beech tree.

Boss, I hope you are not too busy. If you do get some free time, and feel thus inclined, could you shed some light on who I am. Yes, a name would be nice too, but more to the point would be an insight into what I was before I was this thing I am now. I'd jump at the chance of a reassignment? The scenery here is nice but after countless centuries I'm bored to paralysis. Spit's Púca.

DANNY MULCAHY

I pass the day stuck in Dostoevsky counting down the hours till darkness comes, till I can meet up with Nesbit and Bellwhistle. That sentence might sound like Dostoyevsky is a poor companion, he's far from it. I'm on my second round of Crime and Punishment. There's nobody else I'd rather be stuck with – except a woman of course but there's more chances of actually meeting Dostoevsky than that happening. I've never read anything like it. This fellow Raskolnikov might be me, except I was born a hundred years later in the unknown shithole of Spit and he in St. Petersburg under altogether different circumstances. Nobody famous from here and nobody ever will be. Oh, except Matty Slattery's brother who's some kind of Minister. But mark my words. Most never make it out. Bellwhistle talks about it. But he's been a decade talking about it now.

I smoke. Read. Have a wank. Back to the book. Realize I could never be Raskolnikov because I wouldn't have the balls to kill the old woman with the axe. Unless I had a few drinks in me first.

Then I could murder the whole parish. I go for a walk up the hill out the back. Nature polishes some layers of shit from my soul. I come down to the kitchen to eat.

They are silent. You can feel it in the air, this unnameable thing. A force without mass. A mass with energy, but no location, except that it's omnipresent. I eat fast and wait for Nesbit. Seven, he said. Long stretch in the evenings, the summer peaking, the countryside moaning and groaning, sappy and icky from the hungry things of the flesh.

I need love.

No, just the touch of a woman. I'll settle for that. It's been so long.

Time and Nesbit don't get along. Thirty minutes late. Mother throws the holy water on me saying to be home early. She knows well I've the curse. Grunted greetings. Door slamming. It's in the family. On her side mostly. An uncle taken away, dried out. Bits of these whispered conversations fall on my ears and I'm left there to fill in the blanks and paint the picture as best I can. That's how things work in my family.

Nesbit, hair falling down over his eyes as he drives, stoned since morning, stoned since the time I gave him his first joint, well over a year ago. I do feel guilty sometimes because…well you know. He never went to college. He could have but he chose not to. He has no known ambition, never had, and now with the dope it's even worse.

Nirvana on the tape deck. Nesbit reckons Bleach is their best album. Anyone who says that is just trying to be cool by having eclectic taste. Tits. I know this but I don't say this. I'm like the iceberg. What you see is ten percent if even that. Nesbit must keep a lot back too because he's always quiet as fuck and quieter even now since he's gotten a taste for the wacky. What can I say. I bring it back from college, chop it up, sell a bit here and there, friends mostly. I don't make much. Just enough for drink. Drinks my thing. Makes me come alive. Oh, thou invisible spirit thou makes me blossom. Thou makes the wilted flower inside stand up tall and proud and proclaim its beauty to the universe; except, except, somethings not right with the way it comes out – all wrong and broken like a song sung in ten different keys. I have a vague sense of this, but I refuse to believe it. As soon as it pops its head up I hammer it down.

Bellwhistle, sitting on the couch listing to Ten Years After at full blast, blows out another cloud to add to the fat grey waves of hashish smoke that fill the room. Bellwhistle, not a name common in these parts, but his family are generations in the place. Anyway Bellwhistle – the Jap. That's what's he's called round here. Because he's always talking about going there. Years ago, there was a Japanese girl who – god knows why – passed through Spit, and they had some kind of fling. Nesbit's working on loading another bong. I'm half way through my fist can of Linden Village. Cider is your only man. Bellwhistle's rambling on. It's Japan this and Japan that. Most of the people round here can't stand it. They've taken to asking him when he's going to China. That drives him wrong altogether. He's ten years older than us and keeps telling us that the music in the sixties will never be equalled. He has some theories about why this is so but they don't make much sense to me. He's a nice enough fellow I suppose. Nice. Now, there's a word. I finish my can and crack open another. I'm drunk already about thinking about being drunk. Anticipation. You know it can happen, all in the mind.

Bellwhistle's rattling on about *spooky action at a distance*. Ever since he found out I was studying Physics at Uni it's all he talks to me about. He's explaining it to Nesbit who's sucking on the bong like it's the big, luscious tit of the universe:

Particles at one end of the universe, he says, act as if they can communicate with particles at the other end and that for that to be possible the communication must be instantaneous; something which should be impossible because the speed of light is limited and nothing is supposed to travel faster than light according to Einstein's special theory of relativity. It's as if particles can communicate with each other instantaneously. This is the so-called Copenhagen interpretation favoured by Neils Bohr. Einstein, mockingly, called it Spooky Action at a Distance. Well, it turns our Einstein was wrong.

He sits back with a sense of great satisfaction on his face. I suppose any sentence in which one utters *it turns out Einstein was wrong* is bound to have that effect.

Spooky action at a distance, I say, not my field, I branched into fluid mechanics.

It's a lie. How I ever graduated is much more of a mystery than spooky action at a distance.

Great name for a band, says Nesbit.

Fluid mechanics?

No, you gowl, spooky action at a distance.

Great name for my mother, I say.

Bellwhistle laughs. He has this way of laughing – sucks in air making a snorting sound kind of like a horse kind of like a pig – that makes him sound like an idiot but don't be fooled.

What do you think about that, asks Bellwhistle, turning to Nesbit.

Nesbit shrugs his shoulders.

Bellwhistle drinks his wine. Always red and cheap. He refuses to drink beer, unless he's run out of wine, then he'll drink anything. But this is just a phase. Like all the others it will pass.

He really knows fuck all about physics except the big ideas which people like to talk about. But talking about physics without using math is like masturbation as opposed to sex. Of course, I don't tell him this. Iceberg.

You see the thing is, people round here laugh at the old folk, he rattles on. You know, like Paddy Corcoran's wife who believes in piseogs and fairies, and all manners of shite and hokey-pokey, but at the end of the day there might be much weirder stuff going on. That's all I'm saying, I'm not saying I believe in spooks or any of that, or the ghost that many have claimed to have seen on the old bog road, but you know, the fucking universe is so strange man...

I'm thinking if he says Universe one more time I'm going to strangle him, though I'm enjoying him, but I've heard it all before. Bellwhistle, like most people, myself included, is a one-sided album, one-track too many, a one-track pony or is that a one-horse town. I'm already drunk, like I said, on the thoughts of being drunk.

Bong hits bring us silence.

Into it, and the loud music, we drift like wanderers in our own eternal deserts.

The hypnotic rift of Good Morning Little School Girl plasters us to our seats. Along the long winding tunnel of the guitar solo I travel until Bellwhistle destroys it with mention of Japan. He'd bring us there sooner or later. He's on about an Irishman who was famous in Japan for writing ghost stories. He's going to go visit his grave. Lafcadoe O'Hern that's the fellow. He's only really a quarter Irish. And besides half the western world might be a quarter Irish.

When are you going, I ask, calling his bluff.

It's not that simple, he says.

Yeah...hop on a fucking plane.

Nesbit butts in then in that way of his. When he speaks – and he doesn't speak much – one listens. Is it his hollowed-out face, the haunted grey eyes, the tone of voice, or is it purely what he says? Who knows. But Nesbit you could do with a meal. It must get awful lonely here now.

Most people are never happy with where they are, he says, in that tone of voice, lazy, like the words are rolling off a precipice. They're always seeking something else, somebody else's life. But you know what the key to happiness is, he asks, not laying his eyes on us but looking towards the wall across from the couch, sheathed in a wallpaper that he told us his mother bought out of the back of a tinkers' van.

My eyes fall on a silver bracelet that lies to the left of the television where it has marked out its presence in the dust. Nesbit you bastard who are you tapping now, I say to myself.

The key to happiness is sitting right here in my hands, says Bellwhistle, nodding to the home constructed bong. Materials used: a two-litre empty Linden Village Flagon, tin foil, and the empty innards of biros.

Transmuted suffering, says Nesbit.

Transmuted suffering, now that sounds like some kind of brake fluid for a Massey Ferguson, says Bellwhistle in a mock country style accent, the accent he should have naturally, but somewhere along the line he's abandoned it, a move which has only added to his general unpopularity with the local bog hoppers. They hate him and he's happy they hate him. At least that's what he says.

Whatever, says Nesbit.

Explain yourself, I say.

Well, he rubs his eyes. We suffer. We all do. It's unavoidable.

The secret is to get something from it, to turn it into your daily bread. Do we really ever know what's good? There's an ancient Chinese story.

Are you sure it's not Japanese, I ask.

Fuck you, says Bellwhistle wiping his blonde locks from his blue eyes. He swipes his hair back – this particular motion becoming, in recent years, more and more frequent – in an attempt to cover the thinning hair round his forehead. I'll never mention it sober but drunk, well, I could do anything when I'm drunk. Bellwhistle's twelve years older than us, or is it ten.

The story Nesbit, I remind him, after he lapses into a long bong induced pause.

He looks at us, soggy eyed, and perplexed. I'm about to remind him again when he begins talking.

Yeah...there's a Taoist story of an old farmer who had worked his crops for many years. One day his horse ran away. Upon hearing the news, his neighbours came to visit. Such bad luck, they said. Maybe, the farmer replied. The next morning the horse returned, bringing with it three other wild horses. How wonderful, the neighbours exclaimed. Maybe, says the old man. The following day, his son tried to ride one of the untamed horses, was thrown, and broke his leg. The neighbours again came to offer their sympathy for what they called his *misfortune*. Maybe, says the farmer again. The day after, military officials came to the village to draft young men into the army. Seeing that the son's leg was broken, they passed him by. The neighbours congratulated the farmer on how well things had turned out.

Maybe, says the farmer.

Nesbit sits back, sucks on his can of fosters.

Taciturn bastard of a farmer, says Bellwhistle.

Taciturn, I repeat. Bellwhistle likes to use such words.

Maybe, maybe, maybe, he continues, maybe he can fuck off and plough his field like a good farmer, instead of spouting philosophical hobnobs, says Bellwhistle.

This brings a smile to Nesbit's face. First one I've seen since his parents...Well, nobody talks about that. We don't know what to say. So, we talk about these nothings, these vessels into which we can pour ourselves.

Philosophical hobnobs hobnobbing, I say laughing.

Do you have any?

Have any what?

Philosophical Hobnobs?

No. Hobnobbed the fuck out, says Nesbit cracking open another can. You know something though, there's some spooky shit going on round here at night?

Bellwhistle perks up at the sound of spooky.

What do you mean, he says?

Someone's trying to fuck with me.

Like how?

Well, there're throwing pebbles at my windows, making strange sounds, and the other night when I looked out the window, I saw someone out there.

You're smoking too much of that shit, says Bellwhistle. It will rot your brain and take away your drive. I've seen it happen.

The pot and the kettle.

I can take it or leave it, says Bellwhistle.

Bollox, says Nesbit.

Who do you think it was, I ask, my eyes wandering again to the bracelet. It could just be his mothers. I could be reading too much into it.

They blocked the chimney too.

They? I ask.

Yeah, I get the feeling there's more than one.

How longs it been going on?

Started a few months ago, not long after...you know...the mother passed.

The mention of death gets us uncomfortable and I'm looking at Bellwhistle and he's looking at me, and we are both figuring out what to say but Nesbit beats us to it.

I had to call up Radio Molloy, because you know amongst other things, he's the man to call if your chimney gets blocked. When Molloy told me the reason for the blockage I wasn't much surprised. He said years ago it was a common prank. He then asked me who I suspected.

So somebody's fucked up your chimney, asks Bellwhistle.

Yeah, filled it up with a bag of straw and sand.

What the fuck, says Bellwhistle, what depraved cunt would do that?

What did you tell Molloy, I ask.

I said, I didn't know who it was. And I don't. Anyway, there we were standing in the dark of evening, says Nesbit, and Molloy's hat, the dark crabby yoke he's always wearing was crooked on his head against the moon. Somebody wants you gone young Nesbit, he says, they want the ground beneath you, the land boy, can't you see it, and who could that be but those to the left or the right of you. Good luck to you. You know, you'd be better off to sell up, since you're not much into the farming anyway, sell up, take your money and get the hell out of Spit. Shure what would be keeping you here. Easier said than done I suppose.

There he is saying all this, his crooked hat silhouetted against the moon, like he has for the first time in sixty-seven years realized this – that he too could have escaped if he had acted sooner. His voice was all breaking up.

Radio fucking Molloy, blurts Bellwhistle.

He looked up at me with those dark eyes of his, his face fucking riddled with wrinkles, he looked like he was going to cry, says Nesbit.

Now we know why the women are into you Nesbit, it's that poet soul of yours.

Fucking Delahuntys, says Bellwhistle, I wouldn't put it past them. Hungry cunts. And that squint eyed cunt Michael. He puts the wind sideways in me.

Could be the Quinns, I say.

Nah, that's not their way. They'd likely come down here with a few hurleys and bate the shit of you if they wanted to. That Pa Quinn is fucking mental.

Could be someone else entirely, I say.

Could be spooky action at a distance. That hill out there is haunted...that's what they say, says Bellwhistle.

They, who are they when they are at home, I ask.

The fools on the stools, he says.

No shortage of them round here, I reply.

That's where we're headed.

Already half way there. Fools on fucking stools holding up the counter, I say.

I get up and head for the toilet. Once there I check for evidence of female visitors.

The bracelet has got me wondering. Who could it be. Nesbit has always been secretive. Nesbit has always been weird. There's nothing much in the toilet except a big mess. Two toothbrushes, but each as worn and old as each other. She must be here somewhere. I seek a hairbrush. He – my father – trained us to remember number plates of cars, to always get at the details, to root and claw at the surface of things. Clues, he would say, the world is riddled with them. Never listen to what a man says, but how he says it, and his surroundings. There you can find him. What he hides, he is.

Pulling open a drawer I locate a hairbrush which is decorated with long strands of black hair. I bring it to my nose to smell it but there's no distinct smell. It's likely lain here a long time. I once read about a condition called Rapunzel syndrome, extremely rare, usually affects adolescent women. They cannot stop eating hair, their own and others. If they're visiting a friend's house they'll do exactly what I'm doing now, except they'd be unravelling these old hairs and ingesting them as quickly as possible. Maybe I'm not so fucked up after all. Eventually, a large hair ball forms in the stomach and extends into the small intestine. If this happens surgery is required or the effected person can die.

When I come back, they are talking about the festival.

I might head up to Dublin that weekend, says Bellwhistle.

You say that every year. Same as you say you're moving to Ja...

Don't fucking mention that place. I can't stand to think of it these days.

There'll be women there, I say, dreaming.

Just make sure you bring enough hash up from the city. You'll make a killing, he says.

It's not like I'm dealing, I'm just doing you guys a favour.

You forget where you're living, says Nesbit.

Sergeant Mulcahy's son, says Bellwhistle.

Indeed, I say, throwing my eyes at him.

Sees everything, he says.

Never you fucking mind what he sees, I say. There's a sudden rage inside me which I keep well veiled. I suck the remains of my can of Linden village, then crack open another.

The Darky Kelly's are coming, says Bellwhistle, after a minute of long silence. They say that famous Hollywood actor is going to be with him. What's his name?

I hear they're having trouble selling the tickets, says Nesbit.

Going to be a complete waste of money. They're fucking shite live. Ticket my hole. I'll sit out on the road and listen for free. As if five fucking meters is going to make a difference, says Bellwhistle.

Yeah, fucking washout, I say. This will be the last festival.

The summer of love, says Bellwhistle.

What?

This is our 1969.

Bellwhistle you're thirty-two, I say.

Age is an illusion.

No, it's a number.

Number of years Sergeant Mulcahy is going to give you if he catches you dealing hash, says Bellwhistle.

I laugh. But when he says my father's name like that, I don't like it. I don't mention your balding fucking head do I, I say to myself. I've a thing about my father being a cop. Nesbit looks at me. We all have things I suppose. I slug on the can. Fucking baldy cunt. We become silent again. He starts talking again about *Spooky Action at a Distance*. Sometimes I just wish he'd shut the fuck up.

I lie on the nape of the hill, buried in heather looking down on Delahunty's farmyard. The little birds – sparrows, robins, wagtails, blackbirds and tits – are eating the last of the berries from the heather. In the clear sky the sun sits, keeping the cold out of my bones. I've been here hours and I must say the day is as good as you could wish for. I might be close to what one classes content. A slight gentle breeze from the north, rustles my scraggy goat hair. I sit, I chew, not on food, but on my thoughts, and I wait.

In the distance, since morning, the sounds of sledge hitting wood. The Delahuntys out fencing. The silage in, big rush of the summer gone, a brief lull in the busy farming season to allow for this quiet and almost pleasurable work. It was on a job like this twenty-five years ago that the trouble with them and the Quinn's took off. All over a ditch and a bit of land – not enough to raise a brood of hens on – they came to blows. Blood was spilt, hospitals were visited. If it hadn't been for the quick actions of Sergeant

Mulcahy, someone would have died.

There are days like this when nothing at all happens. Lots of them. So, I'm easing back into the heather not expecting much when I see a figure walking along the winding gravel road that twists its way towards the top of the hill. In fact, this roughed out road does not reach the top but stops short and merges into a field about two hundred meters from what we shall call the summit.

About ten minutes later Michael Squint Delahunty, with long strides, is walking towards me, some class of a dog trailing behind him. Well now I say to myself what have we here. He's a tall fellow, taller than his father, taller than the brother that went before him. He walks with a stoop, already displaying signs of a slumped back and neck, his eyes glued to the ground rather than looking ahead. The robins and sparrows and wagtails have spotted him too and are wary of his entrance. A congregation of rooks ride a gust of wind and head west in a hurry. Squint, as I shall now refer to him, moves quickly. The dog behind him follows and though there is something familiar about it I pay it little mind.

I slip out of the goat and follow on in my own form, whatever that is. Many times, I've tried: mirrors, streams, and so on but all I ever see is nothing. Perhaps it's a useful way to be for the work I'm in. Maybe to be nothing at all is the best way to be. All that is, desires — at some level — not to be. Did somebody say that once? No doubt, it has a familiar feel.

I keep up close behind him. Can hear the labours of his lungs. We soon arrive at the treeline, which marks the top of the side of the hill, which the Nesbit's planted half a decade ago. He stops at the stile, gathers his breath, turns around and gazes over the way he came, impressive on a clear day; rolling hills, of ever-changing shades of green, flattening out into a great eastern plateau, then rising gracefully to meet the far distant horizon. Half the country, some says, you can see on a fine day from the viewpoint of Nesbit's hill in the parish of Spit. I don't doubt them. It's a small country after all. If he's impressed by any of this he does not show it. He clears his throat, spits on the ground, then barks at the dog.

Up over the fence we go and in through spruce eight to nine feet tall. The path is not clear and Squint curses the branches that rip at his hands and prickle his legs through his britches.

I turn my attention to the dog again. Look it up and down. A sheep dog but not pure, though mostly sheepdog. Where oh where have I known thee? Could it be. Yes, it must be. If it is, then this event must have occurred before that event. That is nothing new for me. What happens today might really have happened six months ago, or it could well be the case that it hasn't happened yet. I know. Bear with me. We walk on through the thick dense net of branches until we come to a small clearing where two paths intersect. A few minutes later we've reached a large rectangular clear spot, dead centre at the top of the hill where the paths between two rows of trees intertwine. Squint stops. The dog stops behind him. I might as well stop too.

Overhead the greyish white sky peers down on us.

Squint mumbles something to the dog who looks around nervously. I've been a witness to quare things in my time and have sense of when one is coming. Squint opens his Barbour Ashby Wax jacket – bought for him by the mother inside in Quinlan's in Town, only the best for the Delahuntys. The coat must have decent sized pockets because he takes out a carton of milk, then a small silver bowel. On the mossy uneven earth, he cleans and levels out a patch for the bowel. While the dog sniffs around the milk Squint unbuckles his belt. It's the same dog, of that I'm now sure, the one on whose inner ear I tapped melodies.

He pours a little milk into the bowl, babbles incomprehensible doggy talk at which the dog takes to barking. He tells her to shut up then offers it the milk from the bowel. The dog is lapping contently as Squint gets himself ready. Who wants to know about this let alone see it. Nobody that's who. But here I am and what can I do.

Squint then pours the milk over his target and the poor dog begins furtively licking at the milk. It's hard to tell if it's the first time. I have no way of knowing from the dogs reactions but all of a sudden she loses interest in the milk and starts to move backwards. Squint not happy – one hand pulling hard on his milk covered target – curses the dog. Seeing that this reaction only results in pushing the dog back more he changes tactics:

Here doggy here doggy, he says, affectionately.

The dog falls for it. And they're back at it again. She gives a few more licks and Squint responds with low and deep groans while calling out her name:

That's it, good girl. Keep it up.

But it doesn't last. Even the dog knows this is an abomination.

Tiring of the milk Squint turns the bitch round and makes some attempts to bugger the poor animal. It's hard to put a word on how she looks, embarrassed might be the closest, but dogs don't really do embarrassed do they? After a minute or so of these pathetic attempts to enter the bitch Squint realizes the hopelessness of it and pushes the dog away. He leans back and looks up at the sky, moans and grunts and goes at himself with great force crying out as he shoots his seed out into the moss. The dog, being wiser than me, has elected to look away. As he dresses himself Squint curses:

I'll drown you in the fucking churn out in the back yard, he says. No, I know what I'll do, I'll beat you with a shovel until your bones are pulp, then I'll string you up and leave you dangling for the crows to strip the fucking flesh off you. How about that you stuck up bitch yeh?

On and on he goes, with some amusement, buckling up his pants while the dog looks on from a safe distance with one ear cocked. We all have our demons and darkness, and goodness knows I've mine, but Michael Squint Delahunty I'll have to take my hat off to you, you're the first person in decades who's given me a much-needed shock.

Luckily, I don't have to hang around for much longer – you can imagine the state I'm in – for there and then with that incoming shower and the wind driving it I'm sucked out of this scene and dropped above in Paddy Corcoran's wife's room. This time she's really going and for all the time I'd spent with her up till then I'm glad to be there in the end. She was, and is, in many ways, the last of her kind.

*

Well now, young Nesbit, here you are left all alone, parents still wet in the grave, the dark circles under your eyes Nesbit, sitting there like a sponge soaking up these clouds of smoke. Is there trouble brewing Nesbit? Is there something out there stirring in the night? Your dog's kicking up a fuss. You're on the third round of the movie, ingesting that smoke, drag after drag, higher and higher, but there's only so high you can go Nesbit, you'll know that soon enough.

Take it from me, one who's fallen, fallen from great heights, if I'd bones, they'd be spattered into dust, but I'm composed of trickier deities now, fluids and liquids pulled up out of the heart of the very bog herself. Waiting are you Nesbit, glancing at that watch, waiting for who Nesbit, who would be coming to visit you of this hour? Is it the Whiteboys coming to block up your chimney, dressed in women's garb, lips red, faces powdered white, riding dark horses and incanting words of your doom, or is it, Nesbit, some lady on her way over the fields to give herself to you?

Dark Nesbit, hoarder of women's affections. I've a feeling I myself was once like you. Many envy such men but not I, not you, not us who know. Once you're in there's never an out. There's many a body lying undiscovered at the end of it. Speak up Nesbit, and tell me why have I come to visit you this lonely night. I've more to be doing – that's a lie, in truth, that's a lie. Shall we just sit here and wait then, but for the love of god put on another movie.

Whisht! Your dog's yelping is rising to a crescendo. What stirs from the fields, fleet foxes feet, badger's noses, or plodding biped toes. They'll be dew in the morning, fat and thick, silver goblets of it waiting for my little tongue. It's in the stillest hour of night the dew falls, did you know that Nesbit? And what a grand night it is, the moon hangs a sliver short of half, on the wane. I've a pain inside me young Nesbit, premonitions of things to come. I get like this at times. There's no curing of it; a perpetual aching. They say time mends all, but doesn't the very same fellow rip all apart. Fuck time and all belonging to him, that's what I say.

For a moment she returns, her face flashes before me, at once a stranger, at once all I knew. I try to hold her but she's gone. A tormenting ache fills the fluids of my being, if I could smoke like you young Nesbit I would not stop for air.

I wait, I watch, expecting a knock but no knock comes.

Nesbit smokes on, red eyed, suffering without suffering. The dog continues to bark, I wait till the sun splatters the darkness before creeping off to join the goats for a day of loitering round the rocks near the old quarry down by Larry Heffernan's place.

DANNY MULCAHY

Fridays. Never much liked them. Cunt of a day really. I drag myself out of the bed at noon. Sick as a pike, I head straight for the Hurlers near the big roundabout, have two bottles of cider, two double vodkas, sufficient to stabilize the shake in my hands. This time of day sees the place empty, except for me, and a fistful of well-to-do drunks, who will plod along, on their way to death, in an almost comfortable style.

Inside in the toilet I stare into the mirror. I'm fairly handsome when I've a few down. My right eye is still bruised, the cut on my forehead getting scabby. I'm peaceful enough ninety-nine percent of the time. Except for this yoke inside me that comes awake now and again when it's tickled with spirits. I need to stay away from the hard stuff. I've tendencies to go into fits, warp spasms, battle rages. Bellwhistle likens me to Cú Chulainn. Taking the piss of course. This mirror. My grey greenish eyes. My ears eating up the country melody on the speaker. A most pleasant ache coursing my blood, unidentified surges rippling through synapses, neurons firing the embers of my assaulted nervous system. More is needed. Much more. To peak, to reach the place where only absolutes remain. I move my face closer to the mirror. Staring into my eyes, into the places between the colour, I suddenly see Nesbit.

There was trouble at the festival.

Bellwhistle called me the next day. I haven't heard from Nesbit since. I can't recall much about the fight. Blood on my jeans and shirt. The sound of glasses breaking, people screaming. Patches of skin missing from my knuckles. A girl. And she was there, somewhere lurking in the lost hours of that evening. I might have always loved her. Rosie Delahunty. Somebody crying.

Next day the old man threw a fit. I had to get out of the house and so I came down to the city even though I'm done in college. But there's more to it, more I can't recall because I blacked out for hours and have no idea how I got home. It's been days and yet the feeling of dread does not diminish, as it usually does after drinking bouts and blackouts, rather it's increasing.

I push myself away from the mirror.

I fill the sink with cold water, dip my face in it, then return to the mirror, my pupils now narrowed to pinheads.

Outside, the autumn sun's basking in the sky, grand day for the hitchhiking. I've money, a few bob, and a quarter ounce of hash for Bellwhistle, which I can convert into more cash. I could get a bus, but tell you the truth I prefer the hitchhiking. I leg it out past the big roundabout – lovely job done on it, flowers blooming – and position myself about fifty meters in front of it, on the main Dublin road, the tinkers' halting site behind me. Every time I pass here, I can't help but shudder because I remember the day I discarded the army pants I had shat myself in the night before. Luckily, they were of good enough quality to retain the contents of my bowls and not destroy the couch of the unknown house I'd woken up in. They are likely still there, six months later, still in the plastic bag I stuffed them into, hidden in the thick growth of bush and thorns. Behind me, trying to turn my mind to better things, I begin to whistle along to the birds singing and jumping in that same ditch.

Often, you'd be waiting hours. Sometimes you'd get lucky and be picked up in a matter of minutes. It's the unpredictability I'm drawn to. There's randomness too in the people who pick me up: talkers, non-talkers, those who drive brand new cars and those who drive bangers, young, old, smokers, non-smokers, men in trucks and lorries, predominantly men but sometimes old grannies. The Samaritan wears many guises. I once got picked up by the bishop – gave me a lot of smokes – affectionately rubbed my thigh a few times, but otherwise didn't bother me much.

Another time a bunch of travellers let me into the back of their Hiace van, gave a while staring at me, not a word between us, freaked me the fuck out. Scattered on the van floor, billhooks, hammers, and self-constructed machetes. When they got round to talking, I had difficulty understanding what they said, just nodded along. The way they were looking at each other it was obvious they thought me some class of simpleton.

I never use a sign. If they're heading on towards Dublin, I'll jump out at the road that branches off for Spit. It's a wild road, a crooked contrary cunt of a road that snakes its way through deep folds of rugged spruce and pine covered hills, where time gets all giddy, like progress never came its way, like you've suddenly fallen a hundred years. Radio Molloy says it's the worst road in the country. Maybe that's why I like the hitchhiking. Because I can be out here in this loneliness and not feel alone at all. I clear my throat and spit.

A middle-aged man driving a beat-up red Datsun hatchback drops me at Fairport town. He talked a lot I just nodded my head and looked out the window.

Through the town I walk, through the afternoon buzz of traffic and shopping, deliveries, school pick-ups, people coming and going, I walk on, a shadow among them wondering if they can even see me. On a quiet stretch of road just past the local GAA pitch I smoke half a cigarette and stick out my thumb once more. A quiet man – barely a word spoke between us – drops me at the village of Piedcow. Maybe, there was a time when he too walked the roads. I stand at the far side of the village for an hour and fail to get a lift. Only three cars have passed in this hour and I've spent every minute of it resisting the constant lure of the close by pubs. The sun angles westwards. I can't get Nesbit out of my head. The fight. That night. Flashes of memory. The quarry.

I'm hungry, or thirsty or both. I spark up a smoke. Within the walls of the villages two pubs, The Congo and The Rising Sun, the charm of this place hides. Without really deciding to I find myself inside the Rising Sun. Turf on the fire, once evening falls the renegades will come down from the hills thirsty and dirty, tired from work, it's among them I thrive. There is inside me a voice, no, not a voice but a resonance, that tickles me – DNA level – that it is here, among the low I belong, that it's on these empty windswept forgotten roads that I'll spend my life, hungry, not fully drunk, not fully sober, and always in a state of perpetual dissatisfaction unless I can get enough drink to shut off consciousness.

But now the pub is empty save for the barman and an old man seated at the corner of the counter. The light within is so dim I can barely make out my face in the mirror as I lift the pint. The old man wears a hat and mumbles. I scribble words on the back of a cigarette box. Songs, glimpses of things I once knew. Words. The barman and I make small talk. Not worth repeating. Words and more words. The barman's wife comes and asks him to help with something in the kitchen. She does not look happy.

Outside the sun shifts. A beam of sunlight illuminates the old man's whiskey. Dust dances. For a moment I feel the completeness of all things. The old man picks up the sunlight saturated whiskey, empties it, groans, then stands up. He moves in tiny steps but is soon before me, presenting me with the concave hollows of his face. Around him a combination of odours, all adding up to rot. His eyes, big pools behind the fat thickness of his black rimmed glasses, swell. He throws his bony claw on my shoulder.

My wife died thirty-five years ago. She was twenty-four. Cancer in her stomach. A big ball of it.

He holds up his fist which is so big it does not seem to belong to him.

The doctor gave her three months. She lasted two. I had a daughter. I brought her up as best I could. She left when she was eighteen.

He offers to buy me a drink, but I say no, tell him I have to get going before it gets dark.

Goodman. Go home. Get out of this place and don't come back, he says. The stink of smoke, decades old, has settled in his bones.

I skull the rest of my pint.

He offers me a filter less Sweet Afton.

I've got my own, I say.

The dead are dead they're not coming back. Never forget it. Look around you, people are asleep. They think they can escape it, that it won't come to them, but it's right besides us boy, right beside us from the moment we are born. Not the hour nor the day do we know.

I nod. I smile. I get to standing up, reach for my bag.

Who are you, he asks?

The question throws me.

Danny, I say.

Danny from where?

Spit.

Who would your people be?

Mulcahy, I say.

Mulcahy from Spit. I don't know any Mulcahys from Spit. He steadies himself against me with his yellowed fingers. The skin on his face is brown and tarred like he's been dipped in something like molasses, or diesel maybe. He is not ugly; he might even have once been handsome.

Are you sure it's from Spit you are.

Yes, I say, slipping out from his reach.

You know when a man is in trouble?

I shrug my shoulders and smile politely.

I'll tell you, it's when he can't smell his own stink, that's when.

Well, you're in trouble then aren't you, you rotten old bastard.

It was nice to meet you, I say. And what's your own name?

Casey. Willy Casey.

Right Willy, I need to get going.

Outside the sunlight dazzles me to such an extent that for a moment I feel myself falling into a vast nothingness of light, but in time, I manage to steady myself against the wall.

I rarely get picked up by women. Though once, in my early hitchhiking career, I did. I can still remember her clear as the first drink I ever took. Perhaps it was this encounter, which has kept me coming back for more. Most of the time though, it's hours of endless waiting, while hungry and without cash, stuck in the rain and wind, not anybody's idea of fun, but I'm prone to it, like I've known it of old.

Nothing happened. With the woman. Well, almost nothing, but that almost was everything. She reached over and held my hand suddenly. With that touch all the tension went out of my body, the great spirit of gravity that defines my every moment was lifted. Perhaps, if I were braver, I could have taken things further.

Perhaps to have taken them further would have ruined it.

As it stands the moment will never leave me.

Perhaps, I've always been a coward.

I get home by seven, gobble down dinner, assure my mother everything is fine, then head off for Bellwhistle's. When I arrive I find him uneasy. He won't shut up about Nesbit. He says he went up to the house twice during the week and he wasn't there.

I thought he might be down in the city with you, he says.

You know Nesbit, he's an oddball. Likely a woman. You know the way women are over him. As I say this, the bracelet I'd seen at his house last time comes to mind. Bellwhistle's eyes are red. I neck a can of cider in two slugs. Bellwhistle Bogarts the joint. The TV is on but the volume is down. Roadrunner. I ask him to turn it up. He ignores me or else he really hasn't heard me.

What is it, he asks.

What's what?

His secret with the women?

You're asking the wrong boy there, I say. I suppose he's got the look, and then he's kind of mysterious, or gives off the air of being mysterious, that's all that's necessary.

Mysterious me bollox. He's a half simpleton, says Bellwhistle.

I laugh.

Opening another can of Strongbow Bellwhistle takes a slug, sighs, then sits back on his couch. I can't smell his place anymore but when I first came here a few years back the stink was stuck in my nose for hours and not just the stink but the memory of the stink has remained. I don't know what to compare it to. Rot. Maybe that's it. Just general rot. Inorganic and organic and spiritual rot if that's a thing. The rot of a life. Well, that's what I smelt. That I can no longer smell it suddenly worries me because I remember the old man in the pub, his words, his eyes, his sad dead pickled eyes. Again, I think of Nesbit. That night. The blackout. The quarry looming like a great big open scream.

Bellwhistle starts to skin up another joint.

Do you want me to skin up for you I ask? He's all thumbs is Bellwhistle, and when he's agitated he can't function. I think he's on antidepressants. He mentioned it to me once but when I went to follow up on it a few days later he clammed up. He knows me well. I've an eye for the details, I thrive on little half words, and unfinished sentences and the way people say things, not so much what they say, but the way they says them. Fat to a maggot. He doesn't answer but hands me the magazine on which lie the wares, strewn across an almost naked Kate Moss. Tell you the truth, I've fallen in love with her, with that image on the back of the magazine. Half ghost, half woman. Just my thing. I quickly lick three large skins together, hands now rock steady. I'm going for a big one. A tomahawk. As I break open two cigarettes and gather up their innards there's a commotion from upstairs, followed by a voice:

Who's below with you Frank? Is it young Mulcahy?

Mind your own fucking business, shouts Bellwhistle.

How is he these days? I ask with some trepidation.

No change. Bastard can't be satisfied. The more you do for him the more he wants.

His old man speaks again but I can't make out the words. The sound of something banging the upstairs floor continues.

Don't worry, he'll give up after a minute or two. Probably wants me to go up and turn on the radio for him.

Maybe you should check on him, I say.

I'll get up and break that fucking walking stick off him if he doesn't stop, that's what I'll do.

The banging continues constant for about two minutes and then abruptly stops.

I get busy with the joint. After a while Bellwhistle starts up talking shite about Nesbit again.

Mark my fucking words, somethings not right, he says.

We can take a drive up there in a while and see if he's around, I say, putting the finishing touches on what's going to be a perfectly rolled joint. I don't even like the shit, but I can make the best joints this side of the Shannon. I sit back and admire its conical shape, the roach fitted perfectly at the thin end, follow the lines as it thickens outwards and reaches its maximum radius – I estimate at least two and half times bigger than the roach end – where I've closed it off in a nice neat little pig tail. I bite the tail off and spit it on the brown and hairy rug that's sat on the ground in front of the sofa. For no particular reason I've always imagined that the rug was made from a buffalo hide. On the wall behind the TV there's an old Robert Emmet portrait, one of Wolfe Tone too and the men of '98. Bellwhistle's old man used to collect antiques. He can't collect much of anything these days except dust. Behind us hangs a musket that Bellwhistle says was used in the American Civil war. I don't think his old man has been downstairs since the stroke. Lost the use of his legs. Something like that. I don't know anything about his mother, except that she died when Bellwhistle was young.

What happened at the festival Danny, says Bellwhistle turning to me suddenly.

What do you mean, I say, my eyes remaining fixed on the portrait of the men of '98.

You're fucking crazy when you drink.

What did you hear, I ask, trying my best to hide my worry. I can feel my face redden. Another thing I've always hated about myself.

Who were ye fighting?

Look, I can't remember much about it, I say.

Bellwhistle moans.

Hanley's fucked the festival for good, I say.

Yeah, yeah. Don't change the fucking subject.

Silence.

Bellwhistle sparks the joint. I skull another can.

Do you think it might be connected he asks.

What's connected? The money?

You know fucking well I'm talking about the fight and Nesbit's disappearance. I heard Squint was involved.

Squint, I say, an image of the night coming to me. I block it out. Disappearance, I laugh, you're getting carried away there now. Watching too many fucking movies Bellwhistle.

Perhaps it was them?

Who?

The knackers ye were fighting.

They weren't knackers.

Thought you said you couldn't remember.

Weren't you there too...or were you passed out in a heap as usual?

This got him to shut his mouth for a while and he retreated into himself between long audible drags of my tomahawk joint.

You've hidden traumas Mulcahy, he says after a time.

Go and fuck yourself.

No need to get hot about it. We all have them…only yours are…

I better get going, I say.

You only just got here. And you said we'd go to Nesbit's.

I got to make another drop off, I say.

Don't be bullshitting me. You can bullshit yourself all you want but don't come here bullshitting me Mulcahy.

I acted as if I hadn't heard this.

There's a Zen saying, *if you meet the Buddha on the road, kill him*

I ignore him again. This is the only way to deal with his Zen bullshit.

Look, I say, how about we meet up in Quirks tonight and take a drive to Nesbit's after.

Bellwhistle studies me with those birdy eyes of his. Blue as blue could be, but restless like they're on swivels controlled by another entity.

I don't know who's the craziest of the three of us, but you Mulcahy, have two people inside you.

You're starting to sound like an amateur psychologist, I laugh, standing up, can in hand.

Did your old man say anything about the fight, he asks.

Didn't you forget something I say nodding at the quarter on the table.

He lays the joint on the ashtray and gets up and goes to a drawer near the TV, open its. I gulp down the remains of the can, pick up another and crack it open. He's back with the money.

Tonight, in Quirks, he says.

I'll be there, eightish.

Something's not right. I can feel it. I've got a sense Mulcahy.

What are you on about?

I've a bad feeling about Nesbit.

Bad feeling – when have you had any other kind.

I've a sense. The grandmother had it too. It's in the family. The bastard upstairs has it too, he says throwing his eyes upwards.

I follow his eyes and see the ceiling as if for the first time. I've been coming here years I think and I've never looked up to see the ceiling. If I had, I'd have remember it because it's the kind of ceiling you'd never forget, the cobwebs there are deep enough to smother a man.

Though I can't recall with precision I'd say I'm the kind who's always been intoxicated by riddles, who's always followed the sound of invisible flutes, who has sought out dangerous and treacherous abysses. Yet here I am holed up in a jam jar. Marmalade actually. Days, weeks, months mean little to me. The past, the future, the present, I put them in a pot, mix them up, then piss on them. Summer in Spit is the one that hits me hardest. I love it so much, that like the leaves, I wither up and die when it ends. But the festival I do not love. If I can, I keep well away, but here I am again stuck in the middle of them.

Yes, I've taken shelter in a jam-jar – recently used as a wasp trap – on Hannigan's wall. Through the rugged slit in the lid, I crawled. I thought it might lessen the noise, but I was wrong. Missus Hannigan hates wasps, so each summer she places these traps on the high wall outside the shop. It's as good a place as any to observe I suppose. With a single jar like this she can dispose of hundreds. Some glitch in the wasp's evolutionary armour failed to evolve to cope with these jam jar traps. It's so simple it really makes a great mockery of these creatures. When the jar becomes so full of dead wasps all she has to do is open the lid, pour them down the drain, fill it up again with water and sugar and put the lid back on. I'd like to tell her that these humble insects were the first great architects, builders of the first cities, and they outdate us by hundreds of millions of years in the evolutionary time-table. But I know well what she'd say:

That's all fine and good, but they're going about the place stinging children and making a nuisance of themselves. You'd think if they were around as long as you say they are – with your evolutionary timetable – that they'd have copped on a bit and realised they should keep well away from us.

You have a point missus, I'm thinking, as familiar lines of verse fall out of the sky and into my mind.

> It is best to be, good people,
> A stutterer among you
> Since that is what you want
> You blind ignorant crew

The high poets are gone and I mourn for the worlds waning. The high poets are gone, the last of them taken refuge in a jam jar on Missus Hannigan's wall.

Individual snippets of conversations reach me in the jam jar but mostly it's mindless din and intoxicated waffle filling this fine harvest night. The moon flips and flitters a pinkish drunk. I'm unsettled by memories. Menstruation. The smell of drink, a falling glass, the sensual perfume of desire. Girls flicking their hair revealing white feathers of sinew. Blood. Blood on my hands.

Summer in Spit can be a dangerous time for goats. Somewhere

between the first and second cut of silage they come out and hunt down one of my brothers, bring him to the village where a local school-girl crowns him King Puck. He is then hoisted, in a cage, a few hundred meters in the air, and there he remains for three days, while the locals and too many visitors drink themselves into ever descending stages of intoxication. From the cage he watches them dance, vomit, prance about like prats, piss, fight, fuck, roll around in the muck like pigs gone mad. And why you might ask. Apparently, hundreds of years ago, in the time of Cromwell, a goat warned the villagers of an oncoming force of soldiers.

Each year there's a horse fair, a cattle fair, as well as all the usual festival entertainment: swings, bumpers, pillow fighting, tramming competitions, sheaf throwing competitions, donkey races, duck races, three-card tricksters, fortune tellers, candy floss, chippers, ice-cream peddlers, carpet sellers, musicians, clowns, every low-life degenerate from near and far assembles, all with the sole aim of doing each other out of money. Then, of course, for the grand finale there's the main event: the Rosin competition.

Four-hundred years ago a man was beheaded – a man I knew well – and it is in his honour, as well as the goat, the festival is celebrated. As good and wild a man as I've known. He went on the run after shooting down a landlord. Long parts of the year he gave sleeping out in the hills, the sky his curtain, his bed the heather. Indeed, I often slept beside him. A man is both moulded by his circumstances and moulds his circumstances. Eamon was such a man. In the end, love was his doom. The one he loved was called Rosin, and so we have the Rosin competition. But this doesn't make any sense, for according to one version of events she was the one who sold him out. Still, I've been around long enough to realize that sense has nothing much to do with anything.

Down at the dance earlier, place was black with people.

All Spits friends and enemies:

Bus loads from Killballycud, from Templemud, Ballyspud and JohnnyIhardlyknewyou. Droves and hordes from the bogs and hills, from Killbillyguddy and Knockamud and a lonely few from Crownamanagh. From Skinthegoat and Templebeg, out the long boreens of Knockupoldpeg, down the slopes of Foilagoul, Foilduff, Foildarrig, Foilaclug, Foiladuradera and Foilacleara. Yes, from Beattheband, Doaheadstand and Drinkanymanunderthetable, over fence and drain and winding lane, they crawled out of Craythurareyouable. From I'lldrinknomore, Gohometohell the Girlsarewillingandable. All the lads and lasses from Ballydoe, Ballypougemohoin, Lendmeabob, Loboffhisear and Dranktenpints in the morning. From Knockdonee to Tennessey, from Sitonmeknee to Driveonyourass, Dontforgetyourkey and the faithful few from Howsyourmotherforspuds.

Ah what holy hoi polloi hullabaloo, I spit. F the Jaysus lot of ye. Boils down to jealousy I suppose. Everybody else having the time of Reilly and me here sober as a stone, trapped in a marmalade jar, lapping up the detritus.

Safe to say it's been the largest festival so far. That band, the Darky Kelly's must have drawn them all, but the problem is, half of them just stood on the road outside and drank. They could listen as well from there as they could inside. Well, not the end of the world.

A crowd of roughs from Barna started some trouble trying to jump the ditch into the concert. Not my thing at all. I'm the shy type, retire into my own shoe. Madness is the name of the game now. Drunks, and savages, turning their backs on the social norms. All's fair game. Horny men, gone years without, getting the ride, lads too, getting it, that have never gotten it.

It's moving way past late and it's home I'd like to be going. Wherever my home is it's not in a wasp-trapping jam jar on Missus O'Hannigan's wall. The method of death is slow drowning. With six death traps on the go, during the height of summer she could do two-thousand of the bastards a week.

At the base of a wall, Pat Feeney is collapsed into a ball. He's pissed himself and is snoring so loudly that I'm having trouble focusing on anything else. Round the back of the pub, a drunken couple try to go at it, but it appears the man is having difficulty. The woman, not one to give up, is encouraging him with rhythmical hip movements. A few yards in front of me a young fellow is vomiting on the new sneakers his mother bought him last week. I'm about at my wits end wondering what the hell I'm doing here when I hear Danny's voice. I perk up and slap myself awake then slither out of the jar and along the wall to position myself more favourably.

Danny and Nesbit are arguing with a group of men. As I get closer, I make out the unforgettable frame of my old friend Squint. More squinted than usual, a mad look that's usurped both his eyes, he's unleashing some harsh words with Nesbit. Danny, struggling to maintain a standing position is trying to intervene, blabbering all kinds of nonsense, no good to anyone with drink in him, least of all himself. The argument and energy created has its own momentum and quickly drags them through the thronged village centre, past Hannigan's. As it moves others get sucked in, and I too take up position and follow along behind them, through feet, spilled beer, piss, horseshit, cowshit and whathaveyounot.

It's at the gates of the graveyard they stall to a halt. Among them now Rosie Delahunty, accompanied by Mary Cleary, whose brother Frank has now joined the fracas on Squint's side. The shouting escalates. A scattering of onlookers groups together to watch the proceedings.

Squint breaks free from his sister's grasp and drops Nesbit with a punch. Danny swings for Squint but misses. Squint's friend Cleary starts laying a few kicks into Nesbit who's trying to stand up again. I'm having difficulty keeping up with it.

Both Rosie and Mary Cleary are running round screaming and trying to drag them off each other.

Squint and Danny are at it now. Trading punches. Danny goes down. Squint is on him throwing punches quickly. Nesbit meets Squint with a kick. Danny's up again, swinging wildly with both fists he connects with Frank Cleary who stumbles backwards out onto the road. Danny's after him and connects with another punch, this time dropping him. But Squint comes from behind and tackles him to the ground. Back and forth it goes like some ape dance ritual. Nesbit has gone into berserk mode. Foaming at the mouth. But tell you the truth I've seen better scraps in the playground with children fighting over a lollipop. Still, somebody could really get hurt. I was in Hannigan's the night Philly Martin met his end. One Punch. Martin hit the ground. Three weeks he gave dying inside in the county home hooked up to a machine. What I wouldn't give to be hooked up to a machine.

I'm thinking things couldn't really get any worse when the considerable bulk of Pa Quinn arrives, accompanied by Tony Henderson. I assume Quinn's here for Squint, likely to finish off some earlier altercation. But, surprisingly, rather than entering the fray Quinn and his friend quickly break it up, by pulling Danny and Nesbit away from Squint. Cleary remains on the ground moaning.

Get him out of here before he gets killed, Quinn says to Rosie. He's a lucky man I don't finish off what he started earlier, but I'm not one to go beat up a drunk. Get him out of here quick. And the rest of ye fuck off back to the festival.

Pa Quinns a man people listen to.

Rosie and Mary Cleary don't waste any time. They grab Squint by his arms and succeed in averting his attention and he starts walking away with them.

Come on you eejit, Mary Cleary, says pulling her moaning brother to his feet.

Pa Quinn succeeds in calming Nesbit down. Out of his white shirt pocket he takes a packet of Majors and hands one to Nesbit.

That Squint cunt is fucking mental, says Nesbit, slurring his words.

My kingdom for a drink, Danny mumbles in the background.

Squints drunk. He doesn't know what he's doing or saying, replies Quinn.

Why are you standing up for him, I thought the Quinns and the Delahuntys hated each other, says Nesbit.

It's you he hates now. Was looking for you earlier too. What did you do to him?

Hardly ever spoken to him in my life. Fucking Psycho.

Is he ok, asks Quinn, nodding to where Danny is lying.

Just drink, I 'd say.

Get him up then.

On the ground Danny moans and curses.

I look skywards. The day I've had. When I'm with people it's solitude I crave, and when I'm alone it's company I crave. Suppose I'm not easy. Ah well. After a while they gather themselves together, limp back towards the village, Danny's up now, in fine fettle, blood dripping from his nose, singing:

She went down to the chemist shop some remedies for to buy
Have you anything in your chemist shop to make me old man blind
Give me eggs and marrowbone and make him suck them all
Before he has the last one sucked he wont see you at all
With me finnickineerio, me tip finnick a wall
With me right finnickineeroio, we're tipping it up to Nancy O

Quinn, on more than one occasion tells him to keep the out-of-key racket down.

Wasting your time, says Nesbit, he'll listen to nobody when he's drink down.

He'll listen to the butt end of my fist, says Quinn.

Within minutes they're lost in the crowd.

*

You'll most often find me with children or goats. As you know they're not much different. Goats have better manners though, and at times they smell better. But children aren't bad. They are just misunderstood. I've a fondness for the games they play.

After the festival the King Puck is released back into the pack to live his life again as a normal goat. But here's the thing, they can't. Each year I see it. Each year the others in the pack begin to act weird around them. The chosen one has been altered. A king for four days and now he's just another fucking eejit goat. The results are often tragic. They end up becoming separated from the pack, let themselves go, over time go mad, wander aimless, until they succumb to one illness or another and are then picked off by foxes or stray dogs. You mightn't think it, but for a goat there's nothing worse than loneliness. Of course, those in the village have no knowledge of this. How could they.

As well as all that I sometimes sleep on the back of Herons, they have lovely feathers, and grand slender comfortable backs, and besides, they make less noise than a mouse and are all together agreeable hosts. Sleep – yes I can, and lots of it. The only thing that bothers me about it is that I have to wake up. Dream? Well, that's complicated. I do, but they're not my own, I mean I have my own, but I'm often taken into others dreams and that's where I really get to know them. Just the other day I was with Danny hitchhiking the old roads. I do relish these trips. It's only in my dreams I can leave Spit.

These days I report almost everything that happens, yes, write I my accounts on the wet grasses, or on the twirling of the leaves in summer, or I scribble them on the still bits of streams, or in the dirt and muck of the farmer's fields in winter, or on the mane of a horse. Requirement of the job. Who reads them I don't know; all I know is that I have to write them. But it's more than that. The writing comes easy to me and brings me peace. Increasingly, snippets of verse crumble and fall from god-knows-where, land complete in my head.

Each day now there are memories, flashes of what I was before, like I'm trying to get at the taste of something I once ate. Doomed to roam day and night, tied up in the winds, the mists and the rains. I was something grand. Yes, I used my hands, wrote noble words. There was a transgression. A betrayal of sorts. An indelible violence. I have my own journey. Perhaps in the end everything is really about me – my own private universe – and that I'm being led to my own redemption. Who knows? What can I do now but the next right thing.

The thin dawn light bleeds over the black east. Despite being exhausted and craving nothing but a nice bed on the heather, I pick up a stone and force myself to write of the fight I witnessed.

Force myself, not just because I'm lazy, but because I've seen in the past that it's often the little unimportant events, which over a stretch of time, become pivotal to the order of other larger events. Of course, I have questions. Was it her they were fighting over? Is she seeing both of them? Neither of them? One of them? Which one? Is Nesbit ok? Wasn't it all just some silly little drunken fight by some silly little kids in some silly little village? As I scribble the words on a flat piece of limestone at the bottom of Heffernan's quarry, I have little insight into the terrible events that are on the way.

*

A pale fog curtains the morning. An icy breeze struts between the shed walls. Out of nowhere I remember a similar breeze on my cheek, many many years past. It was morning when we walked together in the long dew-wet grass. I sigh. A hundred years is but a day's breath. Will I ever be free of this. Hope can be a bellyful.

Footsteps. This windswept concrete shell of a shed could amplify a falling blackberry. The cattle's ears twitch. What brings them indoors this time of year. Testing. Dosing. Or worse? Aren't they the most curiously dull of animals. Born to be eaten and abused. There was a time when great wars were fought over them, but that was long ago.

The door opens, shafts of light cracking into the dark. In she drifts, each stride pronounces a rare dignity. A queen without her palace, her kingdoms cut out in men's hearts. She wears a dress; white, long and lose, a dress too light for this cold morning, if she shivers, she shows it not.

The cows cannot keep their eyes from her. Nor I. She walks with purpose but for a moment she stops as if to ask herself why she has come. The cattle wait before her. I wait above her. She watches the white of her breath, walks back and forth along the gate looking at the cattle. She reaches out her hand to one, but it jerks back. A brave one edges forward sniffing the air with his black wet nostrils. Little does he know it but today is to be his last.

Good boy, she says. My brave boy. But we can hardly call you a boy can we. Six months ago, I heard your nuts being crushed. I heard too the low desperate moan that followed. You know, in all my life, poor beast, this is the saddest sound I have ever heard. Even the squealing of the pigs as they get butchered is nothing to it. I came in here to talk to you because I had to get out of there, because I don't want to talk to them, because you are a silly beast who understands nothing, and I like silly things. Do you know how much I prefer them to smart things? Silly things I understand. In their ignorance I can lay my head; like it's a fine soft pillow. I wish we could all be a little less smart, especially men, who think they're smarter than they are; in other words, most men.

Pushing off each other now to get a sniff of her hand, the cattle are panting and huffing, as if the words coming from her mouth can offer them eternal grass.

Why does nobody do what they want to do and just be honest about it. You cows are different. I'm like you, I tell you the truth. I act as I will. Look.

All of a sudden – and this takes me by surprise and I'm not one to be surprised – she hikes up her dress, squats down, and starts peeing on the concrete ground.

I fall off my perch on the high rafter.

She sighs. Around her, trickles of white steam float upwards.

There she is, pissing away with not a care in the world. A puddle spreads out over the concrete and makes its way slowly into a small drain which runs along the gate keeping the twenty or so cattle confined. She sighs again, loudly this time. Standing up, dress falling to her knees I notice her lovely calves. Calves to drive men out of their minds.

She then takes to dancing. Round and round, with some grace I might add, her hands waving to some music none can hear but herself, talking all the while to the cows who look on bemused:

Silly eejits. Today ye're all going to the factory. And ye know what that means don't ye? You know, I've a mind to become a vegetarian. I really do. I'm tired of all this suffering. How was I born on a farm? I'm about as suited to a farm as...

She stops.

Footsteps. I hear them; the cattle hear them.

She moves closer to the rail, lays her hands on it. The door opens startling the cattle back a few steps. She does not turn around.

Squint closes the door and stands there looking at her. He stands there for what seems like a long time. She does not turn around, but leans against the rail humming a melody that sounds imported. Her posture, from where I'm now lying, can only be described as suggestive.

What do you want, she says suddenly without turning round. She is leaning with her hips back, her posterior extended.

Squint says nothing. He wears a pained expression on his face, rather like the last time I saw him.

Cat got your tongue, she says, as she twirls round to face him.

He takes a step forward.

Look, she says, turning round, the measure of her voice darkening: Do you remember what happened below in the festival?

I can hear him breathing from here, his face muscles starting to get a life of their own. I imagine his throat drying. The poor bastard, I think, almost feeling sorry for him.

What would Daddy say if he found out you were drunk as an eejit?

His fists tighten to balls.

I knew you'd follow me out here. That's why I came.

She walks towards him. She walks not with her legs but with her sex, this thing between her legs, the epicentre of her being. A rare bird indeed I'm thinking. He does not move. His balled fists. His rage-broken tongue. For a moment I think he might kill her, there and then, right in front of me, and what could I do but witness it? What can I ever do?

Leave him alone, do you hear me?

Squint smiles. His fists uncurls.

You can't even remember can you. The state you were in. Her voice wobbles and she begins to cry. I love him, she says so quietly I barely hear it.

Squint laughs, a gurgling in his throat.

Composure regained, she wipes the tears from her eyes.

I want you to be clear now, that this thing is over, that it was all in your head, and that you have to move on from your fantasies. Do you understand? Now, move out of my way and let me back into the house.

She walks by him, separated by mere inches, pausing as she passes him, so that he can smell that which of he once tasted, that which, with every cell of his body he longs to taste again. She's almost at the door when he turns and grabs her from behind. She screams. He unhands her and steps back. Outside a commotion from the house.

She turns around to face him and in a low calm voice says:

Don't touch me again or I'll tell them about your midnight ramblings.

They stare at each other.

Is it only animals you can bully, she says smirking.

What in the mother of god is after happening, asks a voice from outside.

A few seconds later the door opens.

Nothing mother. Michael's acting like an eejit again, gave me a fright is all.

For the love of god, you'll get your death in that slip of a thing. Go in and put on something decent. And Michael, you should be out in the top meadow helping your father by now. He won't be too happy if he hears you're in here fooling round. Go on now.

For a moment it looks like he's going to say something but his eyes fall to the ground. Face knotted he walks out the door. His mother calls after him but he does not look back.

What's gotten into him lately? Isn't he acting awful strange. Did you notice anything?

Well, he might be in love, says Rosie smiling.

In love? With whom? Not that it would be a bad thing.

I don't know.

Well, wouldn't it be about time he made a move in that department. Come on, we've work to do inside. That boys got a bee in his bonnet. He's not eating right nor sleeping right and the weight is falling off him. Can't you see it?

Yes, mother.

Up in the nights pacing around the place. I'll have to have a word with him.

Leave him be. He will figure it out. You know the way he is.

Indeed, I do; thick or thicker than his father and that's fair thick.

I need to go feed my little ones.

Jesus Mary and Joseph, haven't I told you already we can't keep taking in strays? This is a farm not a zoo.

They come to me mother.

Don't take in any more. He won't stand for it. Keep them well out of his way and don't let him see you taking food to them.

Don't worry I'm good at hiding things.

That you are Rosie...that you are. You know you can be too kind. In this world things come and go, nothing lives forever, the strong must survive and the weak must die. That's just the way it is, and you have to trust that god made it this way, that all things have a reasons behind them. Now, we may not understand the reason, but that doesn't mean there isn't a reason. No. It's just because we are too small to see the reason of it.

I'm going vegan.

You can leave this house if you turn into one of them.

We shouldn't talk like this in front of the cattle, says Rosie, a small smile playing at the edges of her mouth.

As if they can understand, says her mother, rolling her eyes.

Isn't today their day?

Go on now, and feed your little beggars, but come back to me as soon as it's done.

Of course, says Rosie waving her hands, in a way that can only be described as musical.

*

I give the rest of the morning on Rosalyn Delahunty's trail and follow along as she does the rounds, tending to her zoo – as her mother calls it – but hospital would be more precise, or animal retirement home.

There's a small dog, awful looking thing, blind in the left eye, lame on the right hind leg. Might be a cross between a terrier and some breed of sheepdog. It's a cross that should not be repeated.

Terry, she calls him.

Silly little Terry. You must be the ugliest dog in all of Ireland. But you know something Terry, I'll love you, and my love is all you need, you little cute beast you.

She bends over the pallet, pets him on the head. Standing on his hind legs, he receives her attention with much pleasure. In an old barn, filled with round bales of straw, there's a mother cat, her kittens housed between two bales, their location hidden by a sheet of galvanize.

Hush Hush, she says, we must keep you quiet. If father hears from you, you'll end up in the river.

Her voice has a hold over me, a song I once knew, a faint and distant echo.

From the large linen bag she carries, she produces a bottle of milk. She takes to feeding the kittens talking to each one as she does, to each one she gives a name. She talks of silly things mostly, childish blather.

In another out-house there's a rabbit in a cage with a mangled leg. Out from her bag comes lettuce and carrots.

Just when I think she's done she makes for the old house which lies a few hundred yards west from the farmyard. The sky is low and blue and the day has a pure clean glint to its smile. There are days like this in Spit. There was a time I roamed the world as free. I enter behind her. A cool breeze sweeps in the broken windows yet the air inside is thick with dust, mould and decay. Hitting her foot off an old washing board discarded on the ground she stomps on it playfully and curses. She tip toes towards the old staircase which is in a bad state; many of the steps are missing and the remaining ones are riddled with worm holes. Upwards into the darkness she looks for what seems a long time. Out of nowhere the secrets that were once here come to me. You see every house has them, and I've known so many that they all get tangled up in there in the back of my liquid mind. Yes, there was that uncle who came home from America. Back then people were less aware, less cautious. If there are walls, and cement and rooms, there are secrets within them. There is always a world which remains hidden and maybe it should remain that way. It is better, good people, to pass by the doors you do not know what lies behind.

Directly across from us a large black marble fireplace, overhead which hangs a grand mirror, that has warped under the weight of years. Turning around and seeing herself in it she does a little dance, then genuflects. Her great grand-parents built this house. Her reflection is hazy and unclear. Without warning, she laughs. Whistles again that little melody. She moves now, bag in hand, making her way carefully over discarded pieces of wood and broken glass towards the room's exit.

I was here the night her grandmother died.

I do not remember my own grandmother.

Exiting the room she walks along a small corridor. Before us a closed door. She stops and takes to whistling again.

From within the room: birdsong, scratching sounds, rustling. Sunlight and shadow. The days breath on my back. The old door creaks, scrapes off the dusty concrete floor making an unpleasant sound but what really hits me is the smell; something that was once alive. I never mistake it.

Most of the small room is occupied by a large table on top of which are three rusty cages of different shapes and sizes.

My pretties, she says, oh how you've missed me. Mummy has come to see you.

She closes the door behind her.

Wooden shutters cover the window. Light streams in thick fat rays illuminating the room unevenly. On the wall a fading picture; a well-attired man holding a well-bred horse, his fist gripping the bridle close to the horse's jaw. I do not know this picture nor this man nor can I recall having seen this picture before.

My eyes return to the cages on the table. Each cage as far as I can tell contains a bird.

My little baby. Hopping along to see me. Mummy has a treat for you.

From her bag she takes out a jar full of fat pink earthworms. Leaving the jar on the table, she opens the lid, picks out at worm and dangles it in front of the first cage. Inside a blue tit jumps excitedly. She unhasps the little door, then holds the worm so that the blue tit can get at it. Within seconds he's devoured it.

Hungry little baby. Will you have another? Sure you will.

She feeds him another one.

You greedy little monkey.

Along the wall I slither to get a better look at the second cage; a robin – a half-starved looking thing. When done with the first cage she passes by the robin and moves on to the final cage which contains a willy wagtail. As she's feeding it in the same manner as the blue tit my eyes are drawn to the large metal fireplace under the picture, on top of which is a plain wooden box, with simple engravings, perhaps, a container for jewellery. As she feeds the wagtail she talks about her life, nonsense really, she mentions her stupid brother. She asks the wagtail of its news, even waits to hear it tweet and twirp, between mouthfuls of pink worms, then remarks with precise details as if she's understood. Curiously, the robin is ignored.

Despite this more than unusual charade before me, my eyes keep returning to the wooden box on top of the fireplace. All the while the smell permeates. It is not often I get uncomfortable. If

I had my way, I'd be out the door like a rat but, as well you know, I'm useless in determining my own future, and for the moment, I'm bound to her like the dirt beneath her shoes.

When she finally finishes her jibber jabbering and turns to face the fire place I'm hit with a wave of panic. She picks up the box then leaves it down again. My relief is short lived. Fiddling with the silver chains round her neck she untangles one from the other then pulls one over her head. A small key dangles at the end of the chain. She moves towards the box. But just as she about to insert the key, she is like me, startled by the sound of a cry from outside. The distant voice rings out again:

Rosie, where are you? Rosie.

She pauses for a few seconds, as if considering something, then places the neckless back over her head, sucking her teeth as she does so.

*

The sloes are not yet ripe on the blackthorn. This year they are abundant, a sign of a bad winter. As I look at them a memory comes to me. As a boy – and a habit I continued for the rest of my living days – I'd suck on one every now and again. Never much liked them but I ate them precisely because of that, to remind myself. The bitter taste made me feel alive.

This heart of mine is black as sloe, coal burnt in a forge, the print of a shoe on a white wall. A black mood is above my laughter.

In the near distance the dull ache of a saw cutting through wood. Down the easy slope of Wilsons meadow I come, skipping with the waves, trying to keep from the cold wind that snaps at my back. Before me now the hollow they call Corbett's Pond, the water only comes in wintertime, and then only for a week or two. In front of me a thick ditch through which I breeze. I whisp the hairs of a lone mare – Betty they call her – who mows the grass from Wilson's little paddock. The mare twitches her ears in protest to the noise of the saw or is it me and my passing she objects to?

Behind Danny and his father, a tangle of ash, beech, and sycamore limbs. The saw hums idly, Danny is wrestling with a thick long limb of ash, struggling to pull it from the twisted pile. The Serge – I've a thing for giving people nicknames, its's more real and accurate don't you think – looks on, the saw laid at his feet coughing rhythmically. The ash log is long and twisted and Danny struggles as he anchors it on the large beech pine stump around which sits a large bell-shaped pile of sawdust. Danny rocks the log back and forth adjusting the length that is presented to his father at the other end of the holding stump. The Serge picks up the saw and with a touch of his finger sends the engine into a moan. Danny holds the log firm with both hands from his end. Moving round the other side of the Serge I notice Danny's blackened right eye.

Three magpies alight from the cover of a sycamore tree. The blade eats into the wood, digesting and spitting out showers of perfect shaves. There is beauty in all things I think then, if one looks for it, if one looks hard enough. He cuts two blocks before Danny moves the log forward another two feet and the process is repeated until they come to the last section. No words are spoken, no eyes are met. Yet, I observe each of them move with perfect knowledge of the other. Two bees on the hunt for honey, two magpies picking for worms. These practiced movements, the dance of work. The saw hums, the intensity changing from cut to cut.

Between them mere inches, I see the veins on Danny's neck bulge, the one down his tightened forehead bulges too. Winter will not be long now. Turf and wood and long nights. Danny turns the wood around to avoid a knot. Blade and fingers. Arteries. Butter and a hot knife. Fathers and their sons.

A memory returns. Limerick in the time of Sarsfield. I saw a man hanged drawn and quartered. They say it takes but two minutes for a man to bleed out, if cut in the right place. Skilled in their arts they kept that man alive for two hours. At this memory I gasp, or would gasp if I could breathe. Around us the vast fading blue of evening. The sloes heavy in the ditches. This heart of mine.

It's cold but beads of sweat run down the back of Danny's neck. The Serge revs the blade. Between them inches, each inch an infinity. Danny angles a difficult beach limb, holding it sideways so that it comes out straight the other side of the cutting stump. After each cut he angles back to a normal position. Coming down to the last section Danny seeing a knot turns the log quickly. The Serge mumbles, the words eaten up by the saw. A long lineage, a father's father's father. Those born in Spit I know. I never knew my own.

Down to the last cut, Danny watches hands and blade. Half way through the log the engine changes tone. Milliseconds later the saw hops, jerking the log from Danny's hands. Luckily, the blade remains jammed in the log and the Serge is able to control it.

Their eyes meet.

What is not said could fill the vast manuscript of the evening sky. Behind them a car whizzes by. The old neon sign from the pub at the crossroads begins to flicker. Despite the odds entirely against them they collaborate once more finishing off the log. The sound of the saw dies. A clutter of crows croak in the ditch that separates them from the road. The Serge lights up a cigarette. Danny locates the axe, then places a knotty beach log on the cutting stump. Swinging the axe high he buries it deep in the wood. The dull thud cuts through the evening calling all things living to attention. Danny grinds his teeth and stretches his muscles to pull out the sunken axe. It takes another three strokes before he splits the beech log in half.

The Serge stubs out his cigarette and picks up his saw and walks towards the gap at the low end of the wall that leads to the lawn at the front of the barracks. Danny and I remain.

Log after log, swing after swing, groan after groan, Danny works like there's something chasing him. He works like death himself is his master. I can't help but feel that I was once like him.

The darkness of evening drifts in quicker than you'd expect. Covered in sweat; split wood piles around him, Danny buries the axe in the beech cutting stump then lights up a cigarette himself. Same brand as the Serge. As he sits on a beach block and smokes I talk to him telling him my little stories, my little philosophies, giving him bits and pieces of advice. But he pays me as much mind as he does the breathing of his own lungs.

*

Idling away the time, scribbling a few letters on the fresh grass that comes up after the second cut of silage. Mother, of late, I remember. Black hair. Smell of peaches. Music in the courtyard. The Kings chambers. I was once great, wasn't I? Bard. Voice of the people. Highborn. Talent in my veins. Did I waste it all mother? Will I be remembered? Was Achilles right to choose fame and death over happiness? Mother, I am your son. What has become of me?

I'm about to scribble another when a sudden turning of the wind brings me to the top of Heffernan's hill. A fresh shower of rain is falling and in the distance two fine fat rainbows arch themselves over Nesbit's hill. Upset that I've been disturbed in the middle of my writing process I walk around cursing like a cut cat.

I'm pissed with the rain. I can handle it, don't get wrong, but it wasn't raining in Michael Dunn's meadow, the place – not two kilometres from here – where I was engaged in my work. It's the random unpredictability of it that drives me wrong. It's hard to keep dry in this country. Still, half the world is wanting of rain I suppose. I'm pacing round trying to find the reason for my being here – for there's a reason to all of it.

My attention is drawn to a bunch of cattle huddled round a bare wind-whipped hawthorn tree near the top of the quarry, about the only thing capable of surviving up here. The goats are nowhere to be seen, likely scattered by the cattle. As I get closer, the cattle sensing me soon disperse towards the top of the hill. Stupid and all as the bastards are they've better senses than those of men.

Five yards from the quarry's edge I smell blood. Yes, I can smell better than a fox, see better than an owl, and hear just about as good as a bat. Whatever is dead has been dead a while. I stop for a moment not wanting to go forward. I look around me, behind me, checking the run of the place. Did I feel a pair of eyes on me? Did something stir in the ether? Did the pot and the kettle have it out black? The wind soughs in the hawthorn tree. I gather myself then edge forward step by step towards the fall. Peering over the edge I see the outline of a body.

DANNY
MULCAHY

The red blood seeps down my fucking face. I can't get up. I look up at the grand grey clock in the grand grey church in the grand grey fucking sky. Nine-thirty. Morning. A three days drunk dribbling to its end. At first light they kicked me out of the station. They do that. Shift change perhaps or just some perverse cruelty. Think they'd let you have a sleep in. Before they lock you in, they take your shoelaces and belt. First time, it took me a while to figure that out. Slept on a horrible stained green sponge with no blankets nor pillow. In fairness, I've slept on worse. Reading scripture on the wall as they woke me up with rapping on the steel door:

> Tony Ryan's a rat
> Piggy Phelan slept here
> Rachel Murphy's a SLUT
> Up the Provos

Not sure what I did, but couldn't have done too much because they didn't charge me. Glass still stuck in the knuckles of my hands. A big black hole where my memory should be. Another pocket of brain cells wiped out. I wipe my face with my sleeve. The blood flowing from a cut on my forehead seems to have stopped.

I really can't move. Again, I try, but I can't stand up. Is this to be the end? Death on the morning footpath. But not before I've a smoke. Pockets empty. I think I've pissed myself. Yes, I have. Scan the footpath for a few butts. Cars pass by. It's slightly raining. Put a percentage on it and you'd say twenty. I drag myself up against the wall, lever myself into a sitting position. Few souls gather at a bus stop to my left. Nothing much to my right. I don't even know where I am, nothing looks familiar to me, except I can see the cathedral in the distance. St. Johns. The Evangelist or the Baptist? I'm not sure. Hope it's the Baptist. Gave his days naked in the desert. Survived on water and wild honey. Take my hat off to him, he'd know suffering, know what I'm going through. Self-inflicted yes, but still suffering. Wild man. The greatest of the prophets. Related to Jesus on the mother's side. Didn't end well for him though did it. Won't end well for most of us. Might as well fling a few prayers at him and see what happens. What have I to lose.

Might as well put my hand out too because I'm going to need lubrication. John the Baptist see to it that I get myself a drink, I mumble, otherwise I'm going to perish in this desert. Dizzy spells come and go. To my right I spot a few butts discarded on the footpath. One of them half decent. I'm no stranger to any of this. You understand there's a part of me that wants me here. Up, I try to stand, but once again I can't. It's like my legs have stopped working. Some kind of alcohol poisoning maybe. Or a stroke.

Yes, that might be it. I've had a stroke. Up against this wall like a dog, I'll die. So be it.

How'd I end up here you wonder. Well, simple enough. One drink and it's spin the wheel for me. Could wake up anywhere. Footpath. Drunk-tank. Hospital. In another city. With someone pretty. With someone not so pretty. Blackout lottery. Gambling with my bones.

The morning after cutting the timber with the aul lad I woke up with an itch. You see I get these itches and there's nothing that can be done about them. The drunk dies from drink. Simple enough equation. Had a few bob gathered up. Went out on the road stuck my thumb out – early morning your best bet if you going from Spit to the city – got lucky, and was down in an hour and a half flat.

Ask me when am I happiest? You might think I'd say it's when I'm drunk. But not so. I'm happiest when I know I'm going to be drunk soon. This whisp of anticipation. The flutter of the heart. Walking into the pub that morning for the first was the peak of the last three days. One would think I'd know the outcome by now. Keep hitting your head with a hammer and expect something to change. One drink is all it takes. One thing leads to another and here I am beaten to a pulp with neither sense nor direction left in me.

A stick-thin old lady stops and asks me am I ok. She wants to call an ambulance but I convince her I'll be ok if I can get a bottle of water and a pack of fags. She comes back five minutes later with my requirements. I thank her, promising her that I will go home as soon as I'm able.

She chews on her sunken cheeks, adding even more wrinkles to her forehead.

I've a son somewhere in England. Haven't heard from him for

a decade, she says. Her voice wavering.

I nod, trying to think of something to say, but say nothing.

Where do you live, she asks after a silence, during which I study the hell of her face.

I'll need to get the bus. I live out near the uni.

A fine walk.

I'm unable to stand.

Then I really should call the ambulance. The state of you. Your poor mother, she whispers.

For a moment I do think of her.

No ambulance. Give me two pounds missus and your address and I'll come back with it tomorrow. No later.

She laughs.

Chancer. Here, she says taking a blue small purse form her cardigan. The purse must have been bought in Knock, because it's got Knock written on it. She counts out the money, all in fifties and tens. Two pounds, she says.

Thank you, Missus?

Quirk.

I'll never forget your kindness, I say.

I'll say a few hail Mary's for you later she says nodding to the Cathedral. Every day I go there about this time and pray for him. Pray that he's ok, and that if he's not then at least we get some news.

Thank you, I say.

God looks out for drunks and fools.

I'm both, I say, managing a half-smile.

She looks at me curiously for a while, then in her thin hoarse voice says, you need to get the cut on your head looked at.

It's just a scratch. I was grand a few hours ago, must have tripped and cut it on the bushes over there I say, for that's where

I woke up.

God bless you, she says, turning to leave.

The Cathedral, I say, is it named after St John the Baptist or the other fellow?

The Baptist, she says. Did you know there are six Bishops buried within the walls?

No, I say.

In the distance I watch her trickle away to nothingness. I'm glad she came, and I'm glad too she's gone. Just me and the Baptist now. Slowly, I drink the bottle of water and smoke a fag. The rains upped it to forty percent now. I look up at the grand grey church in the grand grey fucking sky and see the hands pointing near eleven.

An hour later, I manage to get up, and start walking.

Four hours later, after frequent stops, once or twice actually falling from dizziness, I reach Paddy Kean's gaff, where I'm unofficially living. Paddy nor nobody else is around, thank God. I'm so sick I really think I'm going to die. I can't even keep water down. Head stuck in the jacks, retching, retching, empty retching. I pray that I can hang on and make all the usual promises, that this will be the last, that I'm going to stop, that I'm going to go down to that place where people go to stop.

Sometime that night I crawl out of the worst of it. I know I'm going to be ok when I start to feel a little hungry. I manage to make some soup. My hands shake so much I can barely hold the spoon. Looking down into the minestrone soup bowl, the silhouette of my head, my long hair hanging down over both-sides of my face. It looks to me like it would make an album cover someday. Very grunge. Generation X. Lord, I say, make me famous and I'll be ok.

Now that I'm well enough thoughts soon turn to drink again.

A few cans to ease off the suffering of a long sleepless night. As always, the demons will come out of the darkness. When I close my eyes, they are there. Hard to explain. Hard to keep them away. Nights like these I have to leave the lights on. Slight dose of delirium tremors.

Nesbit. The festival. My life. My father. What's wrong with me. Up and about searching high and low for some money. Hands down the back of the sofa. Cushions off. All I need is enough to buy something in the shop, the rest I can lift. I'm good at the lifting, though in a state like this my skills decrease.

Either way, nothing for it but to go home tomorrow. Back to Spit with my tail between my legs. Beaten and broken once more. Well, they'll take one look at me and know where I've been. I've been to hell and back mother. Got to keep moving. Stick my thumb out. The restless pursuit. No one knows me and I know no one.

The body is face down, the right arm outstretched, the left hidden, tangled beneath. I don't have to see the face to know who it is. He comes to me in a flash.

Face down.

Frank Liam Nesbit, last of his line. Not really his line, as it's well-known he was adopted. Spits only adoptee, and god did they let him know about it. Old and young, friend and foe knew that he was stained; and all in their own way made sure he didn't forget it. Anyway, maybe that's all beside the point, here he is, dead, face down at the bottom of a sixty-foot quarry. I'll comfort him. Comfort what. The dead are dead. There's not much I haven't seen.

The living, the dead and the dying.

And all of them I envy. At least they can die, while I crawl on, the years rolling off me like a misty shower of a spring evening.

Reminding myself that now is not the time for self-pity I focus in on the work before me. I close my eyes, unleash myself into the wind and within seconds I'm on top of him. The first thing I do is kiss the back of his bloody head.

Good man Nesbit. I liked you, I say. Here you are now having a good old rest.

I follow his right-arm, extended out before him, his hand flat and open, fingers extended to their maximum like he's reaching out to grasp onto something. There's always that from what I've seen: never wanting to let go. As a rule, the living don't want to be the dead.

Or perhaps he's of that small percentage who by their own hand chose to go. Somehow, he doesn't seem the type. And yet, they say you never can tell. It's often the ones you least expect. I'll hang round till someone comes. Little good it will do him, because when the rats come back, I can't even stop them. Most of the time I question why I even exist. What the hell use am I to anybody. Still, I'll pine away to this dead pile of flesh that was once young Nesbit and keep him company until he's found.

I once waited two weeks for a man named Martin Quinlan. Such a wait rarely happens in a place like Spit because everybody's so close; fart wrong here and somebody will notice it. But with Quinlan he lived up the side of a mountain towards the end of the parish bordering Knockaglock. And in truth he was a nasty piece of work and didn't like anybody and nobody much liked him except his poor dog who didn't have much choice in the matter. Still Quinlan had his reasons for the way he was. I knew of them. Others didn't. There is no bad without the good, or good without the bad. I suppose that's my advantage. I do be seeing the things others can't be seeing, hawking glimpses into the inner mechanisms, playing with the ball bearings of individual universes. For as Radio Molloy once put it so well, are we not all our own little universes moving about the place with the divine interpretation that our Universe is the only one that matters.

What can I do now but the next right thing. Young Nesbit dead beneath me. Jumped? Pushed? Dumped? How do I know. There hasn't been a murder here since Ned Ryan, who one evening after milking the cows, took a sudden turn of madness and strangled his wife. That was sixty-five years ago if you believe in such measurements. Back then, hanging was all the go; time ended for poor Ned at the end of a rope. About the only time Spit was in the news.

Adjusting myself, I spread out my form to cover his completely. I reach out my paw and trace it exactly over his, our hands separated by thin films of air and mucus. I vomit up another bucket of my stuff and pour it over him. Mucus. This liquid me. The stuff that's neither land nor water. Touching. I'll be here all night at least. Could be longer. Could be days. Hand touching hand, my form over his, I will wait. It's in the touching I can travel back into their existence. Pregnant women, babies, the dead, the sick, the mad, children on the verge of puberty, these are the best vessels. This is well known.

Nesbit let me into you, I whisper. Let me see what we can find out.

Ah there we are now. You're twelve years old, sitting on the brown couch in the living room. The auld lad is roaring and the mother is in the room sobbing. They don't fight often but when they do they got at it awful hard.

You exist of course but really most of the time you don't exist, like you're just some shadow watching things happen to you. At meal times or when you're missing, those are the times you exist most. Not really missing, but when you go hide in the hills and forests you give hours there until they track you down, or until you get so hungry you just come home. Being alone. Only child.

Not only that but adopted. They haven't told you yet, but you know. Everybody knows.

You yourself are dark while your mother is ginger. Your father is of Norse stock with fairish hair. Your old-man. A head-the-ball. It's well known round here he's a man that can't be reasoned with, one of them that knows it all. You know nothing of him, of his youth, of what makes him tick. He is a man without interest in much, a being that crawls along the days without humour or passion, except once a month he goes to Slattery's in the afternoon and doesn't come back till early morning, well cut, cursing and swearing all things under the sun. Oh, the things he does be saying are the very things that you don't want to hear: the darkest things you can barely bear to imagine in the darkest corners of your little mind. But here they come young Nesbit, lying there in your bed, hearing him through the walls, the whole countryside silent except for the odd owl and the squeaking of a bat if you had ears that could hear bats. Did you ever hear the sun weep? It weeps blood orange tears. Did you ever hear the moon of a still night young Nesbit? A mirror into which you fall, a lake for the pure of heart.

For three days after his drunken violations, he hardly speaks a word. The weight of the air in the house is enough to drive you to the woods. And mother, dear mother, doesn't speak either and all that can be heard at dinner is the slobbing of gobs, the peeling of potatoes, a few sideways sighs and moans. The food in front of you like its own form of punishment. Each time your old man swears off it, but come the end of the month he'll do the same thing. There is no deviation. Relentless. Water dripping will wear away stone, will furrow into your bone, will leave you destitute and alone Nesbit. A boy without love is a man without joy. You know the world is as the world is and it's nobody's fault...and yet. Yet you know there are degrees of fault, degrees of guilt, that some are more responsible, and that you poor boy, because of your age and lack of experiences surely cannot be the one to blame, and yet you do, you do blame yourself. In ways you were a smart boy, weren't you Nesbit, an old soul born into a boy's body. By yourself you've figured out where you came out of and it wasn't them. We've that in common young Nesbit.

What man does not wish, not only for the death of his father but the death of both parents, Nesbit? In the darkness of your room, in the empty bottle of your heart, in the pit of your dreams. How many times did you wish them dead? Yes, in a way it was you who killed them. I know, I know – they died naturally. But who wished for it. Wasn't it you who got what you asked for, Nesbit? Granted it on a plate you couldn't handle it. And thus you took a leap? Did you forget Nesbit that all things are linked. A single thought may turn things arseways, turn molehills into mountains, turn rabbits into rabid rats, turn your parents into dirt. Since they've been gone you've come to realize that you were part of the game, a figure in the equation. We all have our part, Nesbit. There're none that can escape it. You thought you'd be free of it all if only they went away – only when they were gone you were ten times worse off with the way your head was, tapping at you all the time, like that drip of water. I'd know well about torments. No better man. At least that stuff you smoke keeps the edge off things. At least there was that. But you were up to things weren't you, Nesbit, things you shouldn't have been.

This wound on the back of your head is strangely placed for a man who jumped is it not?

Nesbit, did someone do you in?

Come on now Nesbit give me a bit more, I says as I digs my long dreamy fingers into the wounds, into the scrambled eggs of his brain and closes my eyes.

Were there those who wanted your death?

Nesbit did you know there are three who always seek our death. Devil. Family. and Maggot. The Devil seeks your soul. Your family seeks your riches. And the poor humble maggot only wants the leftovers. I whisper a verse into the vaporous air:

> *O Christ who was hanged on the tree*
> *And lanced by the ignorant blindman*
> *Now as they seek my ruin*
> *I wish them choked, all three!*

Or was there a woman involved young Nesbit? They say women were attracted to you. Your darkish looks, your long silences, mistaken no doubt for something you lacked rather than something you possessed. I'd wager being adopted only added to it. They didn't know who you were, they who love nothing better than discovering a man. Aren't those the very dark lands a woman likes to conquer; no boat no plane is needed. And your brain Nesbit. You had a fair sized one they say, but you never did put it to much use.

Sing on now by the empty shores of eternity, smoke on, one after the other, higher now than the highest star young Nesbit. Yet, here you are Nesbit, with me on top of you, broken in a stagnant pool beneath the haven of a tribe of outcast goats.

*

Nesbit gave two weeks *undiscovered*. I gave most of those weeks on top of him, except for the odd excursion here and there, mostly in the company of young Mulcahy. The dead should not be alone. The dead will always be alone.

Heffernan's young lad, Willy, was up the hill with a few greyhounds. On rising a hare, he let the greyhounds loose, but the hare escaped. A full hour later he found the greyhounds barking in the quarry.

Heffernan himself lurked alone with the body before the guards arrived and it was from his lips that certain details made their way round Spit quicker than the mists. His index finger – Nesbit's that is – was extended and pointed west, something that's been the subject of much interpretation since. Other details emerged: empty beer and cider cans scattered near the bottom of the quarry. It was Heffernan too who spotted the wound at the back of the head.

As you can imagine Spit is up in a heap. At first there's a kind of disbelief that a young man, and a nice young man – now he's suddenly nice and his adoption seems to not matter at all – could meet such an end. Nobody's sure what to make of it but they're all doing their best to come up with explanations. Hushed conversations in corners of fields; in the window of Harry Faddon's Post Van; in the late corners of Slattery's and Hannigan's; or below in Patterson's shop, with the smell of missus Patterson's brown cakes cooking, you'll hear any number of conjectures as to the who, where, what, how and why.

Must be somebody close to him. Did you know eighty percent of all murders are committed by someone close to the victim?

Murder? You're reading too many of those books. He was drunk and he fell. Simple as fucking that.

No, isn't it more like ninety percent.

Winks, nods, gasps.

More said in the not saying than in the saying.

More given in the not given than the given.

Around me the words of the good people of Spit, like a great big soupy caldron, smoke, drift and echo.

There was a row the night of the festival outside the marquee. Some of the McCrory's from town were involved. They're a crowd you wouldn't wanted to be getting involved with.

Be-god you could be right.

Nothing surer.

Playing with fire.

No, the row was with others closer to home.

You know, I hear he was mixed up in the drugs too.

So they says.

Was smoking that stuff morning, noon and night.

Hardly left the house the poor chap.

He was never the same after the parents passed.

Awful stress on him.

Wasn't it quare the way they went right after each other.

Who went where?

His mother and father you ape.

Queer indeed, especially, as they weren't very close in life.

They're close enough now; buried on top of each other below in the graveyard.

Wasn't there pressure on him to sell.

There must be some class of a curse on that place.

Pressure from whom?

Shure you know very well the answer to that yourself.

Curse, what curse?

It all got to him. That's the long and short of it. Poor fellow. I suppose he had it hard. People round here might not be so open-minded.

People anywhere. Nothing to do with here.

What fecking curse are ye on about.

There was a man that lived in The Lane, near Wilson's place, years ago. He always maintained that that hill above by Nesbit's was the good peoples land and that any that interfered in it would come to no good.

Silly superstitions.

Silly or not there's none of them left.

None of who left?

The Nesbits. Who did you think I was talking about, the little people?

It was Squint Delahunty that started it all off. Gone mad on the drink.

A Delahunty on the drink? They'd hardly pay for it.

If a man gets the taste for it, he'll pay any price to get it.

Nesbit is gone. And that which is lost is all that truly remains. My heart is a vault for icy winds. Open my eyes, close my eyes, nothing but the memory of her.

After his body is discovered, I go through a spell of depression, well, it's more like existential despair. The days crawl into weeks. If the writing has any value, it might be only to save myself from complete madness. So, at a loss I take to scribbling letters when I can muster up the energy. Most days I can't even do that, I just linger with the goats, or up the top of Coney's hill near the old dolmen. Of late I'm drawn to this place and once there I can't help but feeling I'm waiting for something or somebody. I have a sense that there's a great shift approaching and it's here at the dolmen it will kick off. If there are others like me, whisps, fairies, púcas, wee folk, the little people, the good people, then why haven't I seen any of them? Am I the only thing of my kind. Your immediate clarification would be much appreciated, in addition to being much needed. Do you know I die everyday?

*

My next assignment finds me down in the local Garda station, hanging off the ceiling, the stretch in the evening gone, the smell of Autumn in the breeze, the odd leaf twirling down to meet the ground that's ever waiting.

Sergeant Mulcahy, two detectives, a smoked filled room. Mulcahy, clean-shaven, well dressed as always, has a pale worried look to him that I've not clocked before.

We've set up an interview room in town. Friends, relations, neighbours and anybody connected to him, says the detective, looking at the detailed map of Spit that hangs on the wall opposite the Serge's desk.

The detective has a crew cut, dark thick hair and eyebrows to match. So thick indeed they look like two dead hairymollys crudely attached by glue and a child's hand. He's a face that can only be likened to a cadaver, like he hasn't seen a decent meal since last Christmas. Cadaver it is then. I have this thing, I give nicknames to people I've just met, it's my way of remembering them, categorizing them, puting them into boxes, capturing their essence, packs in more meaning than Peter, Jane or Paul, don't you think?

The Serge sucks on a fag. Outside the window, to the west, midges form a thick meandering cloud against the sun.

The interviews, Cadaver reminds him.

Shouldn't we wait for autopsy report, the Serge says.

Either way, it will have to be done, says Cadaver.

The Serge nods.

Show me the list.

The Serge reads of the list: Michael Delahunty, Rosie Delahunty, Arthur Bellwhistle, Michele Cleary, her brother, on and on he reads, half of Spit might be on it.

The other detective is seated across the table from the Serge. He has lively eyes but a dull round heavy body. Sitting down he looks extremely short. His bald red head gleams. There and then I christen him Runt. Why Runt? I'm not completely sure yet, I'm just going with my gut.

Is there anybody else who needs to be on it.

I'll have a think, says the Serge.

What about this Michael Delahunty?

I just read his name out. What about him?

There are reports that he was very drunk on the night in question.

Already done a few interviews then, says the Serge.

Through the grapevine.

Down in the local then. Nice pint?

This Delahunty?

Half the parish was drunk.

I don't doubt it.

Autopsy report, says Serge, sighing, making a mountain out of a molehill?

Let's forget about this autopsy report for a minute, says Cadaver, and revert back to old fashioned detective work. Is this murder most foul? And if so, who and why? Mr. Mulcahy, as a local you might have more insight into this. Wasn't there an altercation at the local festival, in which our victim was involved. That night was also – as far as we know – the last time the victim was seen alive.

No need for the Mr. Mulcahy, says the Serge.

Cadaver nods.

As far as we know, says the Serge, his sharp eyes, again lonesome for the window. His face is lean and hard like the bark of an old ash. Nasty scar decorating his chin.

The McCrory's from town were involved, says Runt, in a high squeaky voice, one that does in no way suit the barrelish body from which it has emanated.

That was a different altercation. Franci and Peter, they are both up on other charges soon. I can't see how they could be involved, grunts the Serge.

Better to follow it up anyway, squeaks Runt. He's taken to scribbling in his notebook while biting the fingernails on his right hand.

The Serge throws him a look, stubs out his fag in an already full ashtray.

Cadaver clears his throat. What we need you to do is to go over this list, take your time, think of all those who were at the festival that night, his friends in general and anybody who you think might want to do him harm.

Yes, says Mulcahy, again, his eyes gone towards the window.

Is there anybody who would want to do him harm?

The Serge looks at him.

Your gut feeling Mr Mulcahy, says Cadaver – his voice softened – his hands joined in a priestly pose.

Speculation Gentlemen. As I've told you, and some of your colleges already, young Nesbit was a quiet fellow, who was not involved in any criminal activities. Both his parents died recently. He was under a lot of stress living up there alone. He was never much cut out for farming; the land was lying idle.

So, you're saying he likely jumped, squeaks Runt.

I'm not saying anything.

The land...we spoke to a man who said that there were on both sides of his farm people hungry for that land, says Cadaver.

The Serge laughs.

What's so funny?

People round here say a lot of things. You'd want to be careful who you listen to, that's all I'm saying. It's true he owned a strip of land between the two biggest farmers in the parish and there's a well on it. In addition, the hill could have been sold to the forestry. And there are rumours there's big windmills coming, solar powered yokes, that place is prime location, facing right into the west wind that's channelled down the valley. They say you can get fifteen-thousand a year to have one on your land, so all in all, we're talking about a very valuable piece of land. And both these farmers could be what would be described as land hungry, but come on, they've more than enough to buy that land ten times over.

Anything can happen in a heated moment, and if there's drink involved forget it, says Cadaver. And wasn't one of them, a Pa Quinn, involved in the fracas that night?

As far as I know Quinn was the one who broke it up. Besides, I've known Quinn since he was a child, if he was going to kill him, he'd have killed him there and then, and if he had killed him, he wouldn't be the type to try and cover it up.

With drink taken a man can do anything, repeats Cadaver. I've seen it.

I don't doubt it, says the Serge. Look at Hercules.

Hercules, says Runt, looking at Cadaver, who shrugs his shoulder.

Hercules killed his family in a blackout, says the Serge like he's not really speaking to anybody in particular.

The Greek fellow?

Yea, wife and children, the whole lot.

Why bring him up, asks Cadaver not looking at the Serge but looking at Runt.

No reason, except sometimes I can get close to understanding how a man might be driven to that, says the Serge stubbing out another butt and standing up.

Your son, Danny isn't it, says Cadaver. Wasn't he a good friend of the deceased?

I wouldn't say good friend. I don't know if either of them are capable of being good friends to anybody.

Runt stops his scribbling in his notebook and looks at the Serge. The Serge twirls his eyes.

Well, friendship can be complicated. But wasn't he with him on the night of the fracas at the festival, asks Cadaver.

He's on the interview list. He'll answer like everybody else. Is there anything else we can do today gentlemen?

Another round of interviews tomorrow, says Cadaver. Then, we've a meeting tomorrow evening back in Dublin, with the Super, so we won't be staying tomorrow night.

Grand, might as well go have a few pints for yourself. You'd never know what you'd hear down in the pub that might be useful.

Is it really Robbie Slattery's brother who owns that place, asks Cadaver.

The man himself. Humble origins, says the Serge walking to the window.

Robbie Slattery the Minister, asks Runt.

Right, says Cadaver, not taking his eyes off the Serge.

You never tell me anything, says Runt.

You never asked, says Cadaver.

Well, I'm asking now amn't I.

And, I'm after telling you aren't I. Do you see what I have to deal with Mr. Mulcahy, smiles Cadaver.

The Runt throws him a look, then snaps his notebook closed.

I follow the Serge's eyes and see the evening sun sinking over the hills in the west. In another half an hour night will be in.

See you in the morning, says Cadaver, as he's half-way out the office door, Runt following a few footsteps behind.

Right oh, says the Serge, rolling his eyes towards the ceiling. For a moment I swear he's seen me, as he keeps looking at me, but no, there hasn't been sight nor sound of me for six hundred years.

Serge Mulcahy sighs, leans back on his chair, stands up, walks around the table then sits down again and light ups another fag, looking out the window at the dancing midges and the dying sunlight streaming through them.

DANNY
MULCAHY

I've known Nesbit as long as I've known myself. There was always something not quite right with him. Perhaps the same could be said of me, could be said of anybody, if you knew them well enough. And yet, Nesbit had special qualities, ones I, or anybody else I knew, did not possess.

Spencer Daly, the local headmaster at the school, knew all about it. Over the years Daly had perfected a number of tortures that kept us petrified in his presence. His favourite, and most often deployed method, was to lift us a foot clear off the ground by grabbing hold of the hair at both sides of our temples. Sometimes even by our ears. Afterwards, there'd be a dizzy, burning sensation, which I have to say wasn't altogether unpleasant. His punishments were inventive, and most important of all, they were subtle – he left no trace. He mastered the art of pinching and could cause so much pain with just his finger and thumb that it was, in hindsight, rather remarkable. God knows what he'd have gotten up to if given free leash. He was a small man, wore a smig which came out red even though his hair was brown. When he was thinking deeply about something he always took to caressing it with his thumb and index finger, the image of which has stayed with me to this day.

On this one particular morning, he was checking our Irish homework, moving around the classroom, sneaking up behind us, one by one, putting the fear of god into us. It was no secret he nursed a dislike for Nesbit. Maybe because he didn't play hurling, or because he was left-handed. Or maybe he just plain disliked him for no reason whatsoever. Those are the worst dislikes. He stops at Nesbit's desk.

Daly clears his throat and in that playful voice he always used before he launched into one of his sessions, says:

Nesbit did you forget your homework?

No, says Nesbit.

Well, where is it?

It's there Sir.

Where?

Right here Sir, says Nesbit pointing to a blank page.

Nesbit, I'm going to ask you one more time, where's your homework, he says, his voice still in that playful tone.

There, he says pointing to the page again.

There is a pause. In this silence we all crumble – I can still feel it – all that is except Nesbit.

Stand up Nesbit.

The peaceful tone is gone.

Nesbit stands up. There is a short sharp crack, so fast I almost miss it. Nesbit's cheek is red. I'm only two seats adjacent from him.

One more time Nesbit, where is your homework?

Joanne Kiely, seated to my right, cracks; tears start dripping from her eyes silently on to her notebook.

It's there sir, on the page, says Nesbit.

Nesbit, is it a full fool you are?

Yes sir.

Joanne Kielly, fragile as a wren's egg, has the most beautiful handwriting in the class and always gets the highest grades. It is very possible I loved her.

Daly grabs hold of Nesbit and shakes him so much I think his head is going to fall off. He then reaches for the hair at both sides of his temple and lifts him clean off the ground and dangles him there like he's nothing more than a doll.

Now Nesbit, did you or did you not do your homework? Daly's eyes behind his glasses are bulging to the extent that I think they might explode.

Silence. Seconds pass. Nesbit is breathing hard and a fierce look has come over his face.

I did sir.

Then where is it Nesbit.

It's there on the page sir.

Daly looks at him for a long time, not with rage now, but with an incomprehensible expression like he's not quite sure what is in front of him. I have at times since this incident often looked at Nesbit in the same way.

Nesbit, get out of this class and go wait outside my office.

Yes sir.

Get out, he says again, with disgust, as if he's spitting something unpleasant from his mouth.

After this day Nesbit was kept at a distance, seated in the far back corner of the room, far away from the rest of us as was possible. Daly did not care what Nesbit did as long as he kept quiet. Nesbit too, seemed happy with this new arrangement.

It was not like Nesbit was stupid he just had his own ideas, the problem was they were unalterable. He had a knack for drawing, was positively gifted at mechanical things, could take radios apart and put them back together, but he never applied himself to anything. Seemed to have no ambitions.

This was incomprehensible to me as I was rife with them, all of them unrealistic and unattainable. One minute I wanted to be a poet, the next a physicist, then a musician, as well as an explorer, a cowboy, and a criminal. I was convinced I could be all. Whatever mood was on me I had a different ambition.

I asked him about it once, directly, something rare for us. We never talked about what was really going on with us, except when we were so pissed that whatever it was we wanted to say came out all wrong and twisted.

Don't you think you're wasting your life away? Don't you want to travel and see the world, I asked him.

I've already travelled, he said.

Dumbstruck, I looked at him like the way you might look at a chicken whose just after reciting a passage of Paradise Lost.

Bullshit, I said finally. Where?

He lists out a string of countries spanning the five continents. Adds details like his favourite was Italy because of the architecture, and Vietnam because he was totally into that war. During our time in secondary school a series of magazines came out about the war. Nesbit had them all. He liked to collect things and had the best metal collection in Spit. It was he who introduced me to bands like AC/DC and Iron Maiden.

Mouth open, knowing that he's never been outside the country, I sit there. It was useless to argue. That was Nesbit. Prone to bouts of madness. No, madness is not the right word. Delusion. Fragmented realities, something like that. Unbelievable self-belief to the point of pathological denial.

I don't believe for a minute he killed himself.

He just wasn't the type.

He didn't have the part of his brain where he blamed himself for anything. I often envied him for this. Maybe it was an accident but there's no way he killed himself. And who would want to kill him? He never got involved with others enough to give them motive to kill him. Could it really be the land like some people are saying.

That last night there was a bottle of gin we drank at your house before leaving for the festival. Faces, snippets of conversation. Flashes. Made a fool of myself in front of Rosie Delahunty. I remember Bellwhistle driving and talking about spooky action at a distance again. The fight. Something about the graveyard. After that there's nothing, nothing at all until I woke up.

How did I get home?

Did I leave with Nesbit?

Was it even that night it happened?

Nesbit dead at the bottom of a quarry for two weeks. Fodder for rats. We used to walk up there sometimes, smoke and drink, throw the cans over the edge and wait for the sound when they hit the rocks below. Those were nights of stars, nights of long talks with odes to girls we loved or thought we loved. O that sweet easy spirit of drunkenness, layering the world with meaning and precision. Sure, we had troubles, but up there, drunk in our own dominion everything was ok. Yes, I've so much love inside me at times I think I'm going to explode. And yet I know there's a darkness inside me deep enough to swallow everything I love ten times over.

You know the way sometimes you wake up out of a dream that's so good you want to go back into it, but you can't, so there you are clinging to the memory of it, trying to hold on to it, like water in your hands, but no matter which way you clasp it or grasp it there'll be leakage.

Still, something good has surfaced, up out of the nowhere, a memory, a perfect little mushroom, naked in the morning, out of the ether, wilted flower, all I ever had was all I ever lost. Morning in her arms, the sunlight streaming in through the trees.

For a long time, I lie on the heather hoping to re-enter this world but all for nothing. I get up, shake myself into the day, low blood pressured, head melted. Dying moon lingers in the morning sky. One of them days I say as I skip along under the tree line of Devil's Bit, so called because the devil took a bite out of it. Not liking what he bit off, he dropped it about twenty kilometres west, where a large castle was constructed out of it.

Not long out of its form, its nostril undulating the fresh

morning air, I come upon a hare.

Morning hare, I say.

And what a fine fresh morning it is. Sun streaking across the deep blue.

Hare looks at me as if to say who are you when you're at home, then bounds off into the rushes.

Hare, the druids believed you to be a messenger of the gods. Do you have some news for me? Hare, have you seen her?

Getting no reply, I whisper towards a clump of rushes. Well, hare, once caught you'll lose all your charm.

Scuttled along by the morning breeze I end up by the dolmen on top of Cooney's Hill without intending to, where to my great surprise I come upon Squint, on his knees, hands clasped together mumbling words I can make head nor tail of. I'm not here long at all when the mumbling stops. I think he's going to get up, but he kowtows to the ground once more, head touching the wet grass. In this pose he remains his body now convulsing with gentle grunt like sobs.

I've always been on the side of the underdog, the outcast, the hated. If everybody hates a man, I will likely love him and if everybody loves a man, I'll likely find something in him to hate. I've always been this way, these days, even more so. Poor old Squint the dog fucker, the incestuous bastard, and now... worse perhaps.

For whom do you weep Squint? Is it your brother? I spend a fair bit of time down in the graveyard Squint, often see his gravestone, others too Squint, no shortage of them, names, date of birth, sometimes the cause of death. Amongst the others, the crazy Mary's, the drunk Johnnies who pissed their lives away, amongst those, like him, who did away with themselves:

All the broken and frail, I wouldn't give them a thought

Squint, if I wasn't half broken and frail myself.

Who else is going to express their mumblings, their weepings, their lost hopes, their wasted tears?

Who but me, Squint.

Or is it your sister you weep for? Or maybe just yourself?

Or, Squint, is it young Nesbit?

Did you have a hand in his downfall?

Tell you the truth, I feel a little awkward looking at you here in your moment of privacy. I even consider sliding away and giving you some privacy but you're soon up and wiping the tears from your eyes.

From the inside pocket of your jacket you take a packet of fags, light one up, then sit back in the ditch and smoke, your eyes fixed on Knockamoore, directly across the valley from us. Largest hill in the parish. Eight-hundred and seventy-nine metres says the marking stone on top of it. I'll take a seat beside you there, get a whiff of your smoke. I miss the pipe sometimes.

We sit in comfortable silence until he reaches the end of his smoke, then up he springs without warning, heart driven sideways in me, unearths the stout hazel stick he has buried a few inches into the top soil and walks back west in the direction of home.

Squint, I say, the more I see of you the more you remind me of myself, you poor long-suffering bastard.

Old troubles not far away. That I can tell you. Of that you can be sure. But what can I do about it now? Might as well lie back on this ditch, suck the marrow out of a piece of grass, and wait and see what happens. To be useless is one thing but to know it as well – that's a whole other thing.

DANNY
MULCAHY

Round Spit death is on a bit of a rampage. Paddy Corcoran's wife finally passed on. Word of her demise had been a weekly event since ever I could remember.

A week after Nesbit's body turns up, Bellwhistle's old man dies suddenly. Despite being sick for a long time everybody expected him to hang around for much longer. Though he tried to let on he was fine, the death threw Bellwhistle. Despite the exterior hardship of their relationship, they were, in a way, the best of friends.

Of a cold wet October morning we buried him below in the graveyard. His old friend Patsy O'Halloran sang The Fenian Gun. Small funeral, sad and thin. Afterwards, we went to Slattery's. We drank, that's what we do, we drank round the pool table, going outside every hour to Bellwhistle's car to smoke a joint. Everybody knew, you could see the winks and nods but we didn't care. We'd have the craic going in and out, but with Nesbit not long gone there was little mood for craic. We filled ourselves up with so much liquor and spirits that we could no longer put words together. Silence was best. I have little recollection of the night to be honest, but I'm glad to report that I just passed out and caused no trouble or embarrassment. A good night.

I think of Nesbit. The last few weeks I think of little else. But his funeral I'd rather not recall. Somethings are better left alone. Closed Coffin. Two weeks his body lay at the bottom of the quarry. I still expect him to call me, to hear the low tone of his voice, punctuated by long silences, never excited, calm as the nocturnal sky. There are nights I drive up to his house but don't have the courage to stop.

The Guards are interviewing everybody inside in town. Bellwhistle. Myself. Detectives down from Dublin. Saw them around the house the other day. Old man won't be impressed with that. Surely, it was an accident. There's no way Nesbit would jump. He wasn't the type. And who would want to harm him? I can't even remember the fight. It's true we often went to that quarry together when drunk, to scream out across the night, to smoke joints, to drink, to pelt questions at the nature of the universe. Our insignificant voices returned, toned down a notch, humbled by the great vastness that we had no influence on. Once, I remember Nesbit said he wanted to leap into the abyss. I thought he was joking. He said the true measure of a friend is to understand them enough to help them to do something they can't do themselves.

Would you push me if I asked you, Danny.

Cop on Nesbit, I said, because he was so close to the edge.

Don't you remember, he says, that time you pushed me in the river.

We were five, it was hardly a stream.

Still, all in all I could have died. Did you know Danny I've never felt more alive than at that moment, when I thought I was going to drown. The call of the void Danny. One small step, one small shove and I'm into another dimension.

One small step and your dead Nesbit, and there's no coming back from that.

I had not thought much of this incident at the time. But now, every memory assumes importance. Flashes of the night: Squint. Rosie. Beautiful Rosie. Nesbit. The other day I remembered Mary Cleary and her brother were there too. Synapses in my brain reconnecting. The hangovers come, pouring the darkness over me like a black thick vomit. It's not the physical effects; rather it's the thoughts, things the likes of which I have difficulty even writing about. I'm afraid. I'm afraid of myself with it, and without it I'm more afraid. The *it* being referred to here is the alcohol but it's a whole lot more to me, *it's* the Spirit, the thing contained within the bottle, the magic juice of a condensed and distilled universe. Inside my soul there's a hole and this simple chemical fills it to completion. I continue doing what I'm doing because I know of no alternative, or I'm too scared to face the alternative. A bird trapped in the wind of a hurricane. This cage I keep returning to.

Increasingly, after prolonged benders, I think about it, how I would do it. This is a different *it*. At first it appeared as an abstraction, like the way you might think about how those unfortunates captured by the natives in the old Tarzan movies were strapped to trees which were pulled down and formed into a X, then the ropes cut, suddenly freeing the trees and ripping the victim in half. That kind of abstraction. It was never near nowhere real, we saw it, we heard the terrible screams, but as kids we could not envisage its true terror. Or perhaps, as kids we understood terror in the world as perfectly normal. I do not know.

Anyway, here's how it goes. I'm walking up Darcy's hill – the hill at the back of the house – something I often do when I've nowhere else to go and nothing else to do. I come to the deciduous tree-covered little valley that separates Darcy's land from that of the Ryan's on the other side. Lush green in summer, with grasses and ferns up to your belly button, the sound of the rushing stream filling the silence, but it also is the silence. This is my special place. I love the beech, the horse chestnut, the ash, and the hazel trees that have been here long before any of us were.

Of all the places I know, it is here that I think most suitable for my heinous act. Perhaps it's the juxtaposition of the ugly and corrupt beside the beautiful and pure. As a child this place was my paradise and back then I scanned the trees looking for suitable branches for climbing. Now I scan for a different reason. It's dark thinking indeed, and I try to break away from it, but each time, the drinking brings me back.

If it weren't for mother...I couldn't do it to her. To them. But then again, he, the old man, said that I'd be better off doing it. What a thing to say to your son. I know he was angry and probably didn't mean it, but somewhere he meant it, somewhere he thought it, it didn't just come up out of nowhere, the words were formed in his mouth, sent there by a message in his brain.

Wouldn't that be the revenge?

Wouldn't he be sorry then?

But the worst thing of all, for him, would be the talk; the neighbours, the whole parish whispering about it. That's what he fears most. Reputation, outside appearance, that's his great weakness. He is at heart a coward and I, maybe only I, can see that. And for this very reason he hates me.

Shame. O Shame. The shame. Now, there's a word. We know it. What its precise origins are we cannot ascertain. But it's there, always there, since the days of our birth it's inside us, and there's no known way to wash it off. You either have it or you don't and if you have it, you carry it round with you like a big bag of rocks. Wherever you go it comes. When you introduce yourself you give your name, then you introduce your bag of rocks. This is my friend, my friend has no known name, this friend wants my slow and painful death, and wishes me to wither away rather than bloom and grow, yes, he has no name, his name, his name has no name.

Shame.

Shame.

Shame on you and all that you have done and worse still all that you didn't do.

There are but two worlds: the one outside and the one inside.

Who to let in?

Who in their right mind?

Who in the morning, drunk and vomit stained?

Who in the apparel of the fool?

Well-acquainted we are, old friend, see you on top of the glittering stream, in passing car windows, in the iris of the eye you dare not look into. Yes, this mirror mirror on the wall, this old morbid stain.

Shame.

You army of no name, marching all over us.

Trodding us down into the muck.

West wind weeps the willows, I sit by the little stream, hear it trickling down the nape of my neck, breath of winter not so far away now, time when the little robins go around with empty bellies. I give a week here at the butt of this weeping willow tree. Whatever it is that directs me seems not to be in a hurry. Do I get bored, well, not really. I could give all day searching for my reflection in the silver white of the stream, it comes it goes, it comes it goes, water ever moving yet never changing. Do you know, I've no idea what age I am, or rather, what age I was when I ceased to be. Nothing ever really changes. The sky above me, the ground beneath me, the life within me. Perhaps it's rest I need and that's what I'm doing here. But that's the thing, you can't over think these things, you'll just run yourself into a hole. Looking for myself, trying to remember, what it was I was all those years ago. The days blur together into new topologies. A maker of stories and music, this much is clear, it's the rest that has me in knots.

Who was it that employed me?

And who is she, the one who has come to my dreams of late, I know her, but can't recall her, the details, like names and places and times, yet the feeling of her is so familiar to me like she is me, and I am of her, a sister but not a sister, a sister of my soul.

I was human once of that I am now sure. Maybe we all were. Was I wronged or did I wrong. Much of a muchness. Now that she's returned, I suffer daily. It's not that I wish I didn't remember but now that I do I have to make do with this regret. Yes, there is joy, so much – but it is a sad joy. It covers me like skin. No matter where or when I look I see her. I see her when I close my eyes. All the time I long to be with her. That I have wronged her pains me most. How easy to fall in love with your own wrongs.

Yes, it is a selfish love, and maybe not a love at all.

Am I weeping for myself. For my loss. For what I threw away. Because now I am all alone in the world.

Spit's outcast. Spit's slave. And though I mock them and laugh at their stupidity and simple-mindedness as they go about *living*, it is they who have the last laugh. In their ignorance they are happy. In my high vantage point, I'm forever outside. There is no solution that I know of.

Young Mulcahy holds the key. In flashes and little insights, these memories come, catalysed by the falling of a leaf, or the flash of a crow's wing. Is there some way I can help the youth? I fear the worst.

Danny, like most young people, is not afraid of death. No, that's not it, rather he, they don't understand it. They are unaware that in this universe life is the exception. Maybe, it's only us dead that can really know this.

Mulcahy, Mulcahy, Mulcahy. I incant the words to myself, then heave up a large throatful of phlegm and hawk it into the stream, watch as it's carried away on random ripples. And her, young Rosie Delahunty, how familiar she is to me. Yet, when I think of her, I shiver. That room, that half-starved robin, her and her brother in the cowshed.

Yes, the west wind weeps the willows, stream moves greyish, trickling down the nape of my neck, breath of winter upon my back and the little robins go around with empty bellies.

*

I'm hanging upside down from the ceiling of the old barracks. I remember the night it was burnt down. Those were the days when rebel soldiers roamed the hills of Spit, when men, and boys were dragged out of their beds in the middle of the night and shot on the side of the road by foreign forces.

His son sits slouched, head down towards his converse sneakers. Fathers. Did I ever have one? Of course, I must have had, but of him there's nothing left but me. Mother. Yes, I remember. Black hair, the smell of the sea. Seaweed green eyes, and light skin the shade of fat milk. Mother, the touch of her hands, the songs that fell off her tongue were the old songs, the ones that came here with the first waves of people.

You just tell me the fuck what happened that night, barks the Serge.

I told you I can't remember, says Danny, his voice low and difficult to hear.

You and Nesbit. Were ye on the drugs? Tell me the fucking truth and tell me now, because if you don't and it comes out later – and it will – you'll be hung up by your balls and there's nothing daddy will be able to do for you.

Danny continues to eye the ground.

Pat Hennessey, says he dropped ye home. You and Nesbit, at his place. What happened after that?

There's an old typewriter on the desk, some neatly stacked sheets of white paper, an official Garda Stamp – perhaps the most useful item at the Sergeants disposal – a small dark bottle of ink, some red and black pens neatly aligned alongside the paper. Sergeant Mulcahy still has a thick head of sandpaper hair. Even viewed from above I can't make out any of the normal receding lines which should be present in a man of his age. Close to Danny's side of the table, against the wall, there's a riot helmet, a short dark wooden baton. A riot in Spit. Now that's enough to bring a smile to anybody's face.

You know if it weren't for your mother, I'd let them hang you up by your balls. It would be the best thing that could happen to you. Might make a man out of you, because you're nothing near a man now.

The Serge looks away disgusted and fumbles in his pack of cigarettes.

Young Danny clenches his teeth. Breathing hard now, rocking back and forth.

Do you understand you were the last person seen with him while he was alive? Do you know what that means? Is it full fucking stupid you are?

Danny tries to swallow, but I can see the words are stuck in his throat, words worse than any beating. He tries hard to control his shaking lips and twitching face muscles. He tries to swallow again but all the waters gone to the cavities behind his eyes, where it spills over and out, and trickles down his face and into his mouth. The devils a hard man and gods got to be harder if he's to win. Within us all, these two exist. Fathers. Who needs them. What would the world be like without them? A universal father. A mother. A mother of earth. A Father in heaven.

If something happened you better tell me now.

Danny's mouth moves, but nothing comes out. He continues looking towards his feet.

The Serge stands up.

Was Nesbit in the habit of going up to the quarry. Did ye go up there that night?

Danny remains mute.

You're a fucking disgrace. A drunken wino good for nothing. Fuck off across the water and don't come back.

Danny jumps up roaring, sending the chair scraping on the concrete floor. The scream is of the sort that tears vocal-chords. If I wasn't stuck to the ceiling the shock of it would have me on the floor.

Sergeant Mulcahy, worried looking, makes for the door.

Danny darts for the baton. The Serge barely closes the door in time. Tears streaming down his face Danny screams as he beats the baton off the door with all he's got.

Come on, come on, shouts Danny. Over and over, he repeats it, as he smashes the baton into the door. If it were a door of the new style, it would surely be in smithereens but it's an old door made of thick oak.

When he tires of beating the door he moves to the table, picks up the typewriter and sends it flying through the window. He smashes the stamp and ink bottle with the baton then overturns the table sending the sheets of paper flying into the air. If there was music the sheets of paper floating in the air might make sense but to me up here, they seem oddly out of time as Danny smashes the other window, cutting his arm in the process. And then as quickly as he exploded, he clams down, lets the baton fall then sits in the corner of the room facing the door breathing heavily and licking the blood from his right hand which is pouring out at concerning pace. The peel of the Angelus Bell rings out in the distance.

*

Mushroom clouds of grey smoke, blood shot eyes, coughing and hawking, deals done, spit on the floor, calves bought and sold, time and money measured out in drinks. Mondays, Tuesday, long days, in the half darkness, the men of Spit know how to drink, day to day, generation to generation.

Hung up high in the corner over the cigarette machine, all eyes are on the TV.

I'm plastered on the stone wall near an empty corner beside a copy of the declaration of independence. To my right there's a portrait of JFK.

The Superintendent from the nearby Garda College replies to the question posed by the rain jacket clad interviewer:

Yes, that's right, the autopsy report has come back inconclusive, which means that the cause of death is unknow. For that reason, we determine this case to be a tragic accident.

So, the murder inquiry is over.

Officially, there never was a murder inquiry. We now need to move on and bring closure for the family through this difficult and painful time. Like I said, a tragic accident.

What family, mumbles Murty Walsh.

Turn it down, it's awful loud.

The barman, Baldy Lynch, fiddles with the remote and the volume fades. I close my eyes. I'd close my ears if I could, but I can't. The voices of the damned come at me in the darkness, some I recognize, most I don't.

Well, that's that then, says Radio Molloy.

T'was the Travellers.

Are you full fucking stupid, he's after saying it was an accident.

What family is right. Poor bastard. Did he ever know where he came out of? Can they check that when they turn eighteen?

There was nothing stolen. There's no murder. He did away with himself.

How do you know that?

Any eejit would know that.

It's the land...mark my fucking words.

That bit of a hill?

Think about their neighbours.

Indeed.

Will, you stop your shite talk and let him rest, says Baldy Lynch.

There's a woman involved, says Francis Ryan slapping his hand off the counter, which causes me to open my eyes. I soon close them again.

There's laughter.

What woman?

One pretty enough to kill for, one pretty enough to die for.

Who'd that be then, asks Murty Walsh.

There's only one who fits that description.

Well, I can't stay here all day listening to ye're shite. I'm off home, says Tony Macky standing up and walking out the door mumbling to himself as he goes. I hear the door bang.

Lads keep it down, says the landlord Tom Slattery who has just come out from the kitchen into the bar.

Another pint, says Pat Heffernan. I'd recognize his voice anywhere. He's an awful man for talking to himself.

T'was a woman I'm telling you. Jealousy. He was a lady's man, young Nesbit. They were mad after him.

Didn't come from the father's side.

Nor the mothers.

No, there's the dark gypsy in him, wherever they found him.

A regular Heathcliff, says Radio Molloy.

A who?

Never mind, says Molloy.

Did you hear young Danny Delahunty was taken away?

Quare timing.

Drugs they say.

Him and Nesbit thick as thieves.

He was bringing it up from the city.

Bags of it.

Taken where?

Down to dry out.

Is that right?

I'm hardly making it up.

His father won't be too happy about that now will he, Sergeant Mulcahy.

I pull myself off the wall, slither away and make my way towards the fire that's starting to get going in the lounge. The smell of drink has me drove wrong. Looking back at them I sense strongly the wasted years of my own life. Though the details are yet hazy it becomes clear to me that I gave too much time in such places talking about subjects I had little or no idea about.

*

Well now, what have we here. Back seat of a Toyota Savant. Cadaver and the Runt. Smoke intermingling to form a curtain so tick I can barely see out the window. Runt on the Benson, Cadaver on the Major. After a long silence Cadaver speaks:

Don't you feel there's something rotten about this whole thing?

Are we going to sit here much longer, says Runt.

You've a better idea?

It doesn't take two of us to sit here?

Go on then, you can go, says Cadaver.

Runt looks out the window and sighs. They're pulled in off the road at the entrance to the forestry gate. From this position they can see right down into Nesbit's yard. Going to be a long shift here I'm thinking to myself. I'd rather be out with the goats. But you have to take them as they come. There's a dead weight to the day. To the west lightening flickers in the far distance.

The exercise would do you good, says Cadaver. Fifteen miles to the station in town, is it?

Isn't this case closed, didn't the autopsy report put a stop to it.

I'm just saying something's not sitting right with me.

Something's not sitting right with me either because I've a pain in me hole from sitting here, squeaks Runt.

I've got a feeling. You heard what some of the people we interviewed said about that fellow with the squint in his eye, roaming about at all hours of the night.

So here we are busting our balls based on your feeling again. Don't you think it's a total waste of time and resources? Guy with enough alcohol and drugs in his system to knock a bull, falls off, or jumps off a quarry, who cares, case closed, simple enough.

Time and resources, that's a good one, as if you've something better to be doing you wretch. And, look how it worked out last time, says Cadaver, a slight smile gracing his thin lips.

Silence. The Runt chewing on his own jaws. The eyeballs in his head fuming.

Strange weather all the same, yesterday it was Baltic, today you could go around in your t-shirt, says Cadaver.

Fucking world is fucked, says Runt.

I think it's the first time I've heard him swear and it breaks some impression I had previously held. Silence again. Silence. Silence. I'm bored out my brain. When I'm with people I can never properly relax, and thus end up drained. I shout out for them to turn on the fucking radio, but nobody ever sees me let alone hears me.

What exactly are you expecting to see here, asks Runt, the irritation in his voice mounting.

I don't know. That's why we're here.

So, we're here to see if that lad Squint makes a move? Follow him in the night? Take him into the car, rough him up, put the shits under him, see if he talks?

It never hurts to watch. If there's nothing, we'll let it go, ok? Don't tell me you didn't get the feeling he wasn't telling us everything when we interviewed him?

I felt that way about most of the people we interviewed, says Runt.

People are like that round here, secretive, says Cadaver.

They fucking hate us. That much is obvious.

It's not a case of liking or disliking; we're outsiders.

Mulcahy didn't want us around much either.

Well, that's natural given the circumstances, says Cadaver. Number one it's his territory and number two he's worried about his son.

And why the house? You think this Squint fellow is going to come around here?

He's just over the hill, if he's going anywhere, he'll be coming this way will he not.

Runt flicks the butt of his cigarette out the window into the heavy and strangely humid air. Look at those dark clouds over there, he says, nodding his head in the same direction as the flicked cigarette butt. His sister is a fine-looking girl, he adds.

Indeed, she is, and did you not detect that she too was a little tight on the tongue.

Tight on the fucking tongue, you could describe half this god-forsaken place with that nice adjective, says Runt, nodding his head like a piglet about to gnaw on a morsel.

Well, you know the way I have a sense about things?

I know the way you imagine you have a sense about things.

Well, with her, I sensed she definitely knew more that she was letting on. And I even heard talk in the pub the other night about her being involved with Nesbit.

You're getting mixed up here now. Your feelings for this girl are interfering with your rational thought process, says Runt laughing to himself.

I believe too it's the first time I've heard him laugh. It's a strange laugh and sounds rather like he's choking.

You always have to bring things down to the dirt don't you.

The truth is never far from the dirt, says Runt.

Cadaver plays with his long fingers tapping them off the steering wheel, humming as he does so.

A clap of thunder rocks the sky over Nesbit's hill. From here you can really see it for what it is, a barren haunted yoke of a thing. Scarce a tree can survive on it because the wind channelled down the long gorge won't allow it. There's a lone warped Hawthorn tree bent into an awful shape that would remind you of nothing only the mangled figure of a tortured soul, petrified in time. Perhaps that's it. Perhaps there's something inside the tree trapped and punished, by what or whom I do not know. It could be my next station. Things can always get worse. That's one certainty in life they never teach you about.

Another clap of thunder. It's closer than you'd like. A sudden darkness gobbles what's left of the light of evening. The rain is not long in falling, it falls as if in greeting for the headlights of a car that's approaching the house. Cadaver rubs his bony hands together. The car does not stop. Within a minute all sight and trace of it are gone.

Runt coughs.

You're right. There's no reason for us to be here and likely no point. I just want to bring finality to it. You know the way I am, says Cadaver.

You're a rooting, nosey, never satisfied yoke who keeps poking in the dirt until he gets bitten.

Maybe you're right. But I want to get a sense of this place, get a feeling on the scene, drink in the life of the victim, later, we'll walk down to the house and hover around for a while. You know this is where the truth of things is to be found. The pieces have a natural desire to align themselves, the truth doesn't like to hide, no, not in gods world it doesn't. How many times before have I been right, huh? It's not about a logical lead, it's deeper than that…if there are messages for us to pick up, here will be the place to receive them.

He turns and looks at Runt who draws another cigarette, lights it, takes a drag, throws his eyes upwards and says:

I've a thirst on me that you couldn't put a price on.

I'm going to write a book someday about all the cases. People like to read that kind of thing.

Book me balls.

After I retire, mark my words, you'll be in it, so you'd want to be careful with that mouth of yours.

Another clap of thunder rattles the Runt.

Jesus, that's right above us, he says, after jerking in the seat.

We'll be safe enough in the car, says Cadaver.

The rain beating off the roof eats up his words.

I've my money on lust, says Cadaver.

What? I didn't hear you, this thunder, this rain,

Lust, shouts Cadaver, there's webs of it here, the answer never sways far from the deadly seven.

Another ten minutes in the hammering rain, they wait. Darkness falls. The lightning strikes the top of the hill, where the lone skeleton hawthorn tree stands. If it's not dead, then nothings dead. After the rain eases off the thunder moves eastwards.

Cadaver starts the ignition. He drives slowly, like really slowly, like the way a ninety-year-old woman might drive.

About fucking time, says Runt, blessing himself. I hate thunder. I've hated it since I could remember. The mother put the fright of Jesus into us with her stories about lads killed by lightening.

Too much time can be an awful thing, says Cadaver.

Who has too much time?

People living out here in these god-forsaken places. Start making up crazy stories to explain phenomena beyond their comprehension. The nights here get awful long in the winter. You'd be surprised what they get up to.

How would you know growing up in the big smoke.

I'd cousins down this way. Spent the summers here, says Cadaver.

Runt grunts.

What's that supposed to mean?

What it always means. Can't you just drive a little faster?

In your desire to be there you're missing out on the here and now, says Cadaver.

Fuck here, that's why I want to be there, says Runt.

You're a tormented soul, there's no mistaking it.

You got that right, and it's more tormented I'm getting by the minute, says Runt, throwing his eyes up towards the white ceiling where I've been stuck for the last few hours. You look up Runt because you want to be exalted. And I look down because I am exalted.

Outside Nesbit's house they park. Lights off, in the darkness they wait. But nothing happens. Nobody comes. They enter the house, going from room to room, flashlights tunnelling through the dark. Outside in the yard they enter the sheds. I follow along behind them. I'm with Runt on this whole escapade: I just want a conclusion to this so that I can find a nice hole to pass the night away.

We've been here before, says Runt.

If Nesbit had a dog, which it looks like he did, where's the dog now?

Dogs run off all the time.

You see, that's something we missed. Worth our while to come up here now wasn't it.

Yes, says Runt, walking towards the car. A fucking missing mutt. You're always right. Now right me a pint.

I watch them get into the car and drive away. I watch the disappearing light, I hear the engine trickle to nothingness.

*

Foolish and hungry for their doom, moths flicker under the yard light, smell of the last cut of silage lingering in the air. I much prefer the days of hay.

If anything reeked of the destruction of the social fabric of Spit it was the advent of silage. In the days of hay everybody had to help each other more. More contact. More interaction. Look at me. Proof that isolation is no good for no one. Psychologically, things got harder on people after that. It is the youth that always bring a tear of hope to my eye. I'm not one for harking on about the good old days – except for the days of hay making – no not me, I'm with the young. They always know best and are riddled with the right kind of energy. If I could be anything I'd be young.

Inwards I drift.

Rosie Delahunty and Mary Cleary. Sitting on two bales of straw. I've arrived late it seems, party at the tattered end, but better late than never.

Don't you get tired of it here Mary?

You know me long enough now Rosie.

Rosie acts like she hasn't even heard. She's looking into the distance, wearing a sad expression.

Everybody says you should have won the Roisin competition Rosie. Don't feel bad about it, says Mary.

Feel bad? I don't. And I know, she says, jumping up and doing a little dance, naggon of vodka in one hand, cigarette in the other. Who's the fairest of them all? Of course, Rosie Delahunty's the fairest of them all, she says laughing.

You're mad Rosie, says Mary, a slight slur evident, holding her smoke like an amateur.

You don't know the half of it Mary.

I'm sure I don't you mad yoke.

For a while they sit there, passing the naggon of vodka back and fort, sighing after each burning slug. The odd cow moans. The moths flicker. Frogs and crickets add background music.

Won't you go to college next year like the rest of us Rosie? You've had a year off to think things over.

It's America I want to go to.

And what will you do there, asks Mary, outstretched hand taking the naggon from Rosie.

Anything at all, I don't care. Wash dishes. Walk the footpaths. Sidewalks, they say there.

Haha, yes, sidewalks, free of this. Free of all this.

Do you ever get the feeling the dead are not dead at all, but here beside us watching us, says Rosie, stopping her dance and looking right up to where I'm located, perched on a dusty old rafter.

You miss him don't you, says Mary.

Nobody knew him. No, he would not let himself be known. That was his shell. Sad and broken, but inside him there was something so beautiful. I thought I could bring it out, like a little seed that falls into a crack in the concrete.

Wish I was as kind as you, says Mary Cleary. For a moment I study her. All it takes is a moment. A plane Jane, stick of a thing, redolent of a nervous crow, good heart though. I can always judge the heart. The years have made me sharp. I'm good at my game. And what's your game Spook? Telling it like it is. That's my game.

Winter is coming Mary. I don't know if I can last another winter here. Without the sun I wilt.

Rosie, you're too kind sometimes, you know that, you really are, says Mary, holding up the naggon and looking through it with one eye closed.

Leave me a bit, says Rosie.

Mary hands it to her saying, I wish we'd another.

I wish we'd ten.

Rosie puts it to her head, drains what remains, then without warning breaks into tears. Along the rafter I slither to gain a better viewpoint.

What's wrong, asks Mary, surprised as myself.

You don't know me. Nobody knows me, she says.

What do you mean, she asks throwing her arm round Rosie's shoulder.

I'm not as kind as you think. There are some things I can't stop doing. Terrible things. I don't even know why I'm doing them, and I know they aren't right.

What are you talking about? You know you can tell me anything. I tell you everything Rosie, even told you about Pa Quinn.

Forget about it, says Rosie.

I'm sure you're blowing it out of proportion, says Mary.

Does every heart have a dark hole in it?

Everybody's got their troubles, that's for sure, says Mary, now stroking Rosie's hair.

Who would want to hurt him? Did he want to hurt himself. I can't stop thinking about it Mary, round and round in my head like a washing machine.

Don't you think he fell? But the Guards said so. The investigation's over.

What do you think Mary? What are people saying?

Mary's about to say something, pauses, looks at Rosie, then around the barn before answering.

Well, you know the way people talk, you said he was dark and hid in his shell, people will turn that...

His shell? Cracked open wasn't it? That's what the world does to shells. You think he jumped?

No, Rosie...he fell.

No, you're hiding something, tell me, what do you mean, says Rosie standing up watching the smoke from her mouth blow into the air above her, right into my path.

I just hear some people saying...,says Mary her face already full of doubt.

Don't be listening to shite down in the pub. People talking this and talking that. You know the way they are round here. Anything. To escape from their own drudgery.

You're right Rosie. And I'm drunk. God I'm drunk and I love it.

Rosie ruminates in silence. Unsure of herself, Mary Cleary scans the barn.

After a while, Rosie says, you still fancy Pa Quinn, don't you.

Mary laughs nervously, nodding her head, who wouldn't, she says.

He's a fine bit of stuff alright, though he is my sworn enemy. Two houses. Mark my words Mary Cleary there will be no Romeo and Juliet story there, he's all yours.

I think he fancies Deirdre Gleeson.

Maybe. Go find out. A fag, says Rosie, opening the box offering Mary one. You know, we're out of drink. I love it too, this feeling, this hazy drifting feeling, like my brain has made a fog of everything.

I could get used to it, says Mary.

There's more drink in the house but how to get at it. Too risky at this hour maybe. Aren't you sleepy?

Mary giggles. Then Rosie giggles. I've nothing to giggle about.

And who do you fancy, says Mary, in a drained voice....oh, I'm sorry, I didn't think.

It's ok. Who does Rosie? Well, as good as this vodka feels, as good as this fresh night air feels, is there anything better than sex. I can close my eyes Mary, forget about the whole world, it's like I'm falling, no, flying is the word, flying through this white light world where every part of my brain is alive and beaming.

Really, asks Mary?

No exaggeration. I mean, I thought it's the same for everybody?

It's ok, but actually I prefer the hugging afterwards.

There it is. I've not met anybody who likes it like me, so I think there's really something wrong with me Mary.

No. No, you're just lucky is all. I envy you.

You know who I think is cute though?

Tell me.

Danny Mulcahy.

Ah. He's good looking alright, but isn't he trouble.

Maybe it's trouble I like.

They both take to giggling again.

Haven't you heard about him?

What?

They say he's been taken away to one of them places.

What kind of places?

Where alcoholics go to stop drinking.

Well, that would be a good thing. I like him when he's sober and shy, and not when he's drunk and full of waffle. Problem is, he's always drunk.

Here's to that. Why do they always have to be so full of waffle, says Mary.

You know what we'll do now, Mary Cleary, we'll sneak up into the house, pour ourselves a little nightcap, then head up to my room and continue our talk, only you have to promise me not to make a sound. They wake easily here, light sleepers, nerves from the father's side, you know the way it goes. Come on.

As I watch Rosie leading her friend by the hand, an unexpected wave of loneliness saturates me. When the light goes off, on the rafters I remain, no inclination in me to move at all. Darkness of night I know thee well, yet there remains the pleasant afterglow of my encounter with Rosie who reminds me so well of someone I once knew somewhere so long ago. It's a feeling I'd like to grow fat on.

*

I give the night lying out in Corbett's low meadow, near the main road, watching the mushrooms come up. Another perk to this role, I suppose, it's just that I've been doing it for so long, you know.

In like a silent leper the dawn light creaks, soon to be followed by Missus Corbett with her basket and a few grandchildren tugging out of her. She loves the mushrooms. So does the husband. Dripping in butter, fried fresh up. Nothing better. I like to watch them running and talking excitedly when they spot little patches of the small white capped army. For generations, the mushrooms have been coming up in this place. Mr. Corbett says it's the horse manure. His father told him that, and his father was not wrong. There are no better mushrooms the length and breadth of Spit, not that we get many of the white edible kind that people like to get, because mostly the land is not suitable or rich enough. Fairy mushrooms on the other hand thrive here, in the dark groves, coming up out of rotting tree trunks, sprouting all sorts of colours and shapes, red, and orange and yellow, vile and hideous looming things. Children are drawn to them. And more so when told to stay away from them.

I best be on my way, though where I don't know. There are long days like this, rest days, when I've no particular place to be or nothing particular to witness. I hang with the goats, get up to other devilment if my mood permits. If the rest days roll into five or more I start to brooding about the past, trying to figure out what it was that got me here. This gets me to thinking about my future, and that's nothing but doom and gloom. All in all it's better to focus on the now, just live here in this mushroom moment. Since the beginning of time the great wise men have recommended this, what they haven't said is how difficult it is to achieve. Wise men and their wisdom. To hell with them. It's taken me a long time to know that in the end you must make your own wisdom.

As you know, I sometimes compose words, ditties, shanties, little glimpses I catch coming over the hills, in the rustling streams, in the birds calling back and forth. Like my reports, I write them on the long grasses, scrape them in the dirt, finger them out in the big fresh cow shits, etch them into the ice that forms on the pond that sometimes comes at the bottom of this very meadow, scribble them in the fat summer river down by Harney's and ask the jumping trout to punctuate the full stops, comas, exclamation marks.

At times I can imagine applause. Trout jump. Flies disappear. I compose.

I do it for her.

Everything I do – since she has again awoken in my memory – is for her.

She's gone but I've never been so possessed by her.

I do it for her.

I do it to lay traps for her, to catch glimpses of memory, I'm hungry for these memories, I go about the days with my mouth hanging open for them. Restless under barrel-chested night I seek some peace. It's a game I cannot win, it's a game where I'm already marked, and yet, I have no choice but to play, I, who once had everything.

Every day I die.

And I'm glad of this dying for each day I too am reborn.

I go to war every day and every day I lose. And yet I keep going.

I keep getting up. If I've any talent at all, this is it. In these iterations I have found meaning. I have found mushrooms, and mornings with Missus Corbett and wanderings with limping Pete.

I move on, o'er the wet dew grass, away from Missus Corbett and her grandchildren.

I catch up with Pete by the small bridge over the stream that runs down along the big meadow at the front of his place. I walk with him whenever I can, to try to carry his loneliness in the hope that he can carry a bit of mine. A stiff breeze commands the grass to sing, the ditches too, full of whitethorns, moan along in curious harmony.

Summer is near its end.

Pete is white-grey, and there was never a grey hair seen on either side of the family. Sorrow will do that to you. Regret will do that to you. At night, by the fire, with the telly on he sits, but he doesn't really watch it, instead he stares into the fire. I suppose he doesn't know I'm there, though there are times, and with certain people in particular, I get the feeling they sense me. I was with him the night he limped out into the barn with a rope. If I were a gambling man I wouldn't have put money on that he'd limp back out, but limp out he did.

Twenty years now since his mother died.

Twenty years, night after night.

His brothers and sisters are long gone. England. America. One in Australia. Pete works, saves money, and walks. Three times a day, at a frantic pace, he walks like there's something chasing him. Bone thin he eats only bread, the odd egg or two, corned beef from Pattersons on Sundays after mass. Like myself he does not drink. If he'd taken to drink things would be easier to explain.

There was a girl once and only once. A Mary Bourke who lived in Shannon's boreen. They courted for a while, but she was a restless thing and had her eyes on moving away as quickly as she could. Pete got upended. You could say he never got up again. Back then it was not so uncommon. Lack of numbers. Innocent men smothered by their mothers. The Church.

Pete limps on, his breath white in the morning air. I follow along and sing with all my power. The leaves of the sycamore, the horse chestnuts and the ash are falling fast. The beech will fall soon. The blackberries have all gone. The wild plums are rotting on the ground.

Each day I think of them, Rosie, Danny, Squint, just as I think of her. Each year I think there will be a change. This mild autumn gives us late mushrooms, but a mild autumn signals a hard winter. To tell you the truth, I think I die, or some part of me dies each winter; and each year it gets harder and harder to come back again.

DANNY MULCAHY

Thin white streaks of clouds vein their way through the blue peaceful sky. Light my Fire, by the Doors pours out from the tape deck. I spark up a cigarette and think as I round a bad bend, that I wouldn't mind it so much if I were met with an onrushing articulated lorry and were killed instantly. There's some about that expression, *killed instantly*, that reminds me of killing flies; squashing them with phonebooks, with fly squatters, stunning them with the quick flick of a rolled-up magazine, then liquifying them under the soles of my shoes.

We've hardly spoken a word since I came out. He's trying, I'm trying, but there's something between us that makes us hate each other. I know that's a strong word but there's truth in it and I can find no better word. Hate what you love and love what you hate. Something like that. All I ever wanted was to impress him, but whatever I did was never good enough, so I gave up, and eventually I went the other way; if I couldn't impress him then I would do the opposite. And for that – for fucking up – I have, as he himself says, a real god given talent.

All this nonsense came up below in the treatment centre. I never thought about these things much before, they said I buried it, said a lot of things, said I was an alcoholic.

Good, I said, I thought I was mad. Still, a word like that. Alcoholic, surely, I'm too young. What does it even mean? One drink they say and you develop the phenomenon of craving, normal drinkers don't have this, sure they like it, they might want more, but they have the ability to discern when they drink too much. I've never had that ability. Never even come close. I drink and I keep drinking till I fall down or pass out, till I physically can't get any more inside me. When I wake up – and if I still have the means to – I will drink immediately.

Anyway, among the clientele of head-the-balls I met down there I've never felt so at home. Wednesdays was family day. Members of our respective families would come and let us have it in front of the whole group. Fucking carnage. Everybody else was breaking down, crying and the like. Yet, I shed not a tear. Not even for Nesbit. I know he's dead. I know he's gone. But it's like a movie. They said I couldn't get in touch with my emotions, said that I had buried them. I'll go with that. But maybe I wasn't honest. Not bone honest. I wasn't ready. I'm not ready. Of course, I didn't mention shit about the quarry, that night, the blackout, this feeling that I can't shake, that somehow I'm to blame. But I'm not to blame. It was an accident. Yet, there are nightmares. That night in the quarry. I keep dreaming the same dream. A black goat, three-horned, his hooven foots walking over me as I'm buried in a glass coffin. I lie there unable to move, hear the dull thuds of shovelfuls of clay, until the last trickle of light is buried.

Coming close to the quarry I speed up. I tell myself I will not look in. But I do. Goats congregate near the top. The black three-horned amongst them. If they have a leader, it's he.

I laugh out loud to ease the tension of these ridiculous thoughts.

When I get there, Bellwhistle is flopping round the room like a sick butterfly.

So, where the fuck were you? Five fucking weeks and not a word from you. I heard rumours you were taken away...he says his tone and face changing to a look of genuine concern mixed with a bit of fear. Are you ok, he asks.

I'm fine.

You're looking fucking good. Put on a few pounds, can see it in your face.

Clean the fucking place up. It stinks in here, I say.

Yeah, yeah, I've had trouble since the auld lad died. I can't get motivated you know. I miss the auld bastard...I've cans in the fridge.

No, I say. No.

He pauses as if to say something but then reconsiders. He rubs his rough freshly grown beard as if he's confused and trying to remember something.

I see you've found a new supply, I say.

In town, inside in Foleys. Goes in there after the dole and buys a twenty spot. Make it do me for the week. Times are hard.

I see.

So, you can't even smoke a joint, he asks.

No.

Jesus. Must be hard.

It will be fine.

Do you mind if I?

What can I say? The man is in his own house. Staying off the dope is easy enough it's the drinking I'm craving for.

The table, covered in empty cans and makeshift bongs, shakes as Bellwhistle rustles with his toolkit. I should not be here. They warned me about this kind of thing. The smell of it, stale in the air, hanging there like a premonition, inviting me into its vortex. I want to reach out with my tongue and suck it in, suck it in until I can no longer think, until oblivion fills me gill to gill. In my head I repeat that prayer, the one they taught us: *God grant me the serenity to accept the things I cannot change, courage to change the things I can and the wisdom to know the difference.* To drink or not to drink, it is clear to me now, this choice I've never before had. My time down in the treatment centre has given me tools to resist.

You look good man, says Bellwhistle again.

You look like shit I want to say, but I don't.

Nothing stopping you hitting Japan now, I say.

When his father was alive, he always said the only thing that was stopping him from going to Japan was that. Don't we all have these lies. That's another thing I learned down there. Down there they strip everything away, until you're left a bare born ass crying baby.

Well, I will eventually, just got to clear up some issues, he says, not looking at me.

Issues?

Land. The house. That kind of thing. The will hasn't come through yet, he says with a worried look. There are dark circles round his eyes and his face is bloated and white.

I'm going to have one, he says.

Ok, I say.

But he doesn't move. We sit there in an awkward silence. There was always three of us. Maybe he's feeling the same thing.

For a moment we look at each other and realize that we know absolutely nothing about each other. Nesbit. The missing link. Without him, or without any of us, the whole structure of our allegiance comes crashing down. The rules of our game have become meaningless because now there is no game. We must make a new one, but neither of us wants it bad enough to put the effort in. Bellwhistle gets up. There's no music either. I can't remember being in this house without music. Old friends stick together. Those are the rules.

He comes back into the living room with a gold can of Scrumpy Jack in his hand. He cracks the lid, picks up the still smouldering joint in his left hand, takes a slug from the can, then a toke, and exhales with a heavy sigh. The smell sends shivers and ripples all through my body from the tip of my tongue to the bottom of my feet. Overwhelmed with a sudden desire to drink I get to thinking I can just have a few and nobody will ever know. It will just ease this tension in my head. He takes another slug, a deeper one, one like I used to take.

That hit the spot, he says.

He wants me to be with him in his own despair. I'd want the same. Maybe I should, maybe it's where I belong.

I stand up, spark a smoke, and start walking back and forth.

Some music, I say, moving towards the CD player.

Jesus, you're awful uneasy, he says.

I click open the CD player. Pulp Fiction soundtrack. I close it again and skip forward to track eight: If Love Is a Red Dress (Hang me in Rags)

Good tune, he says, before launching into the history of the song.

I sit down. Stand up. Then sit down again.

As he talks, I listen to the voices in my head.

Drink.

Drink.

Don't drink.

Smoke a joint but don't drink. If you smoke a joint you will definitely drink. What about your family? Fuck my family. What about yourself? Fuck myself. There's something better waiting for you, something better round the corner. There's fuck all waiting around the corner. You might as well drink.

Don't drink.

Drink.

Then Something I heard in one of those meetings comes to me:

I can drink tomorrow. I settle on this. I'll drink tomorrow but not today.

I stand up.

I got to go I say.

But you only just got here.

I've shit to do.

Can I hit you for that twenty, he says.

I had a feeling he was going to ask about that. But he's right, I owe him money. I owe everybody money.

I've a tenner on me now, I say, I'll drop the rest up during the week.

I take out the tenner from my jeans and leave it on the table and quench my cigarette in the ashtray.

In the car I take deep breaths and repeat the serenity prayer followed by a mantra I've made up myself: *I have no limitations except those imposed on me by own self-doubt and those restricted by gods will.* What or who this god is I know not, but like they say, I'm faking it until I'm making it.

I turn the engine, the music kicks in, LA Woman. I look up at the sky, it's clear and blue and deep and most of all it's trustworthy. It's a long time since I trusted the sky. For a moment I feel relief. A deep breath, a point crossed.

I don't want to go home, not just yet. I turn left at Tim Mahony's cross, instead of right, and head towards Nesbit's. Dead friends don't talk back. Together the three of us were something beyond ourselves, a delusion that we believed in, that made us more that we could be alone. I miss him. If he were alive and if he were there in that living room, the three of us, then it's unlikely I would have resisted. If he hadn't died, it's likely I wouldn't have gone to dry out. *Why don't you live your life for him. You're alive he's not. Quit crying over it.* That's the gist of what those counsellors told me in the treatment centre. Live your life for him, they say. But they don't know. They don't know what happened that night or what I might have done.

I'm driving directly into the sun now, coming up Griffin's hill, on top of which on a fine day you can see the Shannon in the distance, shimmering and twisting like the fat belly of a silver snake. Packs of clouds hunting the sun across the sky but the sun won't be had and keeps escaping. On the descent, into the valley, Nesbit's hill in the distance, I think I can make out the goats hanging on the west side soaking up the sun. The quarry is in my mind. There is no way not to pass it. Black three horns. Glass coffin. Clay eating the light. I close my eyes.

The road is narrow, the ditches thick, barely room for one car. I slow down, like my father, I've always been a careful driver. I can never be who my father wants me to be.

I drive on, singing along with Jim who's singing about his LA woman, and all this gets me thinking of how I need a woman. Any woman would do, but if I had my choice I'd pick Rosie Delahunty. Nothing unique in that. I've loved her since the day I met her. Have probably told her countless times when drunk, but she keeps away from me like I'm the carrier of some plague.

There is a truth out there for me and when I find it I must hang onto it. I've given my whole life walking around in bullshit and now I've gotten a hint at this truth, and it was given to me down there, and I don't want to let it go. That's why I didn't drink at Bellwhistle's. That's why I didn't give up. Yes, I think, I want that truth. I want to live I want to be. I want to love. All these things, I want. *I have no limitations except those imposed on me by my own self-doubt and those restricted by gods will.*

Freewheeling down the steep hill I pass Roger Ryan's farmyard behind which the old fairy fort lies. The quarry is around the next bend. One hundred years ago the stones were hacked out of there by hand and carried twenty miles on horse and cart to build the railroad line. Nesbit was not the first to die there.

After rounding the bend, I glance down to adjust the music volume, when I look up I see someone step into the gateway in front of quarry. A flash of white. Maybe I'm imagining it. A white dress. Briers clip the windscreen. I slow down even more. Determined to not look into the quarry, I glue my eyes on the road. I've seen of enough of three horned goats for one day. But as I pass, I sense movement, my eyes unable to resist, I glimpse her standing there waving.

I roll the car forward. Still waving, in the rearview mirror, I can see her step out on to the road. Maybe she wants a lift. If I stop, she'll think I'm stalking her. But it seems she wants me to stop. I turn down the music even more and watch her coming. Lord-Jesus, I say to myself. I'm already reading too much into it. Just a coincidence I tell myself, then I recall Radio Molloy's words told to me one Monday morning down in the pub:

There are things in this world waiting for you, he said, planted there by something for you and they will pop right up in your face when you least expect them, maybe if you're lucky, when you most need them. But be careful, the Lord's way is beyond our comprehension young Danny. What appear to us as great ups and downs are merely bumps when seen from a distance.

The wisdom of the fool can indeed be a sharp tool. But if Molloy's a fool, then he's every bit a genius. Aren't fool and genius just words used to describe people we don't understand.

She stands there, her dark hair cascading in the window, the breeze cold from the west sweeping up against my cheek.

Danny Mulcahy, she says, I haven't seen you around recently, a little smile playing round the corner of her mouth.

Well, yeah, I was away for a while I say, my voice weak as piss.

Away?

Yeah. And now I'm back, I say forcing myself to keep looking into her eyes.

She drops them for a second, a kindness, but quickly brings them back on me.

And where are you off to now?

Do you need a lift, I ask.

Depends where you're going doesn't it.

I'm going up by your way.

So secretive Danny, she says, opening the door.

Her white thighs flash through the rips in her jeans. A tight black top displays her perfect curves. Rounding the bend, I could have sworn I saw someone in white. Tricks of the eye, the way the light is falling, I suppose. Illusions.

My eyes fall again to the rips on her jeans and the white of her thigh. Does she see what I'm up to? Is she smiling at my embarrassment?

We drive on.

For a few minutes neither of us says anything. I'm waiting for her and I guess she's waiting for me. I don't know where my new found confidence is coming from but I sense something in her that gives me leeway.

You don't say much do you Danny, not when you're sober at least.

I blush. I've always been a blusher and I hate it. Incidents when I was drunk and made a fool of myself in front of her now appear in all their gory guises. I speed up without intending to. Because I can't think of anything else to say, I say nothing.

You're into the Doors Danny?

Yeah, I say. There's a lot more I'd like to say but it my tongue appears to have lost its ability to move.

Silence.

Where were you, Danny?

Away, I say.

You look different, she says. I feel her eyes burning me but I keep mine firmly on the road. The sky, the game of clouds chasing sun throws shadows and light across the rolling fields and hills.

You were good friends, weren't you?

I nod.

That's where you're going isn't it?

I nod.

I'll go with you. Are you going to go into the house, she asks. Isn't it locked up?

I don't know, it might be, she says with a little chuckle.

I thought I'd just walk up the hill, I say.

Did ye do a lot of walking together?

Sometimes.

To the quarry?

I turn the music up a little.

Minutes pass.

I'm sorry, I shouldn't have mentioned the quarry.

It's fine. I walk a lot these days, I say.

I've heard.

You've heard, I think to myself. Is my walking up and down the hill front page fucking news. But she's right, everywhere I go I'm getting quare looks. They all know I was away but nobody has said it directly, not like her. That's worth something.

Two crows sit on the old chimney and eye us suspiciously. The two cars, inch of dust sheeting them, sit derelict in the yard. Odd weeds poke their head up between rocks and out of the side wall. I turn off the engine. My eyes stop at the dog house. Felix would usually be out barking by now. All these weeks and I've forgotten the dog. Maybe everybody has. In the end we are all forgotten.

Do you know what happened to the dog, I ask?

That mutt, what was his name again?

Felix, I say.

Yes, she laughs. What a funny name for a dog.

He took it from the poem Felix Randle the Farrier by Gerard Manley Hopkins. Felix is actually a bitch, but he didn't care, he loved that name, I say.

I thought you were the only one afflicted with poetry, she says, smiling again.

And what happened to Felix, I react quickly trying to deflect that smile.

I think my brother took care of him.

Took care of?

Yeah, think he gave it to someone who needed a dog. At least that's what he said, poor thing was here all alone. You know, I don't like to come here. There's something wrong with this place don't you think.

Wrong?

The whole family wiped out in a year, she says.

Sure enough death has been here I think to myself but I don't say anything. It comes in three's I've heard said, but there's no need to repeat that now.

Is there anything sadder than an empty house, she asks, looking at me like she expects me to know the answer.

Maybe there's nothing sadder than a full house, I say, turning and looking out the side window.

What do you mean? You talk funny sometimes don't you Danny. I'd love to know what's going inside that mind of yours.

In an empty house there's nobody inside to feel the sadness. The sadness is in the looker; a reflection of his or her own loneliness.

That's so deep, she says throwing her right hand onto my arm for a few seconds. A surge of light travels from my arm right up to the epicentre of my brain.

Something of a poet in you is there Danny. You're always spouting it when you're drunk.

She removes her hand.

When I was seven, I touched the belly of a snake in the zoo. I have the same feeling now, except now I also have a light pleasant buzzing in my brain. I pull the handle on the door. Outside, we sit on the sun warmed bonnet.

What now, she says. Do you want to go inside?

We shouldn't. Isn't it a crime scene.

Was there a crime Danny? I thought...

The sun is eaten by a cloud and the yard darkens.

What's going to happen to this place, I ask.

It's going up for auction.

When?

Soon enough, I suppose.

How do you know?

What's with all the questions Danny, you're worse than your father, she says. Has he deputized you?

She has a different smile for every quirk.

The doors must be locked, I say.

I know where there's a spare key.

I don't ask how she knows. I just note it down in the never-ending catalogue in my head. I 'm good at that kind of thing, or rather, I'm bad at immediate reactions, things often don't become clear for me until hours, even days past the event. Somebody might say something to me – it could be an insult – but I won't figure that out till later. I guess it might be damage done to my brain from all the blackouts. I want to ask her why she is being so nice to me all of a sudden but I don't. Like the kitten I am, I'll play along.

Why do you want to go inside, I ask?

Because it's forbidden of course.

She looks at me like the way one would look at a child. Mother, she is beautiful. The white skin of her face against her black top. Sunlight in my eyes, I'm dizzy. I cannot see. I do not want to see. On top of this I've been struck mute.

Well, come on, she says.

We walk towards the door. The crows seated on the roof depart.

As we get close to the door I see a large grey rat, fat and stoned-looking, sitting in front of the door looking right at us.

Jesus, I say.

She screeches, throws her hands round my right arm. I bend down and pick up a smooth oval stone and do my best to throw it with my weaker left hand. It lands a few inches in front of him, skids along the ground and catches him as he is about to leave. Emitting a thin squeal he scuttles towards the shed and disappears under the door.

Still want to go in, I ask?

She nods.

Clouds catch the sun, and pull the curtains on us, sending black shadows over the yard. I close my eyes. Nesbit's dead rotting face. I open my eyes. Her hands, nature's most beautiful weapons, slender long fingers fish the key out of the crevice, fingers that could pluck harp strings to please the turmoil of troubled men's minds.

A perpetual wheel rolling down a hill, the days and nights they come relentless. Winter is in now quick as you wouldn't believe. Within what seems like just a matter of days the trees go from luscious full things to skeletons. The cold seeks out the weak of bone and mind.

I find myself up by the Dolmen up on Cooney's hill. In summer it's as grand a place as you could wish to while away the time, but in winter it's a forlorn wind-swept barren hole. Not there long at all when along comes Squint. Our second meeting in this precise spot. Why he comes here I know not. Why I come here I know not. Only that here we are, both of us, at some dead end. Behind us a clutter of pines through which the wind howls like a starved cat. When I ask if he has some particular affinity for this place, he does not reply.

He appears troubled but in better spirits than last time. He sparks up a smoke, his bony face, like the knuckle of an old hand, sucks hard. Suppose he's a source of company for me, having not had a conversation in six or seven-hundred years, I've got to welcome the chance no matter it's going to be one way. And I've got to stop this habit of exaggerating. It's only been four hundred years at most.

He sits his behind on the spongy ditch. We're well enough protected from the brunt of the wind and the overhanging pines keep off the misty rain. I suppose he's here to escape, escape work, escape his old man, escape the thumping of his own incessant thoughts, escape the confines of the fields that have him trapped his whole life. Who knows. There's no art to read the minds construction in the face, is there Squint?

He looks ahead. His eyes cast down, maybe at Knockmoore, the big hill that lies the other side of the valley, now half visible in the murk.

Suppose I could talk and he could listen. Or I could talk and make up his replies, like I often do with others when we're alone. One does learn to entertain oneself. And often, to tell you the truth, the process of me blurting stuff out, when its reflected back into my ears, helps me gain a certain clarity.

Squint, I say, I'm beset by a sense of doom that something terrible is going to happen.

Something terrible is always happening. Focus on the positive.

You're right, I say. But what really gets me is my inability to do anything. All I can do is scribble some words and as soon as I scribble them they disappear. Useless. I've no power to influence, not enough to blow your piss sideways Squint. Anyway, enough of that, tell me, what happened the night of the festival?

No reply.

Nesbit, I sigh, were you intent on ending him Squint, because he was up and down on your sister like a yoyo, understandable enough I suppose.

Silence.

He moans, a deep sigh from the bottom of his belly. I'm thinking he's going to break into tears again but instead he clears his throat and hacks a ball of phlegm perpendicular to the flow of the wind.

Ok, I say, what are you doing up this way?

I've a liking for this spot. Can't say why. A man can hide here can he not.

I look at him, his eyes softly blinking, his whole being etched on his face, certainly looks older than his years. I know suffering when I see it. I see secrets and secrets I know. I've been lugging one around these last few centuries; heavy yokes they are, and the longer you carry them the heavier they get.

Unburden yourself Squint, before it's too late, I say.

He closes his eyes and lies back a little on the ditch. Clutching the two sides of the top of his jacket together, I notice a missing button.

Let me tell you about me then, I say, and this maybe not as easy as it sounds because my past is a dark hole; it's only in these recent days is it starting to come back to me. I was, it seems, primarily a man of words but I had a knack for the pipes too. My fingers yet move mimicking the melodies I can still hear, the tunes I composed. In fragments, like the poems I wrote, they come to me, I say. A good night for me is when I get to sit below in Hannigan's beside the fire, soaking up a good session. Monday nights isn't it, the musicians come?

He sighs. I'm thinking maybe he's going to go at himself again but he doesn't. Ten minutes slip into oblivion.

What is that wind doing? I've heard happier banshees. I'd like to fuck off, because sitting here with him in silence is worse than sitting alone in silence, but out of nowhere the sprawling in the wind unlocks something within. A cavity exposed. Raw nerve. A time of loss. She. Tears welling up inside me. Somebody I loved. Somebody who loved me.

There's a woman...she's come up out of the darkness. She's in my dreams, rambling round in there, not that that's bad, it's actually good, but there's something I've done, only I can't remember what it is.

What can you do about it now?

Fuck all, I say.

Exactly. Then just wait. The riddle will solve itself with time.

I ponder his advice.

Are you alone then? Are there others, he asks.

Good question. If there are, I haven't seen them. I've heard stories you know, about the *other crowd*, you've probably heard them too. The old hag who inhabits the willows that hug the stream below in Darcy's, the ghost of the old bog spotted by no small number of men walking the road home from the village late at night, and then there's Paddy Corcoran's wife, god rest her, going on about the hare that goes about sucking the milk from the cows in the fields until they're dried up piles of bones. The old people would know this for what it is. The young people put it down to other causes.

We are silent again. The wind our background. The pine trees behind us sway like they are one great body. The rocks weep with rain. God forsaken fucking hole, I mutter.

As I said all I can do is scribble stuff that doesn't last but seconds. Who knows who reads it, but I've got to do it. Who knows where I'll end up but I have to keep going. That's my advice for you too, put your head down and keep going young Delahunty.

I close my eyes and wish for darkness and silence, tiring a little of maintaining both sides of the conversation, but soon open them to the sound of the sweetest tenor I've heard in many a long year. I stare at him, his hollowed cheeks, the beautiful music so at odds with the man it is coming from. He's up and walking. The thought hits me that perhaps nobody has ever heard him sing, that this rare gift is shared between me and him alone. It's moments like these down the years that have kept me going.

The cold Winds from the mountains are calling soft to me
The smell of scented heather brings bitter memories
A wild and lonely eagle up in the summer sky
Flies high over Shanngolden where my young Willy lies.

The melody is mournful, the words pulled from somewhere deep inside him. If he is a good man I know not. If he is a bad man I know not. All I know is that he is a man, an ugly man, with a beautiful voice, a desperate man, one with enough energy inside to reduce to rubble all he has tried to love. As he walks back the direction towards his home I hear the words fading, sad that he's going, sadder still that his voice and the words are eaten up by the wind.

Like an eejit I stand there for a while, before making a move towards the dense pines, the light eaten by their thick knotted roof. I crawl under some low-lying branches, barely high enough for a sheep dog, I lie there flat on my back, on top of the still dry spongy earth beneath, close my eyes and try to think of her. Yet I can't. I start off well enough but in the end the face that keeps coming to me is that of young Rosie Delahunty.

*

When next I meet her she is naked in the room, her clothes thrown on the ground under the table. The smell of musky rot rubs itself off me in a way a spider might flutter across your skin. She is at herself frantically, between the legs, calling out somebody's name. Boiling with excitement I'm half steam, half liquid and the steam is eating up my liquid. I lie in a puddle on the ground beneath her. What is it I know about her. She moans, her face trying hard to capture something, her body riling in spasms, her hand moving with metronome precision. It must be summer. She is younger than when I first recall meeting her. I call out to her:

Who are you?

For the first time in centuries, I'm tormented by the flesh. Lord, I say – habit of old – Lord, let me up on top of her. She wants what I want and together we'd make a great coupling. Imagine the child. Give in to me this once and let me up on the table. As if she hears my laments, she spreads her legs ever wider, her back and neck arched into unnatural angles and curves, her hand and arm a blur of movement.

With my liquid hands I try to keep up, but there's nothing only tumult and sadness. As she reaches her peak I give up and shake my own obscenities at the uncaring sky above.

Once she's done, she quickly gathers herself together. Starting with her white underwear, she makes moves to dress, talking to the birds in a gentle whisper as she does so.

My little pretties, she says, you won't tell on me will you? I would have went for more but I've jobs to do. Always jobs to do. You know something, soon as I turn eighteen, I'm out of here. This farm is no place for someone like me. Without this little room what peace would I have? None indeed. Nobody sees. Nobody enters. Nobody leaves. They're the rules of this little world, oh, little birds, two must live and one must die. I don't know why but this is so. It is an unholy game.

Humming in a low soft voice she fixes her summer dress, leans down and takes to singing as she puts on her white runners. Two birds jump about. The third cage is empty. Her voice is high and pure, and though not powerful, she has sharp and lethal control of it.

Standing up she examines her shoes and dress, twirls around, gives a short giggle then opens the middle cage. I slither up the wall to gain a better view.

My poor little baby, she says in a whisper.

Turning around, her hands cusped in front of her, she walks towards the fireplace. A falling piece of dried plaster diverts my attention. I count six layers of ripped wallpaper. She places the emaciated body of a small robin on top of the mantlepiece close to the wooden box.

For some reason I'm overcome with emotion.

When she opens the box the smell takes but seconds to thicken. Inside a nest of tiny bones and feathers.

Down the centuries I've seen things that would make stones weep, but I've remained mute of tears until now. Lips and face quivering I speak loud to myself. It's just a little fucking bird, I say. I try to stop the tears behind my eyes, but I can't. She places him in the box, locks it, then with her hands clasped, she says a Hail Mary, slowly and deliberately, like each word contains a separate power with enough force to violate the very laws of matter.

Hail Mary,
Full of Grace,
The Lord is with thee.

Blessed art thou among women,
Blessed is the fruit of thy womb, Jesus.
Holy Mary, Mother of God, pray for us
Sinners now, and at the end of our death.
Glory be to the Father, and to the Son,
And the Holy Spirit.

DANNY
MULCAHY

Out the back of the house, over the wall, into Wilson's small paddock. Through the small gap in the sceach, down under the barbed wire, ashplant in hand, grand bit of a day, sun in and out from the clouds playing hide and seek, peeping tom, how's your mum. Day in, day out, I'm up the hill, down the hill. Two times, three times, often. Pep in my step like you wouldn't believe. Up the long stretch of meadow, grass fresh from the second cut. Over the high ditch that bears the chestnuts, the ash and the sycamores.

Sure, my friend is dead, sure, I've just come out of a treatment centre, sure, I'm jobless and living at home with my parents, and every day, at some stage of the day you come calling to me, come whispering to me that life might be even better if I let you back inside me, let you course through my veins plying your magic cell by cell. All these forces are nulled by one great counterforce, she who's swept into my life and upended all previously held convictions. Sure, I've been in love before. But this is different.

Cross Lannigan's big meadow, tip toe, hop on the rocks, over the little stream, lug myself over the high ditch held together by the exposed tangled and twisted roots of a great beech tree. Easing myself down the other side, I take a moment and look up at the steep incline of the hill before me. Scent of a fox in the breeze, trees rustling with a slight tinge of Autumn, sound of this stream alone could give a man plenty enough to build a dream on.

She took my hand that day, in Nesbit's place, just before we went in the door, and through my body there ran a current that stopped all time, that rendered matter a mysterious entity capable of great feats of fate: I looked up, the sky, the fractured clouds across it, all manifested that life was glorious, spoke out to me that I must live, that I must suck up all that life has to offer, that beyond me there was a great order and structure, that all the ways of my life were holy. My body shook with that great current, that she could love me, that she could take my hand and spark my old dead soul into existence once more. A sudden breakthrough into a different realm.

All sounds over the top, doesn't it. Do I exaggerate. No.

This is precisely as it happened and if I fail to transmit the power of this experience the failure is mine alone. Can the touch of a kind hand really transform the world? Does it have the power to alter the very structure of matter? Why not. We are matter and so is everything else. In matter we move, in matter we sleep, in matter we dream, in matter we create. I'd like to discuss this with Bellwhistle...well, then again, that might not be the best of ideas.

Somethings changed that's for sure. One moment I think I'm fooling myself, the next I'm sure I've been raised to a new plane of existence. The substance has been altered and cannot be realtered. The broken egg will not reconstruct itself. The milk stirred into the coffee will not, even if we watch it for an eternity, unmix itself back.

Up the steepest part of the hill now, to my right the tree-covered valley through which the stream runs, gasping for breath, my heart pounding in my chest, head to the ground, sweat pooling down along my spine. I stop for a break and turn around sucking in the conquered ground that flows east below me, all the way to meet the sky in the far distance, it flows with a precise gradient. Grand bit of a day. Sometimes, I'd like to keep going in one direction without care for destination or return, just walk until darkness falls, then sleep, then wake with the birds, get up and do it all over again and again.

I walk on. No tractors can make it up here. Just crows, and wily foxes.

Manoeuvre myself over another ditch and enter the last stage of the climb. A hare jumps up not ten yards from me and veers off to the left at great speed. In the distance the cattle have spotted me.

Spiritual awakening, spiritual experience, a moment before and a moment after. Yes, I've had one, I had one the first time I got drunk. In Germany on a school tour, a little bottle of whiskey on the ferry over, more once we got there. I fell in love then too. With alcohol. Spirit. *Uisce Beatha*. The Water of Life. Taken out of myself, I saw the universe in its fullness, I felt my own fullness, without care I could soar and be who I truly was. Transformation. What was missing was found, contained in a bottle that could be bought, or in my case, mostly stolen. I had to have it. From that day on without it I knew I was incomplete. But what it gave me, in the end it took away a thousand-fold. The vision was true, but the means were false.

Inputting chemicals might quicken and ease the path, but in the end it's a false method and a fake one. My Rosie O is she too false? I begin to sing, little nonsense words, sure sign of the maladies of a lovesick mind. *O Rosie O I love you so. Will you dance with me tonight. By the firelight O so bright.* Or some such nonsense.

Rosie O will you too take away a thousand-fold what you have given? Have to be careful. Voice of god or the voice of the other fellow. Who's who in the murky minefield of the mind? Most of the time I can't tell my arse from my elbow, shit from a shovel. One day at a time. Yes, one fucking day at a time. All these AA slogans. *Easy does it. First things first. Live and let live.*

Fuck the lot of them. Simpletonians. Amn't I too smart to fall for all of that. Yes, so smart you've almost pissed your life away before you even had a chance to live it.

Why are you walking up and down the hill three of four times a day?

Because I like it. Because I've fuck all else to do.

Because if I sit still I'll go mad.

Because I am mad. Because I love her. Because I'm searching for my god, but that word is out of fashion, higher power is better.

Keep walking, step in step out, feel the earth beneath your feet, turning now to peat, as you near the top of the hill. The rhythm of the soul is found in the feet. My dreams will they ever be complete. If I listen to my feet they will, for there is more wisdom in your feet than in all your philosophy. Somebody said that? I Danny Mulcahy said it. Is that even my name? Who knows? Walk on. Turn off the brain, listen to the rhythm of your feet, the earth beneath contains all the wisdom you have been too distracted to see.

Enter the heather now, sink into the sponge of bog. Lord, bury me in the heather where the bluebells sway. Looking for god on the top of the hill. Hey, have you seen that bastard, he's a lot to answer for. A *higher power*, that's what they call it in AA. You need to develop a relationship with this *higher power* of your own understanding if you want to stay sober.

You need to have spiritual experiences.

Fuck it. I'll give it a try. I don't believe in god but I believe in the devil. Before I went down *there* – I dare not say its name, nor do others – I believed the universe was meaningless and life a series of contradictions that could not be resolved, indeed, the best and only thing I could do in this situation was to remove myself from it, and now, yet now, something has altered. That moment, that glimpse into the nature of things.

O Rosie, O Rosie O, beating out time with my steps, see you tonight see you tomorrow, my waking mind, my dreaming mind, has been infiltrated by your cells, welcome into me, rape and pillage as you will, I give no defence, mine was a land build to be conquered.

Once I reach the top the wind that wasn't suddenly is because there's always some class of wind channelling down the valley of the Slieve Felim Mountains.

Recycled winds that've blown countless times before.

Wind driven over the Atlantic.

The very same winds that winged the Children of Lir, that blew the French off course in '98, that blew over this place when there were no people here at all, indeed the very same winds that blew poisonous vapours over a barren orb when time lingered close to the zero mark.

O wind don't you every get tired.

Have there been others who've come here seeking as I do?

In the long jaw of history, up here like fucking eejits on their knees, seeking outside of themselves what was missing inside of themselves.

Westwards I move, over the top of the hill, where all behind is just more hills, wave after wave of them as far as I can see. Past those hills they say on a clear day you can see the outline of the great river snaking its way to the Atlantic. Someday, I should walk and keep walking until I reach it.

But I am yet too cowardly.

It is here, always at this point, that I force myself to kneel on the spongy heather, the sky eyeing me, the wind daring me, down on my knees, through my teeth I unleash the words: *Thine will be done, not mine.*

Three times repeated, sometimes ten.

To the sun, to the sky, to the bog, to all the dead that live up here, to the winds, I pray. These are my gods. So, I give myself up to them. I surrender.

There's no denying that at times I feel like a great fool, and often make sure there is nobody around before I fall to my knees, as if there would be anybody here, bar the dead, and yet, I feel something here, some greatness beyond me, something more than the dead, some power that could squash me like a fly, my flyness revealed, my insignificance conceived, and yet, at the same time I know I too am part of this greatness, it is here in the middle of these two contradictions that the truth lurks. This is known.

I am a good man. I am a bad man.

No, rather I am somewhere in between at any given moment.

My father is a good man. My father is a bad man.

No, he too, like most men, lurks between the opposites.

Up now and bid goodbye to the west, down the way I came, the whole world below me, standing on the ledge of its great vastness, field after field, green shade after green shade, feeling like I've always known this place, always been here. The beat of my heart, my feet, in the mist and shadows I often can't shake the feeling that something too watches me as I watch all. A guardian.

A spirit of old, some manifestation of the very earth of this place.

Who knows. Who knows indeed, spooky action at a distance. Will run it past Bellwhistle. On and on I move quickly now, thoughts of Rosie in my mind.

We'll meet tonight. We won't meet tonight. She loves me. She loves me not. Every dog has its day. I've had mine. Will it continue? Not if I can help it, left to my own devices I will fuck it up like I've always fucked up everything. Gliding over the wet grass, shower from the west follows behind me, sky clouding and clearing by the minute, changing face of fortune, O Fortuna you old wretch, give young Danny Mulcahy a smile will you, look out for me, my mother Fortuna, look out for me like that old lady who gave me money for the bus that morning. Look out for fools and drunks and those who believe you look for fools and drunks.

Stranded in the dwelling place of rats, looking out a hole not big enough for a skinny cat to squeeze itself into. The first frost of the year came in last night. I've no time for frost or any of her winter cousins, never had. Give me the sun any day. I was surely born in the wrong land. With fat memories I try to warm myself. I was once a great Bard. For kings, I wrote. Yet, I ended up a pauper digging the stones from the earth to till the land stolen beneath our feat.

It's a thirsty task, ploughing this lonely furrow
With a weapon I never employed when I was rich:
This sword-play into the earth has swelled my ankles
And the shaft has martyred my fingers totally.

On cold damp fields my joints blighted. In the end it was the boredom that broke me. A mind like mine tied to a plough. There, Latin phrases moved no hearts nor boulders. I died in January.

Father of Miracles, who made the first things
Earth and heaven and constellations and stars
Spring and warmth, fruit and freezing water –
Avert thy wrath and answer my lamentation.

Beside me the earthworms are shivering too. The bells of Christmas are cracked globes of molten ore stranded in a graveyard for clowns and their ilk. Is this entire earth nothing more than a cruel and uncaring orb hurtling through the vast emptiness.

She was there before I was ever born, and when I met her I knew that I was home. I look out from my little hole and see the tiny flakes journey to the ground. As they fall her names comes to me:

Little Snow.

With the first flakes of winter snow her name forms in my mouth.

Brief illumination.

Little Snow.

Born of the night of the great snow in '49, her parents took it as a sign. Some Christmas eve long-long ago, before the ore was melted and cast, this she told me.

The memory of a night warm in our bed, the moon full and bright casting our shadows against the wall, with her hand she made butterflies, foxes and swans. Later, as I played with her hair I had insight, even then, that the day would come when I would lose her, hell, I even willed it. For, in truth, I've never sought anything with such enthusiasm as my own destruction. I'd lament, but I've grown tired of it. And myself? Tired of myself inside and out, and yet there is no end of me. Space and time and snow and her. She was good. This I know. And she loved me.

Looking up into the vastness – bound we are in infinite space and infinite time – I, for some reason take to wondering how I met my end? Does it matter? Matters to me. I know I died no hero. Did I – too weak to continue – take the cowards route and end up swinging from the bough of a Rowan. Or did I kill her or was it she killed me, or did we end up killing each other simultaneously. Space. The place where time hides.

I look out this hole and wait.

Nesbit is dead.

If there's anything I'm good at, it's waiting.

For whom or what I wait, I know not.

Only in the waiting there is knowing. His murderer goes about undiscovered. Yes, I contend he was murdered. I have my suspicions but no proof. More digging is required. The earthworms are too cold to move. Young Danny Mulcahy is in love. And she keeps half-starved birds and a locked wooden box into which I'm afraid to look.

On this cold Christmas eve Spit glistens. Around me great happiness. And for this happiness I too am happy. Too many Christmas eves spent in similar holes have honed my expectations to levels where nothing disappoints. And yet a man, even a spook, can get used to anything. Merry Christmas Spit. I love you from the depths of my deepest holes.

DANNY
MULCAHY

Bellwhistle's new car – not a new new car of course, it's an old second-hand Datsun – is full of smoke. I let down the window and flick my butt into the cold rain. A vicious wind whips it away. Things get a little awkward when I asked about his travel plans to Japan. He riles off the usual excuses.

Fucking song, says Bellwhistle, diverting the topic.

I haven't even noticed the song until he mentions it. Been too busy with the radio in my head – channel fucked.

It's pretty catchy in fairness, I say, and the lyrics are damn good.

I'm broke but I'm happy. Easy to know she's never been broke. Broke my bollox.

Hating something because it's got mass appeal is no form of criticism.

I like what I like, he says.

You're moved by forces beyond you and you don't even know it, you stupid brainwashed cunt I want to add, but I don't.

It's her voice...it's too whingy, he adds.

You'd give her one all the same, I say to try and lighten the mood.

Fucking too right. I'd give anybody one right now. Been ages since I got the jump.

Yeah.

Yourself?

Yeah, me too, I lie. It's better he doesn't know.

Want to hit Hannigan's?

Well...I...

Just for an hour.

I got shit to do, I say.

I'll drop you home anytime you want to go and make sure you don't touch a drop, he says, starting the engine. Through the headlights thick fat rain sheets down.

Come on. We'll be down and back in two shakes of a lamb's tail, he says.

I'm not staying more than an hour.

Two mineral waters for you and two pints for me.

I stare ahead, hopelessly watch the wipers strain to deal with the rain. Already, I'm regretting saying yes.

Tell me about these meetings again and what kind of things go on in them, he asks.

Why don't you come and find out, I say without much enthusiasm.

What do you mean? Are you suggesting...

I'm not suggesting anything, just that there are some meetings called open-meetings into which anybody can come.

You don't have to say anything?

No.

Nothing?

Nothing.

Not even your name?

No. Nothing, I repeat.

No. I've no business there.

Contempt prior to investigation, I say.

Listen I don't give a fuck what you get up to, but there's no way in hell you're going to catch me in one of those fucking meetings.

I'm taking the piss, I say. I spark up a smoke and offer him one.

Cursing under his breath, he takes it.

I take care of my own shit, he says, a few minutes later.

Good I say. Do that you fucking cunt and wither away up in that house with the ghost of your dead father haunting the bollox off you. You know what you should do don't you. You should sell that fucking house, or burn it and move the fuck out of there and head for Japan, that place you've dreamed of going all your life. And the only thing that ever stopped you going was yourself. That was all, yourself and your lack of balls. Cunt. This I don't say of course, instead I suck heavy on my fag and he sucks heavy on his, both of us wondering what the other is really thinking.

Tuesday night. Place as dead as a weekday mass. Everybody is staring at me because they know I've been away and that I'm not drinking. Most of them would like nothing better than to see me pick up another drink, Bellwhistle included. He's not a real friend. I've never had a real friend, because I've never been a real friend. I prefer to see the destruction of my friends rather than their success. I'm one twisted up little fuck, sipping on my mineral water, miserable as hot dogshit. I won't drink just to spite them. I really want to drink, just to turn my brain off, because it won't stop yapping to me about Rosie Delahunty, whispering to me how right now she's fucking some other guy in the back of a car, or in his house, or in the toilet of some dingy pub, or behind a ditch, or beneath the shades of some darkened grove.

I know it's me. I know I'm going to lose her if I keep this up.

One night we did it against the church, at the back of the sacristy. Instigated by her of course. Then there was the time my parents were away. She rushed down so we could do it all over the house. She even made me break into the barracks where we did it on the big wooden table with my father's typewriter. Anything with any element of danger drove her already wild eyes wilder. She's damn mad, I mutter, and I love her for it.

What's that, asks Bellwhistle.

Nothing, I say.

Up at the counter Dinny Patterson breaks into laughter. His old man laughs too. Whenever Dinny laughs his old man laughs and whenever his old man laughs Dinny laughs. Simple enough infallible law. Six out of seven nights you'll find them at the counter.

Dinny's in his forties. He had a breakdown a while back. There was garda checkpoint stopping cars on the way to the city. Probably close to Christmas. They do that to hit their quotas. Anyway, when they stopped Dinny they got more than they expected, a scenario that they likely had never encountered in all their years of active duty. He was bollox-naked driving the car.

Why are you naked, asks Jim Breslin – the guard in question and from whom this story came down verbatim – stepping back from the window he had leaned into.

Well, says Dinny, it's just an auld habit of mine.

Have you been at it long, asks Breslin.

No long Guard.

Months? Years?

Verging into the years, I'd say.

And why?

Just an auld habit Guard, says Dinny after a minute of silence.

Breslin, after consulting with his colleague, suggests they ring the station in town to get some hint of what they might do. In the end they escorted him home and next day they call up to the house and inform his father and mother who agreed to have Dinny sent down to do a stint in the ward.

Since then, he seems fine, but you never can be sure because he always seemed fine. Looking at them now, you would think they were best friends rather than father and son. Is this the way relationships with your father are supposed to be. I've no fucking idea, but there's something about them I envy. Maybe it's their simplicity, their ignorance or maybe it's just their plain old happiness. Five or six pints a night, that is their lot, no less no more, and with their lot they seem content.

Tuesday night the place is dead. An hour in, Bellwhistle is on his third pint and about to order a forth.

I got to get going, I say.

Just one more, he says, just one more.

One more turns into three more. Bellwhistle is getting all slobbery, lisping his words and repeating himself, talking shite about Nesbit and the good old days. There were never any good days I want to scream in his face; the only thing that makes them seem good is the stuff you're gulping down your throat to delude your brain. I'm at the point of letting him having it. I turn to throw my eyes on him, but in the dim light I see a look of desperation in his face, some aspect of him I've never seen before. It only last seconds but it's there, powerful as a lightning strike. Bellwhistle, defeated and broken and childlike. The drooping eyes, the wasted decades, the receding hairline, the bald spot on top, growing like the ecosystem of a small living pond, the hopelessness of his future. All have converged. He sees it, I see it and of it there's no escaping.

He looks away, lost for words. I feel an inescapable pity for him.

How many times did he listen to me drunk – and I was way worse than him – how many times did he put up with my bullshit.

There and then I decide I'll do my best to give myself over to him for the night. I'll be nice. I will consider those around me. I will accommodate him. I will bury my ego. This feeling does not come with any sense of superiority, rather it's solidarity. I understand him. We may not be the same, but I understand him. His weaknesses are mine and mine his. I look around the pub, at the barman, at Patterson and his father, at Jimmy Burke seated in the corner mumbling to himself under the portrait of Dev. All of them I love. I want to cry I love them so much. And all this without a drink. I must talk about it down in aftercare, but I can't because I'm not supposed to be in bars with other drunks. It's progress surely. According to the counsellors, an alcoholic stops developing emotionally from the time they start drinking. That would make me thirteen. There's no other way of putting it. But I've grown up a bit since then. I can step outside myself and see what's going on around me sometimes, not always mind you, only sometimes, like now, like these moments of clarity. The alcohol sedated fog of my brain is clearing. It takes five years to get your brain back to something like it was. That's what the doctor down there told us. Wet brain, are you going to drive me insane? There are three indicators for people who develop wet brain: blackouts, hallucinations, incontinence. All three in abundance I had.

The Patterson's leave.

It's me and Bellwhistle and Jimmy. And Job the barman. He's been looking after drunks for twenty odd years, and now reaching the limit of his patience, he calls time.

Outside, the rain has stopped but the icy wind has the car windows frosted over. Bellwhistle pisses on the driver side. Reams of steam rise. I cover the passenger side, and my half of the front windscreen, as I convince him to let me drive.

The roads are not yet icy, but I take my time anyway. As I drive, he bladders on.

I can't stop thinking about it, he says Do you really think he killed himself? There's no way in hell he killed himself. He's not the type. Someone did him in. Did ye go up there that night Mulcahy?

I restrain a sudden surge of anger. He's drunk. He doesn't know what he's doing.

How many times have I told you, no.

But you said you can't remember.

I can remember that.

I just can't get my head around it. I miss him so much.

Go Bellwhistle. Get out of here. There's nothing left in Spit for you, I say.

Too late for me. You go. You're young. If you don't get out of here Spit will end up eating you. You, like me, are not cut out for life here. We're outsiders Danny. Spit will chew you up and spit you out sideways. Spit doesn't like people like us, people with ideas and people who read books and question things. Not just Spit mind you, same the world over. Go to other countries and there you can be the outsider, the outlaw, as much as you want and nobody will give a fuck, that's your role, but you can't do it here. No. There's no chance for you Danny. Get out. And stay off the drink too. I'm not just saying it because I'm drunk, I'm jealous as fuck of course, I wish I could have gone to that place where you went. I wish I could have gone to university. I could have but I turned it down. Too fucking late now. You know my old man taught me the secrets of drunk driving. Close one eye, he said. I used to steer home for him when I was a kid. That kind of thing was more acceptable back then. You know I had an uncle who drowned himself in a barrel of water. In head first. Who the fuck would kill themselves like that?

You serious, I say, surprised, because in all these years I've never hear about it.

Would I fuck about with a thing like that, I'm serious as fuck, was winter too, broke the ice off the water to do it.

Jesus, I say out loud, picturing the scene. I can't help wondering what kind of boots he was wearing, or was it the wellies he had one. Surely, he would have put on his best.

Bellwhistle takes a long drag then laughs.

They found him a few days later. The postman saw the legs stick up out of the barrel.

He laughs again, then takes to coughing.

How would you do it Danny?

Pills and vodka, I lie.

Aye.

Things like that run in the family you know, he says.

That's bullshit.

Look at Cobain. Both his uncles topped themselves. He knew it was going to get him sooner or later.

Fuck sake Bellwhistle, can we change the topic, I say.

Last thing I'll say about it is that it's more acceptable in Japan. There it's seen as an honourable way out. I know I'm always going on about it, but I feel like I've been there before, that I existed before this body, before this place, that I had love, that I had beauty in my life.

He lets down the window and flicks out the butt, but it flies right back in his face.

Fuck you wind, he says, picking it off his lap. Fuck you wind burning my face like that. Here you go, you stupid cunt. He throws the butt out again, this time successfully.

You can still go there. You have the money now, I say.

You're right. I will. I'm going back there for sure Danny. You understand it. You're the smartest guy I ever met. I know I haven't met many smart people, but you know shit, not just shit you read, but you have a sense of things. Something like that is rare. Me, I'm going to end up like Radio Molloy. A local character. That will be my lot. Not that there's anything wrong with him but when I look at him, I see myself twenty years down the road, if I survive that long. Children will laugh at me, pelt stones at me, call me names behind my back. I might as well get a dog for company, you know, something to listen to me complain and rile against the world. Better than talking to myself. A neutered dog and a fucking cane, Mulcahy. You go Danny, get the hell out and don't look back. Don't go marrying here and building a big house with eight fucking rooms and only you the missus and the one sprog in it. Fuck that. Fuck paying that off for the rest of your life. You're not cut out for that. Go out there and taste the eternal. Explore the darkness, as the great Freddy N says, *he who explores my darkness, will find roses under my cypress trees*. Good old Freddy. I love that bastard. *Build your houses on the slopes of Mt. Vesuvius* Danny, not on the lonely hills of Spit. Imagine trying to tell that to cunts around here. You might meet your end in some unknown shithole and be never heard from again, there's that. But stay around here and the greasy bacon, the butter and Tayto sandwiches, the ten pints a night, whatever, will clog up your arteries, fatten your fucking liver, or – maybe it's really the unexpressed grief over the state of your loveless and sexless marriage that will tip the scales, and up out of nowhere the urge to rid yourself from everything will see you swinging from the haybarn one windswept Sunday morning. You know it. You've seen it. And everybody around will be saying, Jesus, we didn't see that coming. Sure, he seemed grand. Always had a smile on his face and was up for a chat. But they don't know Danny, they don't fucking know what's going on in a man's soul.

His voice has risen to a shout.

Are you ok, I ask.

What do you mean am I ok? I was never fucking ok, and I never want to be ok. You should know that boss.

Ok, calm down, I say. I put it down to drink. He's had too much. I've never really seen him drunk, because I've always been drunker. Maybe he's always like this, I reassure myself.

The fucking three of us Danny. What a team. There will never be the likes of it again. The shit we pulled off.

Yeah, I say.

Look at that fucking moon over the hill there. Silver bastard. Spooky fucking action at a distance, Danny. Do you know something, the religions had all this shit figured out before the physicists came along and said this is how it works. God said let there be light. Big bang. Reality is one fucked up cunt. Do you believe in any of it, Danny?

I believe in energy, I say honestly. We die, our energy is transformed. Energy can neither be created nor destroyed.

The god of Spinoza. Einstein's god. Would you say that's the first time Spinoza has ever been mentioned going past Packie Quirk's meadow?

Wasn't his grandmother from over Killyballymuck way, I say.

He takes to laughing. But laughing is not the right word, for laughing is a good thing, but in his laughter, I hear no good things. He curses the moon again, then laughs, then curses the stars for betraying him.

The stars betray you, he says. When I was young, I'd look

at them and they'd talk to me, I don't mean I heard voices or anything, but we communicated on some level. They'd tell me to travel, to wander the globe, to do great things. Back then everything seemed possible. In a way growing older is nothing but a steep and gradual reduction of possibilities, don't you think Mr. Physics?

We can't take all roads. One choice reduces the possibility of another way, I say.

There is no anointed way. There is no holiness. Fuck the lot of it.

He is silent a while. The night is vast and empty and nothing else seems alive.

No, that's not right is it. I betrayed them. That's the simple fucking truth of it Mulcahy, he says, I fucking let them down. I let myself down.

The man that made time, made lots of it, I say, aping my father.

No, you're wrong there young Danny Mulcahy, there is rot and decay, and points past which there are no turning back. You should know it well. The second law gnaws and chases us like a starved hound. Entropy. The race is on Mulcahy, the race is fucking on. He laughs again, this time without much energy. He closes his eyes and within minutes is snoring.

When I wake him up outside his house, he insists we go inside for a spliff. The light bulb in the living room is blown. A small single lampshade illuminates the room with a yellow hue. Through the dim light I cannot make out the portraits on the wall. The men of '98. He puts on the Stooges and talks about Nesbit again as he gets to work on a joint.

I remember once, he says, you were there too, that time Nesbit told us the story about the river.

Yeah?

Don't you remember?

There are so many stories. Nesbit and I were thick and thin growing up, I say.

It's the one about the river.

Was it the time we went sticking salmon?

No, says Bellwhistle, way before that. Ye, were much younger.

What river, I say, causally.

I don't know what fucking river. But you must remember it, you almost killed Nesbit there.

A dart of energy shoots through my body which I control with as much calmness as possible.

It was wintertime, the river was flooded. Ye stood at Corbett's bridge, looking down into the flood. It's not a very big bridge is it? But big enough especially when ye were kids wouldn't you says Mulcahy.

Suppose it was.

Remember now?

I do.

And?

According to Nesbit, as we stood looking into the river I stepped behind him and pushed him, I say.

According to Nesbit. So, you deny it Mulcahy...you crazy bastard. What came over you?

That river was a stream, not much more than a puddle. You know Nesbit and his stories I say as calmly as I can, the breath gone from my lungs.

Wide-eyed, Bellwhistle coughs.

He told me himself another time when you weren't there, he says. It happened sure enough Mulcahy.

I laugh.

Is that your answer Mulcahy?

What are you trying to say, I ask fixing my eyes on him.

Well, it's not everybody who would do such a thing. Sure, we might imagine it, but you Mulcahy, you carried it out. Nesbit could have drowned.

Could have drowned me bollox, it was a fucking stream, I say with more venom than I intended.

Bellwhistle looks at me, his eyes swimming in his head, sinking at times, then reappearing. Tomorrow he won't even remember what we talked about.

Relax now young Danny, I'm only having an old chat. Will you skin this up for me, he says handing me the three skins he's managed to stick together.

Sure, I say, but I'm not smoking any.

All the more for me then, says Bellwhistle, all the more for me, he laughs.

Within minutes he's snoring.

I put a blanket over him and head out into the night.

All motivation and desire dredged from the bottom of my glass, I'm down in the dumps, I'm sucked dry to a rotten old tooth. There are days like this, weeks like this even; but this one on me now is the worst I've seen.

Make new memories, Squint says. Fuck that.

How can you make new memories when all you have is goats and fields and bogs and people who can't see you, hear you, smell you, touch you. Feels like I'm stuck in a photograph and I'm the only thing alive in it. How can you make friends with people in photographs, Squint, I say out loud to myself.

When I'm like this there's only one place for me and that's the dark stretch of bog that runs all the way from the village up to Peter Quinlan's house. I submerge myself in the water, in land, in bog hole, up to my eyeballs in peat, my feet in this world my head in the next. Little do the people know it, but this was once an ancient sacrificial site. And what was sacrificed you may well ask? Goats? Sheep? Pigs?

No, says I, Kings were sacrificed. That's right. If they weren't up to the job, they, the common people, were entitled to sacrifice the rulers to appease the gods, and the bogs were the place to do it, on account of their being thought as the place where this world and the next intermingled.

Imagine the following. Crops fail for three continuous years because of bad winters or rainy summers; or there were sudden unpredictable eruptions of plague and pestilence, not at all uncommon back in those days. Someone had to account for these happenings. Kings and other high-ranking members of the ruling class, put in charge to ensure that order was maintained and that people didn't starve, now had to answer for their failures. The details of the selection process are not clear. But what is clear is that they were disembowelled, had their heads cut off, had limbs cut off, had their nipples sliced open, and were then buried with some treasures and weapons in the bog. I do not know if the ancients had knowledge that bogs preserve bodies, maybe they did, maybe they didn't, that doesn't matter. In this spot alone, below me, as we speak, lie the fully preserved bodies of five men, all scattered around different areas of the bog, all at different levels, all killed at different times, sometimes with gaps of hundreds of years between them. All this was long before I came along.

It's memory that has driven me down here to this wretched state. Day and night I'm beset by memories, each one building on the other like a long rusty chain that I just know has little good intention for me.

Little Snow, Little Snow what did I do?

For days, I can't distinguish between dreams and what is real and what is but memory. All I know is that I'm sick, and if there's a doctor or a medication that can cure me the length of the land I don't know of it. I'm beset by visions of blood, brains, broken bones, murder. I'm incapable of work. Fuck Spit and fuck all its inhabitants. The thoughts of it alone makes me puke bile and frogspawn.

After days of this slow molasses existence, no longer able to endure even myself, I drag my being into a heap and force myself towards the dolmen at the top of Cooney's hill. There for three days and three nights I wait, during which the visions, dreams and memories keep lashing at me. I refuse to believe what I'm seeing. I'd like someone to come and tell me I've gone mad. On my knees at the end of three days, I weep and cry out to what I know not. In six hundred years I've never reached this level of desperation. Of course, I would kill myself if I could, but over the centuries I've tried every conceivable method, but as we all know it's difficult to kill nothing.

There's many a greedy cunt in this world. That ye should pay attention too. Little pieces of memories and bits of dreams spliced together have brought me to these thoughts. In everything there's part of me and everything is a part of me. Sure, I was no saint, but neither was I no demon. Six hundred years of relative peace and now this. Ignorance sure was bliss. I can be innocent no more, now that my eyes have opened.

DANNY MULCAHY

Under the shadow of the ash tree that stands near the top of Darcy's haggard, I see the outline of a man. He appears to be looking right into the direction of the setting sun, the direction I'm coming from. Though it's cold I'm down to my t-shirt, jacket tied around my waist.

Leaning towards me on a stick which rests under his armpit, the figure shouts out a greeting when I'm still about fifteen yards away. Being a little short sighted it's only when I hear his voice that I recognize who it is.

I don't say anything until I'm close enough for him to swing out the stick he carries and hit me with it, if that were his desire.

Michael. How's it going?

Going good now, he says, Yourself?

Not too bad, I say. Grand evening.

Not bad now. Lot of rain, land is pure muck.

A silence follows. An uncomfortable silence, because I've never much had a conversation with Michael Squint Delahunty, and I'm not really up on farmer conversations about land and growth. And besides all that he's not taken his one good eye off me, like he's studying me for some purpose. The altercation at the festival is on my mind but as far as I understand it was Nesbit he was after.

I'm about to make a move and say goodbye when he beats me too it.

You're a good man for the walking aren't you.

Well, I say, not sure how to respond, I've been doing a bit.

I do a bit myself, he says. He lifts up the stick, a stout hazel, straightens up, then with a quick and powerful movement he drives the stick back downwards into the soggy earth. Oh, I could be walking out at all hours. You wouldn't think it, but you could be seeing quare things going on around here in the night.

Well, be careful, I say, starting to walk away.

Hold yer horses there now me boy, he says.

He swivels round, pulls the stick out of the earth and twirls it skilfully in his hand.

Is there something you want, I say, my voice wavering.

Oh there is, isn't there something we all want.

You're right there. I want to win the lottery, I say, laughing like an idiot at my own joke.

No hint of a smile cracks his bony face.

You believe in luck then, he says?

I might believe in it if I knew what it was, I say.

Smart man, huh? Simple enough really, luck is luck and a man's luck can't last forever.

Sure, I say, you're right there Michael. Well, I better be off, have a lovely evening.

Every dog has its day, he says, taking a step towards me. I step back.

Is there something you need to tell me Michael, I say, gathering up my courage. I've nothing against you. That night at the festival, I can't even remember it.

You and my sister. I know what ye're at, he says, his voice dropping down a tone.

I don't respond.

He plucks the stick out of the earth again. He lets it swing back and forth in his hands. It's a good six feet long.

Nothing to say for yourself, he asks.

What do you want me to say?

Just understand that it won't last. It didn't last for your friend and it won't last for you. You're a class below her. You're nothing but a stepping stone to her next conquest.

Sounds like you know a lot about it, I say moving back from him.

Oh, I do. I know the state of affairs. I know what my sister is. And I know more about you than you think young Fanny Mulcahy...sorry, I meant to say Danny, he laughs.

I laugh too. My eyes are drawn to his teeth which are a mess of yellow and stain, and crookedness. How they matter at this moment I do not know but my mind has decided to give them great importance.

Is there anything else I should know Michael, I ask with all the determination I can muster. I ready myself. Whatever is coming is coming.

Know this Mulcahy, I'd break you like a fucking twig if I took my mind to it.

Surprisingly, I'm calm and no longer afraid.

I don't doubt you would, I say, but I've no bad intentions with your sister. I love her, I say.

He takes to laughing. When he stops, his gaunt face wrinkles into a scowl.

I go walking in the nights Mulcahy. Somebody needs to keep an eye on what's going on when the sun goes out. I was walking the night Nesbit met his end. I was there Mulcahy. I saw what happened.

Now, within my body there are sudden eruptions involving hormones and chemicals. My lip starts to twitch, my eyes flitter. I watch his hand tighten round the stick.

I hope you've told the cops what you saw, I say, trying my best to steady my voice, but it's gone, like a spooked horse.

I don't think you'd be wanting me to tell daddy what I saw, he says, laughing again.

I don't know what you think you saw but...the case is closed. We all had our say. Besides, I heard you were drunk as ten bullocks that night.

I sobered up.

Good for you, I say, If...

Look around you Mulcahy, he interrupts me, if you scream out here who's going to hear you, who's going to come and save you. Not a house for miles. Only that one down there that's empty, he says, nodding his head in the direction of Nesbit's house.

Works both ways Delahunty, I say.

He takes to laughing.

You're fucking crazy, I mumble as I turn around.

Run off with yourself then. Heard you're off the drink too, he shouts after me, that won't fucking last will it Mulcahy, because you're a fuck-up. And don't forget I'm watching you.

In the forest, a night of dark trees whispering words that form a thin incomprehensible gruel. Here I hang, as always and ever, my inescapable self. A few hundred yards north an owl is perched on an old oak tree. I can't but admire his ability to sit still and do nothing. His eyes two moons born a billion years ago.

Why am I here, owl, I shout out.

To remember, so that you nevermore forget, or so I interpret his hooting.

I remember a forest like this, I say, thick and dark, the trees moaning and groaning, not unlike the sounds of these old trees tonight, creaking and straining, bark breaking, sinews tearing. It was summer, the sap thick and dripping, the crickets singing, the fat frogs croaking. Lust was painted thick across all things living. Lust, owl, do you know of it?

She loved you.

I loved her.

The owl takes to laughing.

You loved nothing. Only your own weaknesses.

In my excitement, I ignore his slight. Have you ever felt loved owl, really loved? God forgive me, I never loved another as I loved her. Yet, I was not good at showing it. This I will not deny. She was kind and good to the bone. Did you know that sometimes after our lovemaking she would sit and cut my fingernails. Other times she would play the harp. While I listened and watched her, I understood the meaning of everything. Why the stars up there in the vast hole of space exist, why the crows gather in the evening. I understood the fish in the streams and seas, the crabs beneath the great darkness of the ocean, the spider spinning it's web, motivated by blind will to try and try again. All of it made sense to me, owl, all of it moved in a delicate and delicious harmony I have not before nor since experienced.

Sounds lovely.

I know it didn't end well, I say, but no need for that attitude.

You really can't remember at all can you?

No, just flashes. Her face. My work. My poems.

Poems?

Yes, bard for hire, I say, a shiver of pride running down the back of my neck.

You might have thought you were, you might even have had talent, but you were more in love with the idea of fame than with work. Ideas above your station.

Cease you prattle owl, I say.

Why is it after all these years you've now come to seek the truth and wisdom of the owl.

Oh, they say you are wise owl, but what are you but another feathered foul stranded here in the night, alone like me, hooting out your nonsense.

And yet here you are hanging on every word of my nonsense.

It's the truth I'm after.

After all these years?

Better late than never, owl.

I'm sure you expect some great drama, at the centre of which, is you, of course. Either the great villain, a vile but somehow justified murderer perhaps, or a story twisted to portray you in some way the victim. The truth is this: in all respects you were an average man, though it is true you were good-looking, and in general favoured by women, who, at first mistook your self-delusions for confidence. You used people and moved on. That's about the size of it.

I feel my throat burning. My eyes watering, my lips trembling.

The trees moan and groan in the wind.

You are right in that, but wrong in that I did not love her, I say after a long silence.

She was that which you sought your whole life, that magic that could have elevated you to a greater and higher purpose. Yet, not long after you discovered her you discarded her as if she were a burden. It was all a game to you, wasn't it. One of them after the other. Made you feel good.

I can't remember rightly, I say, but it wasn't like that.

You don't want to remember.

I'm trying my best, I say. I close my eyes. The darkness moves. Behind my eyes it undulates. Yes, now I see.

Your whole life you were convinced you were special, above others. All this was a reaction to cover up your insecurities, holes you tried to fill. Truth was, she was the most special thing that ever came into your life. She asked you to settle down. You hummed and hawed, then left – a vague promise to soon return – on one or other of your hairbrained schemes, seeking fame, seeking fortune, seeking to escape yourself.

In the darkness I see forms, I hear whispers. Yes, owl, I remember.

Did you know soon after you left, she found out she was pregnant. Waited and waited. Her family wouldn't take her back.

Yes owl, I remember now, her desperation and hunger. The days of rain had the river swollen to ten times its size. Body never found. Washed out to the deeps, food for the crabs, my child within her belly, her song forever silenced.

Tears stream down my face as I remember.

I could not ask for forgiveness, because for six-hundred years I could remember nothing of it. But I ask it now, owl, forgiveness of you, of the forest, of god and most of all her.

The wind, the swaying trees, the trembling leaves, the black moonless night.

She's long dead owl and yet she still moves. Is this my punishment, I cry out, to be banished to the confines of Spit's idle borders for eternity.

You travelled the world pursing your vague dreams, falling further and further into disrepute and degeneracy.

Is this my punishment?

Well, ironic isn't, you confined here, you who roamed the world so free. Ships. Army. Wars. Peace. New Worlds. You saw it all. You might even have gotten what you wanted.

In the end how did I go?

See, it always comes back to you doesn't it. Well, needless to say, it wasn't pretty.

I wait hung upside-down, one minute thinking myself a mouse, the next a bird, flittering between two states avoiding the reality of the bat that I am.

About my end owl? Are there details? Owl hoots, but his hoots are no longer comprehensible to me. Once more the world around me makes little sense. I suppose it matters not how I went, nobody cared then, and nobody cares now.

DANNY MULCAHY

Sometimes, I look into her eyes and I get scared. Sometimes I think she could be fucking anything or anybody and that it has nothing to do with me. She just wants something inside her, and want it she does, like her very lungs will implode if she doesn't get it.

Four times in four hours the other night. My back is a map of claws and fingernails. Yes, in my dead friend's house. She likes to do it there. She did Nesbit too. Yes, that bracelet was hers. She says they were just friends. I want to believe it so much that I end up believing it. They were just friends.

Yet, she knows things, things she's not telling me, things she doesn't want me to know. But what can I do. Truth is I've never been happier and yet there's a nagging sensation I can't put a name or location on.

It seems to me we only ever meet to have sex. I want her to be my girlfriend, but she says we have to keep everything secret. When I ask her why she just says it's better that way.

Because of Franky, I ask. The word sticks in my throat. I've almost never used his first name.

Yes, she says matter-of-factly. There's something cold inside her, like meteorite rock, like out of space debris. Lying there on the bed, his bed, her eyes black and dead as stone, pierce right through me.

When I'm not with her I can't stand it and when I'm with her more than an hour I can't stand it either. Demanding all my attention, she sucks my energy up. Don't get me wrong I'm not complaining. I've been taken to a new world. And yet, after our exertions we might lie together unseparated for hours. That wooden box of hers on the floor. The box she never opens. She'll do things for me, so charming I almost break out in tears, like cut my finger nails ever so carefully. I'm washed over with the feeling that she adores me down to millimetres. Playing the harp for me I watch transfixed as her fingers glide over the strings. She cries for dead birds and the suffering in the world, her heart as delicate as a feathered pillow. I look at her one minute and I see something so beautiful and pure. Ten minutes later she's begging for me to give it to her harder. How to reconcile these two dimensions. Maybe it's me that's fucked. Or maybe I'm too inexperienced. Even if this is so, there lurks a strange presence, no that's not right, it's more an energy, that dances in and out of her. All this in Nesbit's bed. My dead friends bed. Watching us from that hill. That spooky glint of light hanging off it, no matter what the time of day or night, no matter what angle you look at it from.

Stupidly, I've mentioned her in the aftercare group. First off, they were pissed because it's strongly recommend not getting in any kind of relationship for a year. They say we are not mature enough for relationships. I guess they're right. I give whole nights sleepless for things others might dismiss as simple. For example, if she doesn't answer my call or if she uses a certain word in a certain way, or even if she looks at me funny. There are many such nights. The things I do be thinking. Who's she with? What's she doing?

Yes, it must be me, I'm mad. My mind is not right. Yet, when we're having sex I can see her eyeballs rolling beneath the lids, as she eggs me on to drive myself deeper, shouting for me to fuck her harder. Don't get me wrong, I enjoy it, but to tell you the truth I don't like that word. I wish sometimes she'd say make love instead. I'm more romantic. We've never made love. We've fucked each other to the point of wanting to merge into one body. How many has she fucked? The question is in my head like a stone rattling around in a tin can. How many?

Afterwards, when the fucking is done, she'll lie there and talk of marriage and kids and little babies, which makes me so happy. But when she says we can't tell anybody about us, that bad feeling boils up in my stomach.

I've got to be honest. I'm twenty-one and I've never had a real girlfriend. I was always too drunk and too crazy. Nobody could stand me for more than a week. That's the truth of it. I hold my hand up and admit I'm lost, totally lost. She's cracking me up.

These are heights I've never known, worlds with atmospheres deprived of essential elements. Truth is, there's no off switch. I'm high as fuck but I'm dying. She wants to meet again. That's three times in three days. Nine times in three days and she wants more. Sometimes, she lets me come inside her. She has it down to a tee. She says there are times that are safer and times that are more dangerous. How does she know all these things? Who else has she let come inside her? Nesbit of course, but Nesbit's dead. No, not Nesbit, they were just friends. Who else? The others live. It's too much for me.

Down on your knees again and hand it over. Mutter, through

your teeth. God is a good man and will give you a hand if he sees fit. Give me a hand god, for there are times, most of the times, I don't know what the fuck is happening. *God grant me the serenity to accept the things I cannot change the courage to change the things I can and the wisdom to know the difference*

Prostate on the ground, here I am humbled before thee. I love the sex Lord. Lord, I love it. I love her. I want her to be fucked and fucked and fucked until she's satisfied, but I have a worry deep in my belly, and that is, she can never be satisfied, not even if you yourself fuck her. Would you fuck her god? Surely that would do her in the end. Fill that hole in her soul.

Let me hand it all over to you god.

Step three: *Hand over thy will and thy life.*

You take care of it.

Nothing more I can do.

Tip my hat to you Lord.

Go on. Give her one. One she won't forget.

Amen.

I wake up in the back of Danny's smoked filled car. Headlights tunnel into the darkness. Light drizzle falls through the beams. It takes me a while to figure out we are parked at the forestry entrance a few hundred yards above Nesbit's house. Danny takes a swig from a half empty vodka bottle. Lighting another cigarette, he mumbles nonsense, curses, then laughs out loud. It's then I notice a bloodstained knife lying on the floor in front of the passenger seat.

Opening the car door he struggles but on the third attempt he makes it out. When he's steadied himself sufficiently, he makes for the boot. Leaving the vodka bottle on the roof, he opens the boot and takes out a rifle. Cigarette in mouth, vodka bottle in one hand, rifle in the other he returns to the driver door and kicks it shut. Deriving some pleasure from this he continues to kick the door making a large dent below the window. He tries to kick the window in but fails. At one stage he wobbles and falls, then leaves the vodka bottle standing in the grass and the rifle on the ground.

He then runs at the car and delivers it a series of heavy kicks, still failing to break the window. Cursing, but not defeated, he concentrates his efforts on the side mirror, easily knocking it off. Appearing to have sedated his desire to destroy the car he then picks up the bottle and in two attempts drains it. As expected, the empty bottle is flung at the car and explodes when it hits the driver's side window.

Fucking piece of shit car, he shouts, as he leans in the door, turns off the ignition and takes the keys out and puts them in his pocket. He picks up the gun and starts walking.

Outside Nesbit's front door he moves uneasily back and forth, mumbling again. It is useless to tell you what he says for most of it is incomprehensible rubbish. Seeming to reach some decision he turns and walks determinately through the yard, over the gate and into the laneway beaten out by cows, moving up the hill the other side of which lies the Delahunty's.

The sky is starless, the moon muted behind gluttonous clouds. Again, in the darkness he stumbles and falls. I'm right on his heels shouting out with all my might that he should stop, turn around and go back to Nesbit's house and sleep it off. But talking to a drunk is a waste of time, and besides he can't hear a word I'm saying. We plod our way along making our way to the apex of the hill. In the distance I can see the hazy glow of Delahunty's farmyard.

A few hundred yards from the house the dog greets us. Perhaps this knocks some sense into Danny because he suddenly sits down on the wet grass close to a small treeless ditch. He pulls back the rifle bolt and accidently ejects a bullet. Fumbling in the grass he picks it up, pulls the cartridge out, slips in the bullet, then closes the bolt. He raises the rifle towards the house, resting it on the ditch, and gives what seems like a long time looking through the sites. After a while the dog stops barking. To my great relief, Danny, mumbling, cursing and overcome with drink, lies down and is soon asleep. I spread myself out over him as best I can to keep the wet and cold from him. What else I can do. As I can make little sense of this whole event, I assume it's happening some distance in the future. Not uncommon. A rogue piece in the puzzle. Joker in the pack.

DANNY MULCAHY

It's a Saturday morning not long after Christmas. As usual we waste no time in getting down to business. Twice in one hour. Afterwards, she falls asleep her Nokia in the gap between our pillows. A dark strand of hair lying over her cheek she looks even more beautiful, more innocent, no, innocent is not the right word, more honest maybe. I stub out my cigarette. For a while I watch as her chest rises and falls peacefully.

I hate this house. There is nothing but death here, I think, looking at the bland stained yellowed wallpaper in Nesbit's room. Bellwhistle is right. The place is cursed. We should not be here. The dead should not be here. Him, his mother, that wretched knotted thing that was his father.

I edge myself closer to her, checking that she's really asleep. From between the gap between the pillows I fish out the phone, then turning my back to her, heartrate increasing, I input the code, which I've gotten to know by watching her when she thought I wasn't watching. But I'm the kind that's always watching.

Bingo.

There is always a moment before I do something stupid, a moment to save myself. Whatever's in here I'm not ready for it. I turn around and put the phone back, then close my eyes and try to sleep.

But I can't.

Two minutes later I've the phone open again.

Flicking through her messages I notice some of her contacts are entered as initials only. Quickly moving through the last few days, I notice P is most prominent...I open the most recent one.

P: That was so nice.
R: Yes, see you again soon.
P: Can't wait. Same place.
R: Why not. Remember our little secret.
P: Always so mysterios.

Mysterious, spelt wrong. Must be some dopey fuck. My heart's pounding. Peter? Paul? Is it Pa Quinn. Could she be fucking Pa Quinn. Scrolling back further I find an M with the same kind of exchanges. I slam the phone on the bed waking her up.

What's wrong, she asks, not near as shocked as I'd like her to be.

Your fucking phone, is all I can manage to say.

What?

She sits up.

I saw your messages.

What messages? You went through my phone? What the fuck.

Who's P?

Calm down. Your face, Jesus.

Just fucking tell me, I say, my voice changed to a tone she's never before heard. Just fucking tell me, I repeat.

Powerless against the sudden eruptions of my anger I close my eyes and try to focus on my breath, but my lungs are subservient to my mind and my mind is a muddled mess of rage. My right hand is squeezing the phone so hard I think for a moment I might break it. Moving towards me and placing her hand on mine, like a grounded current, she dissipates the vast amount of my pent-up energy.

Calm down baby, it's Paula.

Paula who, I say, suddenly embarrassed.

Paula Sheridan from town.

She looks right into my eyes and they do not waver nor do the pupils dilate.

Baby, you're so crazy, she says, disarming me with her smile.

Why input them with an initial? Whose M?

M is Michelle. We're close. Gang of us from school that used to hang around. Always called ourselves by our initials, like a game.

I'm still panting, trying to keep up with my lungs.

Calm down crazy Danny. She curls into me like a cat. You're so funny. I know what you need. She slithers downwards. Poor jealous baby, she says.

I sigh and am about to push her away, still trying to cling to my anger.

But she mumbles with her mouth full. Takes it out and says, how is that poor little boy, will you check my phone again?

Helpless and powerless now, I groan.

She sucks the darkness out of me.

Later we lie there sedated in the quietness of the room, the curtains inadequate to keep out the shards of daylight that crisscross the dusty darkness. I tell her a story that I've never told anybody. About the time I died. She laughs at first, but when she hears my voice breaking she knows I'm not kidding.

A week I gave drinking, I'm talking about continuously, morning, noon, night. I knew not the day nor the hour. I ended up in the house of a friend of a friend, someplace I had never before been in. Everybody was gone.

I came to, out of a long blackout, lying on a sofa convulsing. I didn't even tell this story down in the treatment centre. It's like it has only now suddenly come up out of my memory. There on the couch I died, I say.

She places her had in mine.

I fell down into a blackness, I continue, a never-ending blackness, a feeling of fright and terror like I've never before experienced. If I screamed or not, I know not, but it felt like my entire body was screaming.

Down down down into the blackness.

Next thing I know there I was from the corner of the room looking down on my body lying on that dirty couch, bottles and cans scattered all round. The only feeling I had was that I did not want to go...there was a force pulling me away from that room, and I only wanted to go back to my body. I was too young. I had yet many things to do, to accomplish. I was not ready. When I came too moments later, I was so happy that I was alive. That day I was as sick as I'd ever been, but I was alive and that's all that mattered.

I feel her heart beating hard against my chest. In her eyes tears gather. She does not speak, only looks at me with those beautiful watery eyes. On my lips and cheeks she kisses me many times. We curl into each other. Soon she is asleep again. In sleep she looks as pure as the dawn. She is pure, if anybody is pure it is her, purely herself, purely her body. That can be a frightful thing.

I believe her yes...but I don't believe her.

I am both awake and asleep.

I do not know what I think.

I don't not even know myself.

I am with her...and without her, what am I?

*

Mother tries to make the conversation lighter when it's only the three of us sitting round the table. Sometimes I'd rather go hungry. He's trying. But the more he tries the less I can communicate. I can't help but get the feeling he's thinking, *why don't you have a job. Why are you lounging round all day doing fuck-all. And here you are at the dinner table eating for free. Nothing in this world is free.* An expression he's fond of mouthing.

I've a job lined up from next week working on the buildings with Patsy Holloran. Patsy goes to the meetings too and is off the drink a year. Drives down to collect me every Wednesday.

Another spud in the gob.

I'm not sleeping well. So, it's up and down Darcy's hill, two times, three times, could be four times on a bad day. Black storms brewing in the hippocampus.

Lovely piece of fish, says the mother.

Yeah, I say, feeling guilty because it's my favourite and she's gotten it especially for me.

Day is looking good. I might go do a bit of gardening, she says.

I'll give you a hand, I say.

No need, he says, not looking up from the newspaper he's already read.

A silence follows.

Same dream last night. Nesbit. The quarry. The Puck. Hoofs over a glass coffin.

We have to go for a drive, he says after a few lungfuls, chest wheezing from forty years of abuse.

Another tree down somewhere that needs cutting. That'll make him happy. Roll up his sleeves, work the day away, earn a few pints that night. I know the way these things go, I like a bit of hard work myself, indeed I like to fuck myself physically into work to the point of falling down. I get off on it. Maybe that's an alcoholic thing, whatever we do we do to extremes, then again, maybe I'm full of shite.

Mother throws another spud on my plate, trying to fatten me up. I put it back.

Stuffed, I say.

Like a skeleton, that's what they said below in the treatment centre. Nuala, the nun assigned as my counsellor, said I didn't have good body odour, asked me how often I took a shower. Once I week, I said. Most people take a shower every day, she said. News to me.

There's ice-cream in the fridge, and trifle.

I'm grand, I say.

Eat it up while it's there.

What time are we going I ask, standing up, taking my plate to the sink.

Cup of tea and a few biscuits, we have hobnobs, says the mother. He looks up at her, about to say something then changes his mind.

Be ready in ten minutes, he says.

Ok, I say, out the door as fast as I can and into my room. If I don't get out of here soon, I'll never survive. Though I know little, this I know with all my heart like there's a still silent pulsar inside of me proclaiming it in regular metronomic intervals.

This age, and still useless, still nipping at the tit. Is there hope for me? One day at a time I remind myself. I'm back down to the treatment centre on Wednesday to spend the day helping Mary out in the kitchen, then making birdhouses in the work shed with Liam the carpenter. Fuck me pink. Is this me lot? I open Nietzsche, Freddy N as Bellwhistle calls him. *The man of knowledge must be able to not only love his enemies but also to hate his friends.* As usual Nietzsche has me upended and confused, like some mad Riddler, still, it's a confusion that is not unpleasant and it helps to take my mind of the realities that plague me. *I sought my heaviest burden and found myself.* I read this a few times trying to gather the sense of it. Nietzsche's like that. Could give the day chewing on one of his sentences. Else I'm too thick to understand.

Few minutes later the horn blares.

Window down, sleeve turned up, arm lying over the open window.

Go into the shed and get the pick and shovel, he says.

Go get them yourfuckingself I want to say but, as always, I follow his orders. When I get into the van, pick and shovel in the back, I spark up a smoke. He looks at me. First time I've ever had the balls to do it in front of him. Our relationship is deepening. I too let the window down. Daffodils dip their heads in the fine spring breeze. Up the back road past Missus Phelans. Up Griffins hill the car labouring in second. When we pass the quarry, I quickly look away when I catch a glimpse of the loitering goats.

There's no chain saw. No rifle. What is he up to. Five minutes pass and not a word. Not unusual for us at all. We could go half the day like that. He once drove me all the way to Wexford for a job interview. I barely spoke a word. Mustn't have been easy for him either, sitting there for hours with a stone for a companion.

Where are we going, I ask finally.

I got a phone call the other day, he says, without much effort.

I swallow. My throat dries. This feeling in my stomach, this same feeling I've had since ever I can remember. Chemicals of trouble well-known to me, brewing. Trouble been following me my whole life. This feeling that lurks in the bottom of your belly, when your name is called out over the intercom in school, when you wake up after a blackout, some primordial knowledge of your actions from the previous night haunting your every breath. When you've gone too far with some cruel words that can never be taken back, when you see the tears welling, their lips shaking.

Straight ahead, eyes fixed on the road, driving slowly and carefully as always. He once pulled two decapitated teenagers out of a wrecked car. Seen things I've not. Done things I've not. Knows things I don't. Father, how to be a man.

The ISPCA, he says.

What, I say. I rack my brain thinking for something I might have done, but the truth is since I've been sober I've not done anything except meet with Rosie Delahunty, and that can't be a bad thing now can it. My mind returns to the night of the festival. The land of the blackout is a terrible land. Two-headed monster dualities, both places at the same time, quantum fucked-up-ness, one foot in, the other foot out.

Do you not know what the ISPCA is, he asks?

I'm not a full fool, I say, I never did anything bad to any animals, I...

Who said you did. Learn to control your mouth before you start blabbering, he says.

Somebody called them up, somebody from around here and reported an incident involving a dog. The ISPCA contacted me and asked me for more information. A representative will come tomorrow to follow up. But I want to get a feeling for the scene before any of them come nosing round. That's the last thing people here need, one of them busybodies coming round the place sticking their nose in where their nose is not wanted nor needed. Trouble for everybody with a capital T.

They told you the location.

They mentioned a creek near Nesbit's residence. Didn't Nesbit have a dog?

Yes, I say.

And what happened it?

I don't know. It was gone well before he...

You heard him talking about it.

Yeah.

How long before?

Month, maybe two.

We park the car at the forestry entrance overlooking Nesbit's place. After getting out of the car he does a quick 360 before taking out the spade and the pick. He then conceals them in a grain sack.

If we meet anybody, all we say is we're out to cut a bit of hazel to make some walking sticks. You got that.

I nod. He walks ahead, the sun, lazy in the blue sky, casts his shadow at my feet. Ahead he walks, he who showed me how to set snares, fire a rifle, skin a rabbit, hold a hurley. Told me there were two ways to do something; the right way and the wrong way. He who never once spoke of his own father. No, not once, even when drunk he did not talk of his own father. Father's father, who before I was born, died. Father's father's father, where art thou? Arth thou in heaven?

We cross the road, then walk down the narrow lane which leads to Nesbit's place. Absence. A void. No human hand to tame the flow of the wild. Yard sprouting buachaláns and thistles. Moss growing on the car roofs. Much time has passed since that first day with Rosie.

Ten minutes later we are in the small creek which sides the borders of the land between the Delahuntys and the Quinns. The willow, ash and hazel tress form a thick canopy eating up the sunlight. An eerie place that before this day I've never set foot in. And I thought I knew right-well all Spits crooks and crannies. We cross the dried-up bed of a tiny stream. Soon we stand before a scene redolent of a crime against all that is good. There on the grass, a skull in death grimace, teeth bared and white, clumps of fur, bones, bailing twine.

I lay the spade and shovel against the trunk of a large horse chestnut tree.

Is it Nesbit's, he asks, lighting up a smoke.

Well, it's difficult to say for sure...

The markings, the fur, are they the same?

Yes, I say.

He's rooting around with a stick now lifting up bones and bits of fur.

Thigh bones. A rib cage. A leg here and there. Some with fur and some bleached bone white.

Interesting, he says.

What's that, I ask.

He reaches down and picks something up. Looks like a button. He spits into his hands, then rubs them together. Once he's cleaned it he looks at it again, then carefully deposits it into his coat pocket.

What happened, I ask.

He doesn't answer.

The sunlight trickling through the roof of leaves. The wind whistling. The call of crows back and forth across the valley.

Here, he says, look at this. With the stick he prods at the

remains of a foot, fur still intact, bound with a piece of blue bailing chord.

Somebody strung this dog up, I say, and...

Left him here to die, or killed him before leaving him, god knows, but somebody went to some trouble to do it.

Fucking hell, I say.

Watch your mouth, he says.

But why?

We could be here till next week thinking about that, he says, looking round carefully, considering something. The real question is who in god's name would call the ISPCA? And who would stumble in here.

Well, I say, but he cuts me off.

Over there, he says, pointing to a flat piece of grassless earth on the other side of the stream. Take the spade and dig out a hole about two feet wide and deep as you can.

I know better than to ask why.

The digging is not easy, rocks and hard ground have me sweating in minutes. With the spade I loosen the rocks, pick them out with my hands, then alternate to the shovel to dig out bigger scoops of the black earth. Plunging the spade once more into the soil, I'm struck by the dull thud. Again, I drive the spade into the earth bewitched by this sound. Like the name of something you cannot quiet recall, it waits, it lulls, it lures, teasing you.

I raise up the spade then drive it down.

Thud.

Once more, I repeat the process. This final thud unlocks the memory.

I'm back with Nesbit near the edge of the quarry. There he is now, standing with his back to me, waffling about his parents, how he willed them to die.

I close my eyes and stop digging.

I reach out my hands to grab him, to push him, to stop him from falling, to save him, to damn him, I don't know. *The call of the abyss*. I too know it. How often do I not know why I do things. There is no scream. Not even a gasp. Just the dull emptiness. A feeling of giddy disbelief inside me...and then the dull distant thud.

Beads of sweat well on my forehead.

What the hell is wrong with you, he asks, his voice throwing me back to the here and now.

Deeper, at least two-foot more. Bury something, then you'd better bury it right, he says standing there looking at me.

I remember something about that night, I say without thinking it through.

What night is that then?

Nesbit. I...I struggle for words. My heart is racing. Beads of sweet sting my eyes.

Listen now, and listen well, that night is past. Bury the past is the best thing you can do for it and for you. Nesbit is gone. The past is gone. And you'll be fucking gone if you don't get that into your head. Do you understand?

I nod.

Now, keep fucking digging.

I plunge the spade once more into the dark earth. Then again and again, putting all my force into each trust. The dull thud of the body hitting the stone below. Distant. Alien. Like it might be nothing at all but a sound soon swallowed by the silence again. Nesbit here one minute, gone the next. The old man's right. I'm going to drive myself mad if I keep listening to it.

I come to in the room again. Three cages. The middle cage is empty. As she feeds the birds she talks. She tells them – her voice unusually sorrowful – that the time has come for one of them to move to the middle cage. I watch her pointing finger dance in the air as she chants:

> Eeny, meeny, miny, moe,
> Catch a monkey by the toe.
> If he squeals, let him go,
> Eeny, meeny, miny, moe.

Her finger falls on the cage with the sparrow.

You've been here the longest, she says. Yes, I've known her of old. She robbed me of my silver she robbed me of my gold.

She reaches in and carefully grabs hold of the sparrow and moves him into the middle cage. Who taught you to trap birds? Tingling in the air the smell of rot. After her footsteps the dust twinkling in the low winter sunlight.

Little Snow is it you, I yell out. My voice an absence centuries long. What has become of you? Forgive me, I yell, slithering up the wall to gain a different viewpoint. There is indeed an uncanny resemblance. Rosie Delahunty, I say, Rosie Delahunty what games do we play?

She makes her way to the black metal cast fireplace. Out of her pocket she takes a white handkerchief, spreads it on the mantlepiece, then takes a small metal tweezers and leaves it on the handkerchief while she opens the box with the key hung round her neck.

Inside the box a bed of white bones, needle thin, on top of which smoulders the mouldy green corpse of the little robin reduced now to nothing but feathers. With her tweezers she picks out the feathers, loosens them to the air and watches them as they swirl slowly to the ground at her feet.

As she works, she hums; variations on the melody, one known to me, one so old I likely had a hand in its composition. I'm not one for boasting but there's hardly a melody played these days that is not a bastardization of one of my own. After the last feathers fall, she begins picking out little bones – ones that have been there longer – and places them on the white stainless handkerchief. When she has collected ten or so, neatly crossed into a pile, she closes the box, wraps up the handkerchief, places it back inside her coat and then bids the birds goodbye.

Emerging out into the cold grey morning she makes her way to the house. I drift along behind her. In the yard her father and brother are loading bags of fertilizer off a trailer. Squint follows her with his eyes. The dog barks and comes running towards her. Stopping for a moment, she caresses its neck, then hushes him back.

Inside the house her mother is manoeuvring a pile of washing from the floor into the washing machine.

I'm going to town in ten minutes to do the shopping, will you come with me?

Ma. I can't, I already told you I've things to do here at home today.

Always things to do. Well, can you get the spuds and the bacon on?

Ok. Mary is coming over.

Grand. Will she be staying for the dinner? Don't forget now they'll be hungry.

No. Popping in and popping out. Want a cup of tea before you go, asks Rosie.

Did I ever say no to a cup of tea.

Rosie puts the kettle on.

Mother, tell me about your father again.

No Rosie. Why do you always want to talk about those things that are better left alone.

Well, I want to hear it.

Sometimes I wonder about you Rosie Delahunty, did the fairies swap you when you were a child.

Where else did I come from, Rosie says, smiling.

Her mother laughs her fat jolly laugh.

I've known her the length of her life but in this moment, her laugh has shaken me. It is beyond comprehension that in a life like she's had, that she should be capable of laughter, yet here she is every day with a smile on her face.

Have we time to brew a pot?

Teabag will be fine.

Rosie puts the tea bags in the cups and pours the hot water from the just boiled kettle.

Seated at the small table covered in a white table cloth they drink the tea, the silence between them broken only by exclamations from Missus Delahunty.

Ah, that's grand now. Lovely little cup of tea.

After her mother has gone Rosie takes the blue teapot from the cupboard and sets it near the cooker. She then takes out and unwraps the handkerchief and crushes the bones against the counter with the side of a large chopping knife. She sets the kettle to boiling, and when it starts singing a few minutes later she gathers up the dusty powder, moving it slowly into the palm of her hand. She drops this ash into the blue teapot, then adds tea leaves and water and puts it on the side of the counter to brew. All the while I watch her, her every movement inveighed with an uncanny familiarity. My skin, if I had skin would now be riddled with pins and needles, or it might peel off me like the way a snake's does when the new skin is bursting to get out. After a while of sitting at the table with a blank expression on her face, looking out the window, she rises and heads for the tea pot. She then returns to the table and pours herself one cup of tea after another until I presume the teapot contents have run dry. Needless to say, I do not know what to make of any of this.

Mary Cleary arrives in the door, silent as a rogue stream of air; a breeze Rosie seems well in need of. She's kind of like myself is Mary, nobody really notices her, at times a rather potent tool. Non-stop they talk, hardly a moment silence between the pauses. I've trouble keeping up. Plans here, plans there, the future, the past, topics changing so fast I'm getting dizzy here on the ceiling. Rosie brews another pot of tea.

At some point things turn serious, the pace slows, vocal chords tighten:

How long? I'd no idea.

A few months. I just don't want people knowing about it. You know what people around here are like. You know the way people talk. It'll be slut this and slut that.

As long as you're happy, says Mary, don't worry what they say, she says putting her hand across the table and holding Rosie's.

I am, I was, I mean it was so good, but Danny can't handle keeping it secret. And he's starting to get really paranoid. Doesn't trust me. Checking my phone. It's starting to drive me mad, feel like a little bird trapped in a cage, she says, her voice starting to wobble, and if I'm not mistaken tears already flowing down the sides of her lovely cheeks.

Have you told him about it?

I've tried. Sometimes he's so lovely, then out of the blue he'll flip over the smallest thing, his face changes...it's scary, like there are two Danny's, one I kind of know, the other a whole other world I don't want to know.

Just be careful Rosie. Take care of yourself.

Men, what the hell is wrong with them. Look at my brother, weirder he's getting. You know I think he's really cracking up.

Michael? He always seems so sensible.

You're forgetting.

Ah yes, but that was drink, and he almost never drinks, right?

Lately, he is. He's not right...I don't know. Something's not right. I'm worried about him. Nothing good is coming Mary.

When we're stressed out our brains start turning against us, piling up problems, making things bigger than they seem. I don't doubt your feelings, Rosie, just it helps me when I'm like this to be aware of them, says Mary drinking from the blue tea cup.

You know, I wish I was more like you sometimes, sighs Rosie, so sensible.

Me? Haha. I'm not popular like you Rosie. I'm just plain old

Mary. I wish I was more like you.

Rosie pulls back, straightens her back, looks at Mary quizzically:

You don't. You know I'm foolish, deep in your heart you know it, you know I chase foolish things, foolish men, romantic notions, you're different, wise Mary, says Rosie, in a voice without rancour.

I don't think you're foolish.

You may not think it, says Rosie, but you know it, deep in your bones you know it. Maybe I too know it.

I don't know what you're on about, says Mary with a chuckle, where do you get these notions at all.

You're right, says Rosie her eyes drifting towards the window. A good person can sometimes do bad things, can't they Mary.

None of us are perfect, says Mary, looking at Rosie who's still lost out the window.

I can't figure that Danny out at all, says Rosie. He lives in another world all-together.

At least he's still off the drink, right? That must be a good thing.

It's great. I'm so happy for him but he's just like a little boy sometimes, it's cute, it was cute for a while, but now. Men. God help us Mary. He can't control his emotions at all. Maybe it was something to do with all the drinking, that's what he said. I think the whole relationship thing is too hard for him now. It might be better for him to focus on himself.

You could be right Rosie.

Another cup of tea?

Go on then.

Something a bit stronger in it?

Are you mad, too early in the day for that. And I'm driving anyway.

I never heard the car.

I parked up on the hill and walked in the lane.

One won't kill you.

Just the tea, says Mary.

And a few biscuits?

Hobnobs?

Of course.

Well, who could say no to hobnobs. Oh, I meant to say when you were talking about your brother, I saw him out walking the other day. He looked well enough to me.

When's he ever going to meet somebody who's going to be able to stand him. Things have changed Mary. We've changed. We want more. Who wants to be chained to the kitchen the year-long and be a servant for men who are nothing but hungry all the time. Not me, I'll tell you, no no no, not Rosie Delahunty. But that's what he wants. That's all he knows I suppose. But who, who could love him.

There's somebody for everybody, says Mary.

That's it, there isn't. Look around. How many single old men in this place.

But he's a fine big farm of land, he'd make a great catch, says Mary laughing.

Is that what you're after Mary Cleary, says Rosie, pouring the boiling water into the teapot.

Everybody's after something.

And there's somebody for everybody, says Rosie.

And nothing lasts forever, says Mary.

And empty vessels make the most noise, says Rosie laughing.

DANNY MULCAHY

I've a feeling like I'm cusping water in my hands trying to contain it, but sooner or later there will be nothing left of it. I keep messaging her but the more I message the less she replies. It's like she can smell the desperation. On Saturday nights she goes into town with her friends. I don't go out much anymore. Without drink, it's torture. I lie sleepless, twisting and turning the nights away.

Once, she asked me had I ever fucked in the nightclub? In the toilet? Is that what she's at? She suggested we try it and then laughed. The way she laughed. I didn't like it but as usual I ignored my feelings. That's what I do. Most days I think about ending it. Most days I want to be rid of her. Then two minutes later I think she's the best thing that's ever happened to me.

Entropy always increases, a restless degeneracy, one mad switch in my head flips another and the dominos pile up on top of each other. Here I am, roaming the hills in the night with a flashlight I bought inside in Quinnsworth. Out the window I sneak and foot it the few miles to her house.

I know it's mad.

Rain, sleet, snow, eyes of cattle, fox's eyes, rabbit's eyes, goat's eyes, my eyes.

I should confide in someone, but where to begin.

Truth is, I've always been like this. I've always been drawn to the things which are forbidden.

On top of all this, the lure of drink is as perpetual as the sky. I go to the meetings and there all I keep hearing is; *you have to be honest.*

The honest alcoholic doesn't drink.

The grateful alcoholic doesn't drink.

Am I even an alcoholic? You can't be honest about everything. I'm only twenty-three. The whole thing is a scam, a psychological trick, fucking fools going to meetings seven days a week – brainwashed. They'd be better off drinking.

Humility is key, they say.

Humble yourself and pray.

I've been humbled my whole fucking life. I'm walking around dragging a millstone of shame round my neck. Have ever since I can remember. That's not going to change in a wet week.

Humble insect of the night, I creep and crawl all the way to her house.

From a distance the lights in the house make it feel like I'm not really there but rather I'm an actor trapped in some strange movie. Leering through the ditch I immerse myself in their world. After tea, Eamon plays with the newspaper, Maureen knits and watches the soaps. Squint, that brother of hers, does be in and out of the house like a yoyo. He wears a torment well known to me. I'd go closer but their dog is on to me. They can't figure out what's wrong with him. In my hands a good lump of a blackthorn just in case they forget to chain him up for the night.

Yes, I do feel like I'm doing something wrong, but fuck it. What else have I to be doing, night after night, discerning pattern after pattern, piling woe onto woe.

Soon as she's done with the tea, she helps the mother washing up and then she goes up to her room. Often, she does not draw the curtains. It's like she knows I'm out there, or she knows there's someone out there, in the darkness, desiring her.

Maybe there are others out here, hidden in the trees, dug into the hollows, perched on the electric cables, armies of us.

That she is sick is obvious.

That I'm sicker I don't deny.

Here we are, desperate sex starved cunts huddled behind the ditch trying to catch a glimpse of that which has been denied us. She is our great liberator. I sleep but two or three hours a night. The days I spend walking up and down the hills juggling great visions in my head but doing absolutely nothing about them.

To haunt the same rooms, the same hills, hollows and streams. To be one with the birds of the air, the animals of the field, to get bored to the point of oblivion, to scream up at the uncaring skies. To squeeze precious drops of memory from your shrivelled up brain, then once remembered to wish one could forget, to be helpless and clueless, to be at the cul-de-sac of one's wits. To be sometimes rent with a sense of tired satisfaction after a hard day put down in the trenches, a hard day at the office. In the end I'm little different to any and much similar to all.

Spook of Spit, here I am, again stuck up on the ceiling of the local barracks watching the Serge watching the swallows play on the laurel hedge that hugs the stonewall that marks the boundary between the barracks and Wilsons paddock. Nothing is easy, and anything that is you can't very well trust, can you.

Not long here at all when a shadow crosses the window.

The Serge takes out a smoke, cracks a match.

A knock on the door.

Come in, says the Serge.

Squint, long and lean, lurks into the room.

Michael, says the Serge, thanks for coming down. Take a seat.

The Squint nervously throws his eyes round the room.

Fancy a smoke?

Squint shakes his head.

Go on and sit down, says the Serge. Your father doesn't smoke either does he? Nor drink. Hardworking man. The Delahuntys were always hardworking were they not?

I never said I didn't smoke, says Squint sitting. His eyes like rumpled sheets. Sleepless Squint, I know well your quagmire.

Hardworking man yourself Michael, though recently I hear you've started having a few, says the Serge nonchalantly.

No law against it is there, says Squint, straightening himself up in the chair. Still, he keeps his head lowered and looks up at the Serge with darting eyes.

There's a law against running your mouth though isn't there, says the Serge, his tone of voice darkening.

The Serge does not take his eyes from him and does not speak. Squint begins to squirm. The silence continues.

Was there something you wanted to talk about, asks Squint.

Oh, right, says the Serge, there was something, what was it again. That's right, your jacket.

My jacket, says Squint, confused.

Did you buy it in town, Preston's?

I don't know. The mother got it.

Decent woman your mother, not many like her kind left. Did you ever hear of that Oscar Wilde fellow, interesting fellow, he had a few good ones, what was it again, ah yes, *the tragedy of every woman is that they become their mothers, and the tragedy of every man is that they don't.* Bit of a genius all the same.

Squint doesn't reply.

Don't you get it?

I'm sure Danny would agree with it, says Squint, a little smile breaking his face.

The Serge laughs. No flies on you Michael, and half the place thinking you a bit on the slow side. Misunderstood, that's the word. What was I talking about says, the Serge rubbing his freshly shaved chin, ah yes, your jacket. Looks like the top button's missing?

Hardly need that one, closes up well enough without it.

Any idea where you lost the button?

If I knew that, I'd go looking for it wouldn't I.

Well, no need to go looking for it Michael, I found it for you.

Squint holds himself well, indeed he holds himself too well.

I found it with the bones of a dead dog.

If you look close enough, you'll see fear bleaching Squint's face.

Here we go, says the Serge, fishing in his pocket. The button, now inside a small zip bag, he places on the table.

A call from the ISPCA the other day, one of them down yesterday, they've taken the remains for tests, the button's already been analysed. DNA, fingerprints the whole shebang. Them boys don't mess around. Tell me, says the Serge, what I don't understand is what the poor dog had to do with anything.

Squint is silent. The Serge is silent, now not even looking at Squint but out the window at something neither of us can see.

Circumstantial evidence, says Squint.

Fancy words for a fool, says the Serge but you're no fool, are you Michael? Indeed, you're not. Your brother was a very smart fellow too. Terrible waste. All that potential.

Squints entire body, led by his head, is nodding back and forth pendulum-like.

I heard a man once say that he'd like to live twice, said one life was not enough, says the Serge. Said he'd like to live in the lonely cities, in starved villages, to look all the evil in the eye, to stare at the decay of bodies, dead dogs too, try to stick his foot into the laws that govern it all, as if he could do something to cease these hungry howling laws. Well, what do you think of that Michael Delahunty? Funny isn't it, how some would like to stick around forever, and some can't stand it at all. Would you like another go at the wheel?

Not twice, thrice, quadrice, quince, not six times, seven times, I shout out. Let me tell you a man will tire of all that is humanity. The wheel of blindness turns and turns and turns.

I don't know what you mean, says Squint.

Ah forget it, I'm only thinking out loud. I'm only talking about the law: gods and mans. One we can do something about, the other we can't. Isn't that the way of the world?

Am I arrested, asks Squint.

Well now, says the Serge, that depends on you. If you're lying about the dog then you're lying about what happened that night young Nesbit met his end. Now here's the problem. I'm after hearing some rumours, no rumours is the wrong word, for these are facts. I've sources reliable as the earth itself that have informed me you're going around mouthing, after you've a few drinks inside you, that Danny was somehow involved in this tragic accident. So, here I am and here you are, and now you've a chance to tell me what you were saying below in Hannigan's.

All I said was the truth.

Is that so? Then why didn't you say it when you were interviewed by the detectives?

I...I was confused...afraid...because of the fight. I thought they'd blame me.

Listen here now, I'm going to give you a chance to tell your side of the story. Go on now and tell it, and tell it right, for this may well be the last time you'll every speak of that night again.

Squint is silent for a while, his eyes darting here and there looking for an escape, thinking of possible answers, weighting and assessing. In these recent days I've come to know him and never a word spoke between us.

Danny and Nesbit went up to the quarry together that night. And?

Well, only one of them came back.

Tell us something we don't know. The mind Michael is a terrible thing. Most of all, you'd want to be careful listening to yourself. What you saw, what you didn't see, the whole thing mumbled up inside you, a man often sees what he wishes to see, and pushes down that which he doesn't. In truth, everybody's bat blind sometimes, especially in the middle of the night with a heap of drink down, wouldn't you say. People can fall, take a tumble, hurt themselves easily enough, there's no denying it, no predicting how a man might suddenly lose the run of himself. Did you see anything else?

I was tired. I went home.

I see, says the Serge taking a pen and paper. Tired indeed. Who's to say it was not you that went to the quarry after Nesbit. Who's to say it was not you who helped Nesbit over the edge, assuming that is he didn't help himself over. This whole thing is a mess isn't it. But it's a mess that's already been solved Michael. And here you are trying to open it up again, picking at a scab, reopening a wound. What good will it do? I'll tell you what I'm going to do and I'll tell you what you're going to do. You're going to stop talking shite about that night, you're going to do the best thing for your family. Your father and mother are good hardworking people. Do you think they want the whole village to know their son's been stringing up dogs and doing god knows what to them. Is it a dog fiddler you are Michael?

The Serge stops, his breathing heavy.

Squint narrows his eyes.

A dog fiddler, repeats the Serge, not taking his eyes from Squint. Do you know they're cracking down on that sort of thing now. You'd likely get prison. The world is going in a direction where it cares more about dogs than it does people. You'd get more for the dog than you would for Nesbit. What do you think of a world like that?

Squint clears his throat: The truth will out in the end. Danny, he's trouble.

The Serge take a deep breath, considers Squint like he's not done before, sighs, stubs out his cigarette.

You're right. His mother made him weak. But all that's beside the point. He'll learn. There's no need for you to worry about Danny. I'd be more concerned about yourself and your own. Haven't they suffered enough Michael?

Now Squint is breathing hard.

Did you know it was me that cut down your brother. Frosty morning, everything white and frozen. Peaceful like you wouldn't believe, like a post card. Three days he'd been there. In some strange way I've never been able to get my head around the fact that he was part of the postcard too. The construction of some sick God, that's what came to my mind that morning. The dead, are they ever really dead, Michael, hordes of them huddled together, mustn't every field and ditch and dyke around this place be full of them. Or more precisely aren't they as much a part of the fields and ditches and trees as we are, more so even. There are things you can't understand, things you never forget, says the Serge, and things you never hope you have to do again.

Squint stands up, the chair squeaking off the linoleum.

Do we have an understanding, says the Serge still sitting.

Squint looks at him then nods.

Good man. There are dark yokes indeed that haunt the night and those that go about roaming in it will sooner or later bump into them. Safe, tucked up in the bed is the best place for any man. You don't have it easy, who does, we all have our crosses Michael Delahunty, a man's greatest burden is always himself, but who else can you be besides yourself. This is what it comes down to Michael. Acquaint yourself with yourself.

DANNY MULCAHY

Danny, he says, do you remember? Danny, don't you remember? And why Danny?

I wake dripping in sweat. Attic light. Clouds of dust. I open the skylight. Old dead moths drop to the carpet. Dead or not dead, who but the moth can tell. Stacks of books. Old photographs of people whose existence permitted mine. My grandfather, the one I never met, stands beside a horse and cart. There I am, in his face somewhere. Will I be old someday? I came here for the gun. What memory drove me I cannot say. But here I am before the closet. A musty smell. A memory of childhood. My other grandfather's walking stick. It – the gun, a .22 rifle – lies in the corner hiding behind old coats.

Father taught me how to use it when I was ten. He taught me ways to trap birds, how to place the snare between the rabbit hops. And how to net trout out of the rivers of a summers evening. He taught me how to listen to old men in smoke-filled bars on cold winters afternoons; their songs, their stories, still, and always will remain, songs and stories that cannot be found in books. He taught me how to rise a hare and turn it with the hounds, stories of Tombstone and the O.K. Corral, taught me that dead-men tell no tales, nor neither do little boys. He, my hero, taught me of greater heroes, hurling legends, men who wore the blue and gold, the black and amber and the rebel red.

The sights are likely off, I think picking up the rifle, feeling out its weight. It was heavy then and it's heavy now. Yes, I have loved it more than anything I ever loved. Those countless mornings and evenings, moving across the fields, gun in hand, hunter of an ancient land.

Creeping up behind a ditch, snow on the grass. The sky a thick heavy grey. My first ever rabbit. Field shaped like a bowl, the rabbit's brown body against the snow on the far ditch opposite me. I rest the gun on the low hanging brow of a hawthorn branch. Hands shaking, lungs jumping, the crosshairs jiggling on my target. I take a breath, try to hold the crosshairs right behind its shoulder. Pulling the trigger I see the rabbit jerk, instantaneously followed by the thud of the bullet, the echo ricocheting across the empty evening.

While the rabbit tries to drag itself towards the ditch I race down the slope of the field then up the other side. A trail of red in the white. Not two feet from its burrow when I stand over it. In short sharp intervals it squeals, the volume decreasing with each cry. I lay the gun on the snow, pick up the rabbit by the back legs, dangle it while I aim my blow. On the back of its neck, hard as I can, I bring down my open hand. Nothing but a small crack, like that of a snapped matchstick. Too simple. Too quick. Its eyes fixed now and will ever be.

Everything changes they say, but they keep forgetting death. Death never changes. The master of all irreversible processes.

Excited now to show off my catch I set off for home. As I walk, my feet crunching the snow, I can't keep from looking at it. Seeing little black fleas running in chaos from the ears I'm disgusted to the point of wanting to throw the rabbit away, but I don't because the desire to impress my father is greater.

Why are they running?

By the time I get to the road I've figured it out.

Their house is on fire.

The death of their host has brought chaos and they must now figure out what to do. No death is isolated.

All boys should hunt, for the world is a hunting ground.

It's not my first time skinning a rabbit, but there's something strange about this one. Firstly, it's unusually big. And secondly, as I take off the skin it secretes a white milky substance.

When I open her up, I find her young.

Three foetuses.

Purple and decrepit.

If it's my imagination or not I don't know, but they look like they're screaming. I dump the three foetuses with the head, feet, fur and guts in the bin where those things go. The rest I put in the pot with some cabbage and a chopped-up onion.

Though shocking, this event does not stop me. The thrill of hunting outweighs any disgust I may have felt. Watching the movies, you think something shot – animal or person – dies quickly. Sometimes they do, if it's a head shot, or a spine shot, or a heart shot, but more often than not it's messy. There's squealing, bleeding, kicking and gasping. Death throws that go on and on.

Sometimes I can't help feeling that there will be a reckoning, sooner or later, somewhere down the line, some eternal recrimination will hunt me down.

Two episodes stand out.

It was summer, tall yellow buck weeds covered the fields. A stomach shot which caused the innards to explode. He tried to escape by using his back legs, but his legs soon became entangled in his guts, with the end result being that he completely eviscerated himself.

The other incident that refuses to bury itself in the past is somewhat similar. A shot to the face caused the rabbit to circle in hysterics, round and round, like it had completely lost its mind. It could easily have escaped but all sense was gone. The screaming – more intense than anything I'd ever heard – drove me into a panic. Nearby, lay a storm-downed beach tree. I picked up a stout limb, broke it again to adjust its height. I imagined it would be over quickly. I aimed my blows at the head thinking one would be enough. But one, nor two, nor three sufficed. The more blows it took the more I wanted it to be over. Please understand, I'm no sadist and derive no pleasure in suffering. I couldn't kill him and the more I tried the more he wouldn't die. One of his eyeballs popped out, then the other, but he was still alive. At this point I got real scared and for a while I couldn't move, I just stood there watching it gasping. Eventually, I forced myself to pick him up and end it with a rabbit punch to the back of the head.

As I said there will be consequences.

Perhaps there have been already. Perhaps the fact that I recall it is consequence enough.

The newspapers, the media people, always say that the victim felt no pain and must have died quickly. I know differently. Think about it. A rabbit is tiny compared to a human. And their small bodies fight until the last. Did Nesbit fight. Did he linger long?

Skull crushed.

Rats at him.

Crows at him.

Badgers at him.

What was he thinking as his eyes dimmed and the world around him bleed out his ears?

I sit on the chair in the attic and wipe the dust from the gun with the wet cloth. I pull back the bolt, check the barrel is clean, push the bolt into firing position, undo the safety button and pull the trigger.

The click is clean, the action good.

How long we have been parted.

How long I have neglected this aspect of my soul. No more. A three-headed goat haunts my dreams. I open the skylight window and aim the gun out into Ned Ryan's field focusing in on a lone heifer grazing along the ditch. Gun steady against the tiles, I have no problem holding the crosshairs precisely on her eyeball. I wouldn't mind shooting one of Ned Ryan's heifers, just because it's Ned Ryan. But I might feel bad for the heifer. Still, I could save her the trauma of that journey to the factory and the bolt gun. She could exit now without notice, happy doing what she loves best.

I wake up on Cooney's top field again near the dolmen, slapped in the face by a bitter little bastard of a wind. As usual, I give a while waiting. My whole fucking existence might be summed up as dilly-dallying for something or other. Not long here at all when I see a familiar tall gangly frame making its way along the treeline.

Squint, I blurt out, what's happening?

No matter where he is he seems out of place. No matter what he wears it seems not to fit. All hands and feet. Down on the ditch he throws himself, taking a deep sigh. Beside him, I plant myself. In some way I know they can feel me, those who are in need of me most. Yes. He sparks up a smoke, takes a deep breath, exhales with great exaggeration.

Things are coming to a head, I say.

He looks into the distance, eastwards, unaware of my jabbering.

Your sister, Rosie Delahunty, is eating the ground up bones of starved-to-death little birds. Robins and the likes. What the hell is going on over at that house of yours?

The day I've fucking had, I say.

He nods his head.

Busy day myself. Picking stones off the top meadow, getting it ready to spread slurry on it. We're the same you and I. Both trapped.

I nod.

Eating the dead bones of birds – what the hell is wrong with her?

Everybody's got their box. May not be the bones of dead birds in there but there's something dark lurking in the soul of all.

You might be right, I say.

Too fucking right, I am.

Squint, I say, with great tenderness, what is it you want?

I've never lived my own life. I live the life and dreams of my father. The land is all he cares about. It's not my dream. But I'm chained to it now.

Is there more trouble ahead, I ask, worried he might be planning something drastic.

Isn't there always.

I had a strange dream last night. Somebody decapitated that old goat with the three horns. Down at the quarry. Wasn't you was it?

Me? No. I've no qualm with goats.

Forgive my asking, but after the dog...

I can't be staying here long. He'll be shouting out my name soon. We've to spread slurry this afternoon. Never ends does it. Work. Work. Work.

He stares into the distance, his face a grimace. I'm sure he's going to start weeping again, or he'll scream, that might be better.

You should scream, I say. Let it all out, scream till the air is gone from your lungs. Nobody will hear you here. If you don't, it's going to turn inwards and fuck you. Tell me a story Squint. I've a great need of one. Tell you the truth, since I've remembered her, I can't forget her. I'm sad and lonely now as I've ever been, no, more than I've ever been.

So, you want to forget again, now that you've remembered.

Wouldn't you?

I really have to go. It's not my place to give any advice, but when I look at you, I can see myself. You've a hole in you and there's no one else that can fill it. You have to fill it yourself.

How?

Self-improvement, helping others, taking on challenges, stop thinking about yourself all the time...that kind of thing.

Before, I can reply, he's up and humming a melody familiar to me, though a name I cannot put on it. The little time spent here seems to have revived his spirits. Company I do provide. It's the lonely I love best.

After a while of staring into the numb emptiness I crawl under the dolmen and wrap myself up in myself, wishing somehow I could escape from myself, but it's not to be. She is gone. Yet part of me still hopes that somewhere, someday, we will meet again. It comforts me to think she has come back as Rosie. These delusions ease my pain for a while.

Does this kind of weakness exist in all people? I've no idea. I've no idea of fuck all. Life is hard, they tell you, but what they don't tell you is that this afterlife can be harder. Squint is right. I've really got too much time, too much time mulling over myself, feeling sorry for myself. It's people I need.

DANNY MULCAHY

My body aches. For hers it aches. Her voice, her touch, her smell. When last we met, at my touch she turned cold, how these tables have turned. The body is incapable of lying. And yet, the body is entirely a mire of lies the mind must obey. Something was off. No words needed.

Lord, what have I done.

For your own good, she said.

Danny you need to focus on yourself.

Fuck off, that's the last thing I need. To escape myself is what's needed. A blind ape would know that. Well, she'll see, she'll be sorry. They all will. You know there's part of me that's glad of it, the sick twisted fucked up part that's more than well-able to throw its weight around. Throw yourself into the shite and roll around in it, it says. Time to indulge this little voice that's been echoing in the back of my mind since I came out of that place. *Poor Danny Poor Danny Poor Danny Pour Danny a drink Pour Danny another. Yes, Danny needs a Drink. A drink will fix all your troubles.*

Hear it.

Drip.

Drip.

Dripping.

Restless, irritable and discontent.

Danny it's time to take a little drink for yourself. And why do you want a little drink Danny?

Is it because of her?

This pain?

Is it because you can't sleep?

Maybe all of those but most likely none of those. The alcoholic drinks because it's his nature to drink. It's not like the movies where they always pin it on a particular reason: his wife died, she was abused as a child, he lost everything. Got news for you, reason has no place in any of this.

You drink because it fills the void inside you, the empty aching in your chest, the dull thudding nothingness. The restless, irritable and discontent.

A few drinks and you go from restless, irritable and discontent to fearless, invincible and omniscient. That's some fucking jump. Man would pay a lot for that.

Go on.

It's just the one.

Hear it.

Drip.

Drip.

Dripping.

You can go back on the wagon after a few days. One last bender. What harm could it do?

Call somebody and talk about it.

Go to a meeting.

One is too much and a thousand never enough. A head full of AA and a belly full of beer don't mix. Yeah. *FEAR*: Fuck Everything And Run or Face Everything And Recover. Ah, it's all a load of bollox. What harms a few drinks going to do. Few pints of Ale. Maybe a few shots. Whiskey. Vodka. Bottle of Rum. Naggon of gut rot. Three-litre flagons of cider for a fiver. I can hear them. I can smell them. I can feel them warming my gullet. Old friends gather round me, light the bonfire on my tongue, stoke the ambers in my mind, my whole-body aching for it, the cells within demanding chemical fulfilment. Fucking drown me in it they shout. Just one more little trip into the realms of the gods; to once more merge into one, I and the spiritual elements of this coincidental universe. All our particles liquified into self-fulfilling prophesies.

To drink. To not drink. She loves me. She loves me not.

What does it fucking matter? Down to Mulligan's. Up to Hannigan's. Never know who you'd meet. Or go at it alone. Hiding bottles. Give a week on it. Could be over in a day.

Blackout and wake up in a different city.

Wake up in a cell. In a hospital bed. On the footpath soaking up the rains. Naked with some girl in some never before and never to be seen again room. All the better. Buy a few bottles inside in town. Give the night in the ditch conversing with the birds. End up under the bridge with the winos. People like you. People for whom god is one thing and one thing only – purists – god is the next drink to wet your mouth, simple as. Life is reduced to a singularity. Give a few days there, on the outer circles. Keep going on like this, and it's either the rope or the river.

Out there the wind knows you, sings for you alone. Weeps for you too. Life is a watery dream where all the edges are taken away, a molten state is achieved. It's there I long to be. It is among them I belong. My trajectory seeks its own end. I belong to that class. Poor Danny. Poor Danny. Yes, pour yourself one. Just the one mind you. Lies, coil of snakes, snakes on the tip of my tongue. Hiss. Hiss.

Hear it Drip.

Drip.

Drip.

Dripping.

Poor Danny, Poor Danny, Poor Danny.

Pour Danny a drink.

Pour Danny another.

I don't speak goat. And goats don't really speak. But after hanging out with them for so long, I've learnt a bit about how they communicate, basic shit, like anger, hunger, loneliness and fear. It's about all you need really.

So, when I see a congregation of them, bleating and baaing at the top of the quarry I sense something is wrong. Before I even get to the edge of the quarry I pick up the scent of blood. When I reach the edge and look down, I'm greeted by as strange a sight as I've ever seen in Spit.

From the large quantities of dark thick blood near the front of his body I can safely deduct that this job was done here. Besides this blood, near the ground where his head used to be, there's a large wound behind his right shoulder. I feel round it with my tongue. I am able to stick it a good length into a small symmetrical hole. It takes little deduction to assume that he was shot from his perch atop the quarry, from which he fell. On the ground, he was decapitated. As is often the case I am clueless as to the who and the why, but surprisingly I'm not so surprised. After what I've seen with young Rosie nothing much can surprise me.

From the top of the quarry, they take to wailing again. This infuriates me. Fucking hypocrites. Now you're sad, now that he's dead and gone, you want him back. But for a decade you ignored him. You're no different to humans, I want to shout out but I bite my tongue and remind myself I'm a witnesser not a judge, and my witnessing does not judge, and my judging does not witness. Hard to believe it's a decade since he was crowned King Puck. Like many before and after him this led to his ostracization. And for goats there's nothing worse.

As is my wont, I lie down beside old three horns and hope that I can get a bit of rest. I offer him some consolation and shout out a few prayers to the powers that be that things won't get any more fucked up.

*

For days after the discovery of Three Horns I lurk around the dolmen expecting news of some sort or other. But I'm blind as to the who's and why's. Danny's on my mind. I've been expecting Squint too, but it could be weeks since I've seen him.

Indeed, this is the very thing I'm thinking before I'm transported in a jiffy down to Hannigan's, holding up the wall with Radio Molloy, who's crouching to light the pipe against the wind, maintaining that the wind is neither a good thing nor a bad thing, only the direction you're propagating in gives it value. Good if you're going with it, bad if you're cycling into it. More discriminations of the mind, he says, puffing now, dark reams of delicious smelling pipe smoke, pouring out through his blackened teeth.

Why is it we have to label everything? Couldn't we just let things be the way they are?

Was a grand short mass, says Archibald Hamilton, in a delayed reply.

Nosey Quirk nods, puffs on the butt end of a fag, eyes watery like he's been a week weeping. We stand there watching the mass crowd indulge in quick chats and salutations, then disperse in patterns which I hold could be determined if one stood there week after week and studied them for long enough. Within five minutes most of the cars have gone and silence returns to the village. Us now, and the crows and magpies perched on telephone wires and the roof of Slattery's. Two magpies warily watch the movements of the crows. Father Flannagan beeps as he drives past. Sudden shower of rain drives us into peat and whiskey.

Quirk buys the first round. Top shelf. I perch myself on the fag machine under the TV near the door for the toilet. The three men sit on the high stools facing the bar. Molloy and Archibald talk, while myself and Nosey Quirk listen.

Did you hear about Squint Delahunty?

No.

Sad. Very sad. Poor chap.

What happened?

Took three to mount him. Two hours, they says, Ambulance seen going in and out. Heard he wrecked the place. He'd have fierce strength, amplified no doubt when in that state.

Nerves?

The very man. Kitchen destroyed. Mother in an awful way. Chairs out the window.

Went for the auld lad with a spade. Spent a month below in Headersbridge.

Is that where they're taking them now?

Aye, a new place down there. There's more. He was spending a lot of time with the wild goats up there by the Dolmen, was heard talking to them even. Running with them. Might even believe he's one of them.

God help us. What brought it on?

Who can say. All I know is he'd taken to the drink recently.

Doesn't suit some.

Doesn't suit a lot.

Awful hard on the mother and father.

Lovely fellow when he's right.

He is.

Just the way he'd look at you sometimes, with the eye wrong in his head and all that.

I'm not saying he's dangerous, I'm just saying you'd want to be careful is all.

Same way with a bull. Never let your guard down.

T'was the drink.

Never did us any harm.

Right you are. And, sure, he'd only recently started on it.

Didn't suit him at all.

Chain reaction.

Kicked something off.

Now that you mention it, wasn't the mother's father afflicted in the same way?

Lafferty wasn't she? Her father would have been Paddy Lafferty.

That's right.

Old Eamon's had it hard.

Some families bear the brunt.

Comes to us all in the end.

Don't know about that.

Some bear a greater burden, there's no denying it.

You're right, some have a heavier cross.

The sister is off to America I hear?

Really.

New York. Job lined up and all.

Lovely girl.

Smashing.

Rumours tend to follow her around though, don't they?

No smoke without a fire.

Same again, says Radio Molloy.

Have I ever refused, says Archibald.

No, begorra that's one thing you haven't done.

He was good on the fiddle, says Archibald.

Who?

The Squint.

Is that right?

So, they says, but doesn't like to play, shy about it.

You know, says Radio Molloy, I've always had a soft spot for Nero.

Nero, says Archibald taking the cap off his head then refitting it again, an action he repeats at least once a minute.

I don't think he was as bad as they make him out to be. Scapegoat.

If you say so, says Archibald.

Our biggest mistake is to think old Nero never loved. I put forth, says Molloy, that he not only loved, but that the poor bastard loved too much and that's what drove him weeping up the hill to watch the flames usurp his kingdom, because he could stand it no more, this kingdom wrapped round his head like a millstone. Do not all men fiddle to mock their own destruction?

For a while nobody answered.

Maybe it wasn't even a question.

Then up speaks Nosey Quirk, a man who rarely breaks the air, but when he does you know to listen, cause Nosey Quirk knows, though bat blind and victim of a life swimming in whiskey, he swallows books whole, dines on numbers and facts. Nosey clears his throat.

There were no fiddles yet invented then, Nero, if he played at all, played the lute, he was thirty-five miles away when it started, for six days and six nights the fire raged, immediately he cut the price of corn, paid for much of the relief efforts from his own pocket – much thanks he got. No one knew who started the fire, of course, mostly likely an accident. Nero blamed the Christians, never liked them, fed them to the lions and worse. The Senate, crowd of bastards, spread the rumours it was Nero, they never liked him, spent too much on the plebs. While the flames surged, Nero stood on his private stage, sung of the destruction of Troy, he was awful fond of concerts and musical activities, a case of wrong man in the wrong job, artist he was, politics beneath him. His mother poisoned Claudius his predecessor. His wife his own mother. Would you lot do better?

Nosey Quirk picks up his glass, drains the malt and is silent.

Good man Quirk, says Archibald. That was a fair spake. A spake that deserves a drink.

There you go said Molloy, there you go, he repeats, I always had a feeling about that. You can never know a man unless you know him can you?

The news of Squint upsets me more than I could have imagined. My heart is soft, and my love is great. I was happy, but I only realize it now that I've become less happy. Oh, after all these years I'm still as stupid as I ever was.

I have no wisdom, no faith, no skills.

Is there no learning in this valley of a small, dark river where I was born.

I close my eyes and wish that I could be there with him, wherever he is, to comfort him, because who else is there to comfort him. Don't misunderstand, it's not because I'm good, but in the comforting I myself get comforted.

*

Panicked and confused Danny comes to in the early dawn light. Slobbery eyed, he fumbles around mumbling to himself, trying to make sense of his predicament. Despite my efforts he's wet and cold. His eyes dart over the gun, over his hands, his clothes. Delahunty's chained dog takes to barking again. Does it sense what is coming? The large two-story house, a hundred yards ahead, lies quiet and lightless.

Danny groans, picks himself up, staggers, and almost falls. When he's got what he wants, when he's found his bearings, we begin to lurk our way slowly back towards the top of the hill. The drizzle continues, droplets rolling down his face, the sky is all stained with different moods of grey. Curious cattle eye us from a few hundred yards. Renegade rooks frolicking on the sycamore trees down near the stream have spotted us too.

We stumble on.

When he finds his car and the damage done to it, he curses out loud, but is relieved when he discovers the keys still in the ignition. Passing the quarry, he stops for a minute but does not enter nor even look at it. At this hour of the morning we encounter no other traffic.

He parks the car a few hundred yards from his house. The morning has brightened and the blue sky from the east spreads.

I'm relieved when he leaves the gun in the boot and goes by foot to his house, moving with a newfound sense of purpose.

When he comes out twenty-minutes later he walks straight to the outside shed. Inside the shed he locates a piece of old rope and rolls it up neatly into a loop and then puts it inside his jacket. For a while he roots around for something else but seems unable to locate what he's looking for.

Once he leaves the shed, he heads straight across the lawn in front of the house. At the corner, where the long laurel hedge and the lawn intersect, he hops the small stone wall. As he makes his way through Wilson's haggard he has to hush back the dog three times. Head down, to shield himself from the drizzle, he moves quickly up the slope of old Darcy's big meadow. I follow, hopping in and out of his footsteps in the wet grass with the frolicsome energy of a kid.

*

He sits, feet dangling over the mud sloped precipice looking down at the fast-rushing stream that twists and turns its way through the valley. For a small stream it makes a lot of noise, indeed nothing much else can be heard, except the birds, but you can only hear them if you listen hard. The sun beats broken, jutting out in beams through the clouds, the drizzle ceased, a low crawling fog hugs the ground. Mild and ancient bracken spring from the moss-covered sycamore and beech trees. You'd get the feeling there's something watching you here. I mean there is something watching you, me, but it's also like the very place is watching you, the trees, the stream, the bed of dark granite stones through which the water rushes. In a clearing directly below Danny, a lone horse chestnut tree spreads its long random arms without care for order. A quiet morning sits on Spit.

Danny holds his phone in front of him, typing deleting then retyping. I could crawl up behind him and have a look at who he's messaging but I've manners enough not to snoop too deeply, and besides I've a fair idea anyway.

He throws the phone on the ground.

Out of his jacked a short naggon of whiskey. He smokes cigarette after cigarette and sucks from the naggon, moans occasionally, mumbles something, then goes back to staring into the stream below. Out of nowhere, startling me, he jumps up, throws the empty naggon and watches it shatter on the rocks by the stream. The phone taken from his pocket soon follows. He then turns west, towards the hill behind him where the sun ever sets, and falls down on his knees. He rocks his body back and forth, for what seems like a long time.

When he stands up, a quiet calm has overtaken him. He takes the rope from his jacket, negotiates his way down the muddy path, etched out over the years by cattle coming to the stream to drink. Under his feet beach nuts and twigs crackle against the rushing noise of the stream. Not far from the bottom of the steep slope he loses his footing and ends up on the mud. He laughs out loud, lies there for a while looking up at the sky muttering words I too have somewhere heard before.

Oh thou invisible spirit of alcohol if thou hast no name to call thee by;
Let us call thee devil, that men should put an enemy in their mouth;
To steal away their brains.

Ten yards past the large horse chestnut there is a fallen ash, up turned in a recent storm, which someone has been at with a chainsaw. A pile of cut blocks are heaped to one side. Danny struggles to pick up one of the large blocks, so instead, he turns it on its side and rolls it towards the horse chestnut, positioning it under one of the low-lying branches. He returns and picks up a smaller sized block. During the long summers of his youth, I used to watch him playing in this very tree. Horse chestnut leaves are large and thick and provide the best cover for boys playing games of war. He carries the smaller block and places it on top of the first block. When he stands up on them they wobble, but not so much that he can't control it. Nearby, the barking of a dog distracts his attention. He jumps from the blocks.

Go home you fucking eejit, he shouts.

The dog, still barking, shrouded in fog, looks down at us from the top of the embankment.

Around us the bird's flit and sing, and though they notice us, they do not deign to change any of their routines on our account.

With the blue rope he makes a simple slip knot. He climbs up on the blocks, shouting at the dog to go home as he does so. Over the lowest of the branches, he throws the rope. The dog starts to descend the mud path. I call out to Danny but my voice yet has no grip on this world. It's true that any man's death might diminish me because we are all one. I don't disagree with the poets, but the mass of the world remains constant no matter how many live or die. This, I have come to realize.

Up the tree after him in a jiffy I slither. Danny adjusts his apparatus. The dog, now but a few feet away barks furiously.

I'm sorry, Danny says in a voice that's barely audible, before stepping off the block.

The branch strains but does not break.

Oh that I had some mass but I weigh less than a midge. Still, even a midge might tip the scales, might contribute to the fracture point. So, I start to swing, pulling and pushing the branch while

Danny, his face bright red, his eyes bulging in his head, clasps at his neck. He's looking right at me but of course he cannot see me.

The branch goes up.

The branch goes down.

The dog protests, tugging at his feet. The sun moves an imperceptible amount from where we hang but move it does. The stream below us rushes on. Around Spit people are waking up to another day. Death is natural as the air.

The branch goes up.

The branch goes down.

Horse chestnut tree I say, horse chestnut tree bend and break to me. He's too young I shout out. The dog echoes my sentiments. Why it matters if he lives or dies, I know not.

The branch goes up.

The branch goes down.

Danny's legs kicking uselessly. Purple is Danny's face. I pull down with all my being. Six hundred years I scream, six hundred fucking years. I curse the gods. I curse the very nature of existence.

The branch goes up.

The branch goes down.

A crisp cracking noise lands us in the mud. Danny, still conscious, gasps, claws at the rope burning his neck. For a long-time afterwards both of us lie there in the moss and mud looking up at the sky, the dog beside us, licking Danny's hand.

Visitors from an ancient place, the ferns nod back and forth in a gentle breeze.

*

No rest for the wicked. I'm fucking plastered with exhaustion. Pleasant is the life where novelty is a rarity. I'm back in the barracks, hung off the ceiling, looking down at the three below me. Little did I think I'd see those two again, but here they are, seated opposite the Serge, who's tucked in snug behind his desk near the old heavy door. Runt next to the window, as he was last time if I recall it right. Outside, a frosty clear morning peacefully waits for the day's events.

A decapitated goat's head left outside the church. This kind of thing is no good for anybody, says Cadaver, his tone playful.

What was it the Super said again, asks Runt.

Let me see, it went something like this: Gentlemen, go down to that shithole Spit and establish some law and order, says Cadaver. Fucking ISPCA onto him daily. Firstly, something about a strung-up dog, and now a decapitated goat.

The Wild West, weren't those the words he used, says the Runt. There's something like a grin taking control of his face.

The Serge takes the smoke from his mouth, grimaces.

Eighteen years I've been stationed here, says the Serge, his voice lazy and untroubled. Round here it takes at least three generations before you're in.

Cadaver clears his throat. So, about this goat. Are there any suspects?

Hardly thought I'd see you back round here again, says the Serge not even looking at them. Official business gentlemen, or did you just grow fond of the place, he adds with a half-smile.

Tying up knots, says Runt.

The Serge looks at him funny.

Don't you mean loose ends?

Oh, yeah, I suppose I do. Loose ends. Loose cannons. Plenty of them around here.

Is that right, asks the Serge, nodding his head. Ye've been spotted more than once snooping around. Nothing happens here without everybody knowing.

Well, that's debatable, says Cadaver. Places like this are rotten with secrets.

That fellow with the squint, says Runt, looking up.

Eamon Delahunty's son?

The very man, says Cadaver.

Brother of Rosie, says the Runt.

Spit's Rose, says Cadaver. Would have, should have, been crowned, but they couldn't give it to her because she was from here; they'd have been accused of bias. As if the whole place isn't rolling in bias, in connections and nods and winks, in I'll scratch your back if you scratch mine. You know, I've had this feeling all along, about the people here, it's hard to explain, but it seems like everybody is protecting everybody else, and nobody is willing to talk, says Cadaver.

Gossip, it's not healthy, that's the problem with gossip, it's not the gossip itself, it's just that swallowing it is not good for one, says the Serge.

What do you make of him, asks Cadaver.

Him, and his sister, adds Runt perking his head up once-again from his notebook.

Since you asked lads, I'll give it to you straight. Hard working people. They keep to themselves. Poor Michael's taken ill, down in the ward for a month, but he's back at home now. His father is a hard man, works from dawn to dusk. Not everybody's cut out for that, especially nowadays, people like the soft road.

For a moment I forget there are three men in the room. Runt has melted into the furniture. It comes to me that this is his great talent, his ability to say nothing and to be nothing at all, serving, one could say, as a mute sponge sucking up the ego spillage of those around him.

Cadaver clears his throat again, positions his hands together like he's in prayer, like the way priests do. His thick eyebrows twitch and move inwards.

We have to tell you something, says Cadaver.

It won't be easy, says Runt.

I've idea enough about what ye're going to say. Come out and say it and let's get it over with. We've all better things to be doing.

We've good reason to believe your son Danny was responsible for the goat, says Cadaver.

Good reason? Asks, the Serge.

A witness, says Cadaver.

And who would that be?

We're not at liberty to say.

Gentlemen, this is my parish. These people are my flock, I know what's good for them even if they don't know it themselves, so I'd advise you don't come here with that attitude. I've nothing to hide, so neither should you.

That may well be, but a witness is a witness, says Cadaver.

The Serge nods thoughtfully. You're right, he says, sighing.

And speaking of Rosie Delahunty, we've reason to believe Danny was romantically involved with her.

The Serge laughs out loud, opens his cigarette box, takes one out and lights it.

Is there a law against that?

She was involved with Nesbit too, says Cadaver.

And?

Cadaver looks at Runt.

She might have been involved with half the parish, says the Serge, what's that got to do with anything?

Neither Runt nor Cadaver respond.

If you've got something to say spit it out, otherwise don't

be wasting my time. And if you're making accusations about anything, I'd be very careful. As for Danny, my son, he's a fucking eejit, he might even be a full fool, but that's our problem, me and the missus. Indeed, it was he who shot the goat, it was an accident of course. The decapitation thing...well, he was drunk. He got carried away, was trying to butcher it for the dogs. Drunk out of his mind, didn't know what he was doing. He's gone to the owner of the goat, apologized and compensated him. By god, he'll work to pay it off.

Wasn't the goat wild, asks Cadaver.

Wild? No, there's nothing wild left anymore. Go up to Heffernan and ask him whose grass those goats are eating. Mr. Heffernan is a reasonable man, as is Father Flannagan. They won't be pressing charges, the Serge says, exhaling a large plume of smoke.

Cadaver looks at Runt who is writing vigorously in his notebook.

Now, says the Serge, how about you tell me why you've been snooping around this parish. And fuck your inuendo out the window there, if you've something to say about Danny and Nesbit then fucking spit it out.

Cadaver looks at Runt, both men shake their head.

No, there's nothing of the kind. We're here because of the goat, the ISPCA are kicking up a fuss.

Don't you worry about that says the Serge. I'll take care of them boys.

This is coming all the way from Dublin.

I know well where it's coming from and I've ways and means of making them boys go where they're really needed.

We just thought it would be better to put all this on the table.

The Serge takes the cigarette from his mouth and crushes it in the ashtray, his face tightening.

On the table me bollox, he says standing up. Gentlemen, let me go and see if my son, the prodigal one, is in. We can clear up this misunderstanding and all move along and do something more productive with our time. Young Nesbit is dead, a tragic accident, let the boy and his family rest.

Whatever happened to the land, asks Cadaver.

Was left to a nephew who auctioned it off last week. Of course, the Delahuntys bought it. So, if there's any tree you two should be barking up, I'd suggest that one, says the Serge walking out the door.

They watch him walking past the window.

I told you he'd not take it well, says Cadaver.

Short fuse but forgets his anger easily. This type is well-known.

And what type are you, asks Cadaver.

Oh, I hold onto it, let it rot and fester, then I feed off it. It keeps me going through the hard times, says Runt, a smile brightening his pudgy round red face.

That's as good a description of yourself as I've ever heard. You've always reminded me of a parasite of some kind or other. You'd survive along with the cockroaches after a nuclear holocaust, says Cadaver.

Not a very nice thing to say to your college now, is it?

We're not in the habit of saying nice things to each other, are we?

No, thank god we're not, you long streak of miserable shit, says Runt.

That's more like it. Even the hollow nut desires to be cracked.

What the fuck is that supposed to mean? Hollow fucking nuts?

Work it out, says Cadaver, rubbing his hands piously.

*

My best friends are places. I idle about from one to the other discussing old memories shared to us both. For these last centuries we've seen a lot. I can't deny there's been happy times. Our memories etched into each other. The dead, the living. We have no words, only the crude etchings of our mother and her ever changing faces. The frost comes, then goes, then comes back again. There's a morning of snow, and there are days of rain. There are pockets of glorious sunshine and, as always, the sky is a conundrum of changing faces.

It is on such a morning, when I'm moping about moaning about all this to the goats, that I spot Squint, more slouched than usual, walking at fifty percent his normal pace, making his way to a rock near the spruce trees where we are gathering a bit of shelter from a teethy wind. All this time wondering about his wellbeing, I'm overcome with a sudden surge of joy to see him. The joy is short lived.

His face his puffed, his eyes no longer shifty and jumping, rather, dull and lazy. I notice too that the large, long restless fingers on his oversized hands no longer dance. The goats disperse.

What's happened to you, I say.

He reaches inside his coat pocket.

I heard they took you away. Are you on medication is that it?

We are silent for a while. I watch the goats move north-westwards towards Nesbit's hill.

He inclines his head east, towards the village below us.

Your sister, I say, Rosie. I've fallen in love with her. Well, maybe not. You see, a long time ago I loved a woman myself, and she me, but I did something unforgiveable. Your sister she reminds me of this woman. The woman's name was Little Snow.

Who knows but perhaps she's some kind of descendent. It's a small country. Generations removed, who knows who's who? In the end we're all related. Tell you the truth Squint, I'm having a hard time figuring it all out. My place, my purpose here. My job. I suppose you have the same worries. Things will work out won't they, in the end.

I wouldn't hold my breath.

I'm six hundred years dead what use have I with breath Squint.

He sucks heavy on the fag, an unbearable mien of sadness gripping his face.

Sing for me Squint. Your voice such a beautiful thing. It was a long time since I was so moved as that day the music came up out of you.

This Little Snow, he says.

I see my reflection in his beady eyes. I'm dressed in silver rags. No longer goat but something else entirely.

What of her?

Maybe you never loved her.

What do you mean, I ask, my blood quickening.

You don't seem the family type.

The mention of this drives me to pacing back and forth.

Look, he says after a minute of this. I know you loved her. All I'm saying is, it was a long time...

Enough I say, continuing to yoyo. I want to lash out at him, to scream, to beat a rock off him, but all this is swallowed by the knowledge that he is right. I never loved her, or rather I did, but I couldn't show it. I drove her away because I can only love what's gone. I'm in love with the memory of her, rather, than her. It comes to me now, that it's very likely I've never loved anybody. I stop moving, stand there, my eyes fixed to the ground beneath me, the rain dripping down with grim determination.

As you know there are considerations operating beyond us. There are pictures being painted much bigger than we can comprehend. You and I, what are we but mere specks, he says.

I look at him, mouth open, tip of tongue extended, saliva drips stupidly out the right corner of his mouth.

So, this is it then, I say, a perpetual posting at Spit.

It's not about you. It's not about me.

What the fuck is it about then? Don't give me that universe bullshit. Fuck the universe. What's the universe ever done for me? I clear my throat and spit on the wet grass. If he notices he doesn't show it. The silence returns. The wind. The goats. The sky flexes her thousand faces. Squint stares into the distance.

Squint, I say, I need to talk to someone about her. I need to...

I'll be here, no leaving of this place for me now. No good end in sight is there? A dog fucker I have been and a dog fucker I will remain.

The tears race up the backs of my eyeballs. My face contorts. I hate to harp on about it, but I need to get it straight in my mind. I need to tell somebody, I say.

Yes, yes, let it out, it's normal in these times, he says. Men cry nowadays like it's nothing.

I clear my throat again and speak in a soft and low whisper. I lost her, and in the losing of her I really found her. I did not appreciate what I had. Now, I can only appreciate what I lost. I lost what I am and in the losing I found who I am. Squint I've been humbled, cut down like a fucking buachalán. You may not know it, but I believe I was once a great man of words, a poet, a man even kings feared. But I ended up like you Squint, a plougher of fields, and then, as if this wasn't enough, when I died, I ended up banished to this outpost – the Spook of Spit. Yes, I've had happiness in my life, much of it, sadness too, more of it.

Squandered happiness. There remains a low steady hum through my days, ever reminding me. Maybe happiness will come again. It will. She will not.

My throat dries up. The words won't come. I cough and spit and breathe in and out. I'll be here beside you Squint. You feel lonely, don't worry, I'm here. This is my place. This is my home.

Squint lights another cigarette with the butt end of the one he's just smoked.

You're the only one I can be honest with, I say. I mean that. I look forward to your visits, our conversations, I know you don't really talk, but that's ok. You being here enables me to see myself, my shadow. Without a shadow nothing can live.

When he leaves, I feel the vacuum, and as always I can't help but seek her to fill it. My eyes fall over the fields before us, covered in craters, dents, small hollows, like it was once a battlefield pounded by huge mortars. But there was no battle here, these were once dwelling places, where families lived in small stone and mud cottages. During the time of An Gorta Mór, when the potato crops failed, I saw twenty-nine families leave Spit in one day. They left from this very field in the year of 1847, and their decedents return looking for the place where their ancestors were born. I've always wondered what hungered in them, what vacuum in their life drove them thousands of miles to return to these very fields. Now, I know.

For a long time, I stand there numb, unable to do much of anything but exist. By the time I snap out of it dusk has crept in and the heat from the meadow below us is gone. The cold of the forest tingles off my back. I welcome the night like an old friend.

*

Wherever it is I'm deposited there's something to learn. One learns to keep an open mind about these things. Sometimes, I've to interpret what's been said, if anything has been said. Sometimes, I've to see with a different eye to what I'm seeing with my other eye. Sometimes, I've to use my tongue to lick the very earth where I'm standing, or lick the necks of those standing around me, to get a true feel for the situation. Sometimes, I'm bored out of my balls, the length I have to wait, the shite I have to listen to. Sometimes, I've to play with me own balls and interpret the signs. All men will know of what I talk. And sometimes I don't know what the fuck I'm doing. No, it's more than sometimes. More often than not I've little idea what the fuck is going on.

As I've said, it's the usual mess of bits and pieces, scattered here and there, and me, poor fool that I am, have to try and put them all together to make some kind of sense of it. I give senseless things the appearance of sense. Order out of the chaos. But even an insect aspires to this. And am I above or below this insect? In truth, I do not know. Sometimes I'll swing one way, then the other. That's about all I can say on it.

Anyway, here I am in a pub full of noise. I see everybody but nobody sees me. I crawl along the floor smelling the cow shit from their boots, the sweat dripping from their holes, their unused, unwashed farmers cocks. Who do I choose? Who did I come to listen to? It's late and the pub should be closed, but this is Spit and things don't go according to plan in Spit. There is in this land an ability – natural or composed I know not – to make its own rules. This world is dying, this old world, and I witness the new birth. It has died and been reborn many times. The son of the father, the daughter of the mother. New Spit is a place I'm not very fond of. I've sense of many changes. Many of them for the better and many not.

Am I not like those old men who complain that things aren't what they used to be. Old men should be quiet and go about their business. Mouths without teeth cannot bite. Nobody needs to hear what they have to say. There are those who will say old men have acquired wisdom. Maybe. Yet, their wisdom is also an anachronism. They've had their time. This, I truly feel about myself too. Because what we old fools say, is more often than not motivated by regret of things we never did, or chances we didn't take, of choices we took motivated by desires to remain warm, dry and safe. But did it save us from the glue factory, the old folks home? Where we'll end our days staring out a window whilst being surrounded by people who want nothing to do with us or each other. Is this to be the end? Is this to be the memory of life lived?

Still, who am I to talk, a man – not without his talents – a man who not only forgot his Jerusalem, but killed his Jerusalem, a man who spent most of the last six-hundred years in the form of one goat or another. Anyway, where all this philosophy is coming from, I don't know. I get like this at times. Maybe it's to distract myself from the fact that I'm slithering along a pub floor.

I head for the lounge, less feet there and more peace. When I get there, I hear a familiar voice. I slide up the stone wall to gain a proper view and am happily surprised to see the Serge seated at the bar. In front of him a small glass with a lick of whiskey remaining, beside it a half pint of ale. White shirt, ruffled, he wears a three-day beard. The proprietor, Matty Slattery, beside him.

In the end, little we do matters, says the Serge.

How do you mean, asks Matty.

Isn't their character set from the day they are born. Same way with a dog or a horse. They're either good or bad and no amount of training or proper feeding or education them is going to make any difference.

But surely it would help wouldn't it, says Matty, adjusting the thick dark frames of his glasses.

Maybe it helps a bit, but it all comes down to this, if the ingredients are not there then there's nothing that can be done.

Will you have another, asks Matty.

Do I look like I'd refuse.

Matty laughs.

Whiskey and sulphur. I float in and out between them. The hum of twenty-seven drunks. Maudlin bullshit and lost dreams. A chorus of frogs belching at the sky. Come up and come down. I crave a lot of things you know, but nothing so much as smoke and whiskey in late night establishments. I was in my youth famed and never had to put my hand in my pocket.

Mary, another round.

Mary, indolent against the counter moves with resistance. The air itself does its best to avoid her. She reminds me of someone I once knew. A barmaid too. I crawl over the stone and place myself right between Matty and the Serge so I've good access to their mouths. The pub is a swarm of noise.

Do you know the aboriginals?

I do, says Matty. I've a brother out in Sydney. Forty years out there. Did well for himself.

Publican?

Building business at first, now he's two places in Sydney: The Fiddler and The Blackbird. Sometimes, I wish I'd gone out there myself. Great country. The size of it. Did you know you'd fit one-hundred-and-ten Irelands into Australia.

One-hundred-and-ten, repeats the Serge, before he reaches for his pint, angles it to his mouth in a slow lazy movement, leaves it there, sometimes drinking, sometimes not, the process, intimate as a kiss, his neck muscles moving, his Adams apple undulating, the liquid in the glass decreasing, then increasing as he adjusts his gullet.

You all did well for yourselves. Robbie up in Dublin, a man of influence who never forgot where he came from. Tell him I was asking for him, says the Serge.

That I will.

Leaving the empty pint of ale back on the table the Serge sighs, runs his hand across his face.

Well, they had unusual ways of dealing with issues, he says. Way outside our realm of thinking.

Who's that?

The aboriginals.

How do you mean?

You know the way some people just won't play according to the rules.

There could be good and bad in that I suppose, says Matty.

I'm talking about the bad. Those, who, even though given every chance have proved themselves irredeemable, bad to the bone types. You know the type.

Yeah, I'm with you, says Matty adjusting the black cap that is ever on his head.

Life in those circumstances, in the deserts of the outback, was very harsh, if one person wasn't pulling their weight it might affect the safety of the whole group, says the Serge.

Matty coughs. I've a feeling you're going to tell me something awful. You know something Serge, you're fond of these awful stories. Last time you told me about the Mongols and their punishments, and one in particular I've never been able to get out of my mind. You know a man can read too many books.

Was it the one concerning animal fat, the maggots, a cross, and a fine hot summer.

Jesus, grunts Matty. Why not kill a man and just get it over with. I can't understand the unnecessary torture, says Matty.

It strikes fear into the masses, acts as a deterrent. Anyway, my point is the aboriginals would mark out these troublemakers at a very early age; they would kill and cook them, then the whole tribe would then eat them.

Lord Jesus Mary and Joseph. I hope the Garda Siochana is not thinking of implementing such drastic measures.

The Serge laughs, showing his missing right upper incisor, a tooth rarely seen.

It would fix a lot of problems Matty. But seriously, going back to what I was saying, we know these things from an early age don't we.

But is it not often the case that the very worst turn out to be the best?

It's rare, says the Serge, rare indeed, he repeats.

Mary places two fresh pints on the wooden counter in front of them.

I'll fix you up later Mary, says Matty.

Mary acknowledges this with a slight nod, then goes back to serve another customer at the other end of the bar. A minute later she returns, comes out from behind the counter and shoves a few more sods of turf on the dying embers. Mary, says I to myself, contrary Mary, where have I seen you before? She has a face that's difficult to like. Yes, the English came and took the land, the old Irish families crumbled and I and my ilk lost our way of living. Bye and bye I came to a place then where devils inhabited the wind. In lonely fields picking stones, my hands welted from spades and shovels. My back ached and the damp and cold invaded the seven joints. That's how I ended my days, much like now, among the uneducated and unrefined, begging for a few potatoes to keep myself alive. I was refused drink in taverns where they once threw it at me. Mary, you remind me of that woman I once penned a poem about. Here it is, up out of nowhere, fresh in my mind, as yesterday's kiss:

A Glass of Beer

A shrewish, barren, bony, nosey servant
refused me when my throat was parched in crisis.
May a phantom fly her starving over the sea,
The bloodless midget that wouldn't attend my thirst.

If I curse her crime and herself, she'd learn a lesson.
The couple she serves would give me a cask on credit
But she growled at me in anger and the beer nearby.
May the king of Glory not leave her long at her barrels.

A rusty little boiling with a musicless mouth,
She hurled me out with insult through the porch.
The Law requires I gloss over her pedigree
– but little the harm if she bore a cat to a ghost.

She's a club-footed slut and not a woman at all,
The barrenist face you would meet on the open road,
And certain to be a fool to the end of the world.
May she drop her dung down stupidly in the porridge.

I take a bow as in days of old. Though nobody has heard me it feels good, a great relief sweeps over me, like I've just shed an invisible weight. This memory gladdens me, as if I've been looking at myself in the mirror for years in a darkened room but now somebody's flicked a switch.

The Serge suddenly opens his eyes.

He's gone Matty, he says looking into the distance.

Who's gone?

Danny.

Where's he gone?

I don't know. England first, but I think he's going out to the east somewhere.

He'll make his own way. You have to remember his age.

I was never like him, says the Serge.

You had different circumstances is all. But you are like him much more than you know.

He'll be the death of his mother.

Didn't he stop the drinking?

He did. But he's back on it. At least he was. Tell me, what are people saying about the goat.

Well, you know...

Tell me straight. Is there talk?

Isn't there always.

And?

You wouldn't want to listen to that.

People listen to precisely that.

He's not a bad lad, says Matty. I was always fond of him.

What do they say of Nesbit?

Accident mostly, some say he fell, some say he jumped, some say he had a little help.

What do you say Matty?

I'm not qualified to say.

Where would you put your money?

It's the question I'd like to ask you Serge.

The Serge mumbles. Picks up his pint and angles it towards his head.

There's something I need to ask you Matty.

Go ahead.

A favour.

I'll do what I can.

It's your brother Robbie in Dublin. There are two detectives down here snooping around causing trouble when there's no need for trouble. The ISPCA have been onto them. Now you know it, and I know it, them fellows have no business round here. And young Nesbit, God rest his poor soul, is long dead and gone. A tragic accident Matty.

Matty blesses himself.

I know the fellows you're talking about. Didn't much like the look of them.

Matty takes a black notebook from the inside of his coat pocket and leaves it on the counter. Say no more John, write down their names and leave it with me.

The Serge takes the pen and writes in the notebook. When he's finished, he hands it back to Matty, who puts it back inside his coat pocket.

You can tell him to count on votes down this way, says the Serge.

Good man John. He'll be happy to hear that, votes was all he ever cared about. Maybe he's right. Look where it's got him.

Never forgets where he came from, says the Serge raising his glass.

You know, it will be good for Danny to get away. Let it go, let him go, hand it over to the good Lord. And when you do see him again hold out your hand to him and love him. We all need a bit of love.

It's discipline he needs, says the Serge.

That will come when he loves himself enough to practice it.

Loves himself enough, scoffs the Serge. You're getting soft Matty.

Look around you, all these problems in the world, all these troubles come from a lack of love. There's too much hate, self-hate, too much envy, too much of wanting and not enough of giving.

You sound like a Priest. You sell whiskey Matty, not salvation.

The same thing, says Matty.

They both pick up their pints, and in perfect synchronicity, take a long hard slug, return the pint to the counter and sigh.

Did you ever hate your own flesh and blood, asks the Serge.

What, asks Matty, turning his head to look at his companion.

The Serge repeats the question.

We all have those moments.

Moments. Eighteen years I've given to this place Matty.

No matter where you are, you'll meet the same people in the end. The people here are far from fancy, they're the dirt of the earth, closer to it than in most places.

His mother is in an awful way.

She's a strong woman. He'll come good. There's a goodness in him. There's great goodness in every drunkard only they are ashamed of it, so they try to bring out their bad side to hide it. Trust me, I've seen enough of them down here over the years. I can almost spot one straight away. I saw it with Danny. The look, the change in character, the bravado, the transformation, the lack of control. I know all the signs. Though it must be said that even though all vary in certain respects, they have at heart a common feature, and that is, they are seekers, they are men with something missing, and that is what drink gives them. There's a loud drunk, say like Willy Patterson, and then one like Blondy Henderson, who'll sit there for days and just drink whiskey after whiskey, hardly uttering a word but staring into a place no other men can see. He'll get up suddenly and leave politely then be back again as soon as the doors open in the morning. Then there's the man who will have to be carried out screaming, and the man who will fall asleep and so on and so on, but what I'm saying to you John is that at heart they are all good men, kind men, perhaps great men who are forced to be little, men who tie themselves into cages too small for themselves, when they should be out there throwing themselves against the world, and that's what Danny is doing now. It will do him good to test himself, to stand on his own two feet.

That's one way of looking at it...you could say they're a bunch of self-indulgent selfish bastards too, says the Serge.

That they are, I'm not denying it. And neither am I denying what I just said. Both exist and that's the mystery.

If he goes on like that over there across that water, he'll meet a bad end. That's where the mystery will be. Mark my fucking words.

You can go searching for everything in the world, except for love and death. These things will come find you when the time is right. Isn't a man's destiny eked out for him and there's not much that can be done about it, no matter how much we may try, says Matty.

Do you believe it?

I know it. What else is there?

Go up and tell it to my missus because she's me drove wrong about it.

*

Around Spit the daffodils are popping their yellow heads up along the ditches and roads, along the haggards and farmyards, the well-kept lawns, and in patches over the gentle rolling slopes. Sitting here by the top of the quarry with the goats lazing in the sun a man could forget his worries, could almost be content.

To seek something is to already have found it.

Somebody said that to me once.

Can't remember who, can't remember when.

In the distance engines come and go. Occasionally, birds break the silence too, but really they are part of the silence.

Into this silence breaks a familiar whistle. The hairs on my neck tickle. It's a tone well known to me. The goats shuffle and make for the pine forest on top of the hill behind us. I slip out onto the grass and slither quickly to the blackthorn tree that stands forlorn above the quarry.

Her dark hair weaves in the wind. Swiftly her feet over the grass. On her face an easy smile, her eyes sharpened with a knowledge beyond her years, beyond even all mine. She is just a girl, I remind myself. What could she possibly know? Yet, as she stops by the blackthorn tree and twirls round on her feet, dancing almost, still humming the tune, I think she might be as ancient as the limestone rocks of the quarry. There and then I envy her her freedom.

Slung round her shoulder a green cotton bag. She takes off her shoes and socks, places them by the tree, stretches her arms up towards the sky, arches her back and takes a deep lungful of the fresh March air. She picks a white blossom from the hawthorn, crushes it in her hands then smells it. Her whole-body shudders at the chemicals contained therein.

I call out to the gods to let me be a man again, to let me take her in my arms. Kneeling on the ground she looks over the quarry towards the sun moving west towards evening. Over her head she moves the strap of the bag. Oh that we two could remain here forever on this hillside. Feet behind her back, head buried in the ground I hear her whimper, then sob.

I'm sorry. I'm sorry Franky. I never meant for any of this to happen. I loved you, just as I loved the others. I can't help loving you Franky you know that don't you. Don't judge me. Please don't judge me.

She puts her head down again and sobs. I slither round in front of her to have a better view. I want to lay my hands on her, to hold her, I want to lick the salty tears from her face. I want to slither inside her and never leave her. I want to tell her that she never has to change, that she, in all her imperfections, is perfectly herself.

My love, I say. My love. I'm sorry. But she hears nothing. I'm inches from her face but I might as well be at the far side of the universe. Then I too begin to weep at the memory of her. Together, prostrate, Rosie and I weep and we continue to weep until the weeping is done.

She wipes her eyes, dries her face with a white handkerchief, sighs, then from the bag in front of her she takes out a small object wrapped in a white table cloth. She then takes out a small shovel with which she precisely cuts a foot-sized rectangular sod, she loosens up the earth beneath but does not remove any. Reaching into the green bag once more, she brings out a clear plastic bottle filled with a greenish liquid. Beginning to hum, she removes the cap, then replaces it with another which is pierced with holes. She sprays the dug-up earth until the bottle is almost empty. Judging from the smell, the liquid is some kind of soap, likely the one they use in the kitchen to wash the cutlery.

She continues to hum, breaking it once to say, hurry up you

little monsters.

Within minutes the dug-up ground is crawling with earthworms of all shapes and sizes. She picks out the fattest longest ones and puts them in an empty jam jar. Soon the jar is so full that she has trouble closing the lid. With the remaining water in the bottle, she washes her hands then dries them with the handkerchief. When everything is in the bag, she stands up, twirls around in a complete circle, the wind rustling her hair, the sky a peaceful lazy blue. After another twirl, she kneels down, kisses the grass then rises up quickly and begins to walk round the edge of the quarry.

I ache to follow her.

Rooted to my spot I watch her make her way down the side of the quarry, and helpless, I see her emerge at the bottom and climb the old, rusted metal gate near the road. There she waits. About five minutes later a car stops. A voice. Laughter. A male voice. She opens the passenger side door. I count the seconds until the sound of the engine fades to nothing.

I fall back on the grass and will the wind to dissolve me.

Later, much later maybe, sun declining, I force myself up. As always, when desperation has almost finished me, I take to scribbling.

What can I do? And what can't I do? Within the answering of these questions is the key to a more content existence. I'm going to get my ass in gear this year and get more proactive. I'm done moping round feeling sorry for myself. So, what to do? I pick up an old crow's feather and on the wettish earth 'neath the hawthorn I scribble a list. Take some classes. Invest in yourself. Spend more time with Squint. Develop a new skill, one that doesn't require a body. Start going back to mass, more specifically hit the confessional. Take some time away from the goats. Go outside the comfort zone. Be more proactive with regards dating, they won't come falling out of the sky! Actually, given your condition, that's the only way they will come for you. Nothing lasts forever. There will be an end.

I will read these at the beginning of each and every day, and sometimes in the night before I retire. Yes, I say trying to convince myself, but within moments I come to realize that it was scribbled in a moment of optimistic idiocy.

Your job is to mope around the holes, the hollows, the cracks.

Your job is to wear a dour face of greyish mist. Your job is to haunt lonely windswept half-starved hawthorn trees.

You are to linger in the unwashed skin of goats, in the rotting carcasses of the abandoned and the unloved. You are the hope of the desperate the last embrace of the shunned, you are here, at your station, to wait for the man who has reached his end. In short, you have your place. Somebody's got to do it. Don't be getting ideas beyond your station. Embrace and accept.

*

News of Danny has been scarce to none. Might snatch a few words below in the pub, or chance upon someone who mentions him when I'm on one of my little assignments, though it has to be said, things have quieted down and I've been returned to my normal schedule, which is both good and bad, bad in that I might go months without doing a single thing. I was below in the kitchen in the Barracks one night when he rang but to be honest, I didn't hear much, mostly his mother on this side giving him the run down on the local happenings.

So, when I find myself in Bellwhistle's living room of a night I'm both excited and fearful. An awful mess greets me: cans, bottles, contraptions, litter the table and floor, and the room's filled with reams of smoke so thick I can barely see. God rest his soul I knew his father well, as good a man as you'd hope to meet.

Bellwhistle, struggling to keep his eyes open, lies on the couch with the TV blaring. He's mumbling to himself between slugs from a can of cider, and if I can believe my ears, I hear him mention Danny's name. Well now, I say to myself, what brings me up here of a cold winter's night.

I'm just beginning to gather my bearings, when up he stands, too sudden for my liking, and slouches towards the small bookshelf that's under the photo of the men of '98. Mumbling, he fiddles around for a while then picks up an envelope, takes out the page inside, then returns to his prostrate position on the couch. Fags, ashtray, beer are all within reach of his right hand, and all too close to the big rug that looks like the hide of a buffalo. He reaches out, grabs the box of Bensons, lights one up. With his left hand he holds up the letter.

Danny, you bastard, he mumbles.

T'is knowledge I crave most of all. I'm up on his shoulder before he can take another breath and what he reads I've read before him. The page is well-worn, stained a little with spills of what looks like coffee.

Dear Bellwhistle,

I write because, between us, there are things unspoken, things I need to say. I write because the writing is easier than the saying. We're both no good at the calls.

There's something I've never told you. A little story, silly really, never told anyone, not important at all, but I wanted to tell you and ask your opinion about it, because I think you'd understand.

When I was a kid, I came cross a picture of the dome in Hiroshima in an encyclopaedia. Looking at this picture an unaccountable feeling came over me, that one day I would be there. It was as if in that moment the future, the present and the past collapsed into one. I know you're interested in such phenomena. Come to think of it I've never told anybody about this experience. Somethings are better kept inside. And somethings not. They say we are as sick as our secrets. Here's another one, but please keep this one to yourself.

For fuck sake Danny you're getting soft in the head over there, you sentimental bastard, Bellwhistle says, his words louder than they need to be. I should burn this shite, he continues, extending his arm, looking at the paper from an unreadable distance above him.

No Bellwhistle, I need to read on, I say.

He brings the paper down again within reading distance but no sooner has he done so he raises his hand again. I've no idea of what he's at but he repeats this process a few times. My worst fear is that he's going to crumble it into a ball and cast it into the mire that is the room. But luckily the words on the page catch his attention once more.

Remember the last time I drank, just before I left Spit. You'd just told me you'd seen Pa Quinn and Rosie together. Well, I was dating her, had been for a while. I didn't tell you, because she wanted to keep it quiet, on account of Nesbit and all that. Suppose seeing her – or hearing about it from you rather – might have tipped me over the edge, but I was heading for the edge either way. Long story short, I ended up on a three-day bender, most of it I can't remember. Suppose you've heard about the goat, I'm not denying it, all I'm saying is I can remember little of it. That's why I don't drink Bellwhistle, surely you can see it's for the best. Anyway, when I finally sobered up I was in such a state that I decided to do myself in. Don't misunderstand, it wasn't a sudden decision, I don't know how those things usually work but in my case it has been there looming round in the back of my mind for a long while. You know the valley that runs down the back of my place, I tried to do it there, but the branch broke. I know – just like me to fuck that up.

Bellwhistle starts hissing and gurgling, sounds which I assume signal laugher of some kind. He flips the page around, looks briefly at the densely covered text on the back side, as if checking for something, then reverts back to the front.

When I came to, in the mud, beneath the tree, I was so happy I was alive. Right there and then I had, I suppose. what many refer to as a moment of clarity: I had to leave Spit and I had to leave soon.

When I tell this story in AA rooms, which I rarely do, people always come up to me afterwards and say that was your 'higher power' looking out for you. I know, I say. And I say it to myself too. But soon as I say it, I feel silly, and take it back. I was just too heavy. You know the way people get carried away. The breaking point was violated. The branch broke. Simple mathematical relationship. If it hadn't, I wouldn't be here. Suppose it's about ten thousand miles to that tree. When I return, I'll give it a visit and give thanks. I know you'd laugh at such shit, but there it is.

Do I miss it, you asked last time on the phone? And I couldn't really answer. Well often, in the night, before I sleep, or when I lie there restless, I'll close my eyes and walk it step by step, ditch by ditch, hill by hollow, up that valley, and all the way up to Nesbit's place. This might sound fucked up too, but I miss the weather. The weather here is calmer and much more predictable. Seasons come and go like clockwork. I miss wet November evenings, with the wind howling in from the west, the excitement of being out in it, the satisfaction when you return home to a blazing fire and a hot mug of tea. No, I'm not over here singing sad songs and weeping for the homeland but you know what I mean. And yes, I miss her too.

Fucking horseshite Danny and you know it, Bellwhistle says, taking a long drag from his fag.

We were together for a few months only but it changed me, changed me for the better Bellwhistle, despite all that I suffered and still suffer. I've been alone. Long loneliness. I've grieved long for her and still see her in my dreams, in all my waking hours. But it's here in the darkness of the night when I cannot sleep I've come to know myself more. Even, to love myself more (I can hear you laughing out loud at this shit Bellwhistle. I don't mind. It's the truth).

Well well Mulchay...I'm happy for you, I really am, Bellwhistle says in a voice which has dwindled to a slurred whisper.

Somehow, when you told me she was pregnant and getting married to Pa Quinn, it was a great relief. We could never have lasted, the energy between us was so great it would have destroyed us.

Keep me informed of the going-ons in Spit. I seek the local news, the gossip, the fat of the land. Send me all you can. How's Radio Molloy? And the others that hold up the high stools? You know, I never planned to come here but when I was in England the chance of a job came up and here I am, in the place where you always wanted to be. Like I said before you're welcome to visit anytime.

It's late and I have to get up for work soon. Yes, there are nights I can't sleep at all. It's true we rarely get what we want but sometimes we get more than we can imagine. My nightmares for the most have ceased. Nesbit fell. Nesbit was pushed. Both are true. Depending on the day I'll believe one or the other. Or, now, increasingly I may go a whole day without thinking about it at all.

Stop fucking moving Bellwhistle, I want to shout because the paper is all over the place. I think he's about to pass out. Just a little more, I say, just a little more.

What I love most about this little place is that it's entirely mine. I'm sitting here listening to Nick Drake's Five Leaves Left. The Cello song. Three hours to London. Dark minor chords mingle with a sweet innocent voice weaving words that hint at a mind on the precipice. You'd approve. I've just lit another Lark – the smokes here are three times cheaper. You'd love that. I'm reading a bio of Rimbaud. Hard to believe I'm gone so long, but then again it's not really that long is it. What is time but masses of days lumped into one giant stew, and memory is merely the violation of this mass, the instances of difference.

The sliding paper door is half ajar and light beams from the street lights outside shaft through the clouds of smoke. Moving and shifting, the smokes here then gone. Or it's there, then not quiet here.

Yes, Nesbit both fell and was pushed. Sometimes we just have to save ourselves. He sought the void. You know that, Bellwhistle.

The paper falls. With it the half-smoked cigarette. I'm down on the ground before it lands, and thank fuck the paper lands the right way up for me to continue reading. To tell you the truth – and what can I do about it anyway – I should be paying attention to the fag which has fallen too close to the big rug.

I read on as Bellwhistle begins to snore.

It could easily have been me. Sometimes I think, in his drunkenness he jumped. For a dare. To test the boundaries. Probably thought he could survive. You see, it's better to think of things like this, Bellwhistle: life is a riddle, a game to be played. And the rules, are in part, up to us.

For the dead we should live, Bellwhistle.

For Nesbit.

Remember that night you asked me about the time when we were kids? Well...

The paper starts to turn brown. Little yellow flames flitter over the corners. The rug is up in flames. I look back at the letter, see the words disappearing...*yes, by the flooded river, and me behind Nesbit...*blackening to a thin film of carbon the paper crumbles to smoke.

I turn towards Bellwhistle.

Wake up, I shout. I go into a frenzy, trying to create some commotion to wake him, but he's snoring away, and what use have I ever been in these situations. A black thick smoke oozes. I go to Bellwhistle, lay myself over him, and say, if this is to be it Bellwhistle then let it be it, there's little either of us can do about it now.

*

Of the black earth, the peat and bog I am a faithful son, and someday to the bog I shall return. But not quite yet. Not now. There's work to be done. Wind furls the long grass. Taking in the fine weather, moving with the goats, I've spent the better part of the afternoon sucking up the sun's energy. To the west low embers begin to burn, a lone star winking.

I'm not surprised at all when Squint comes to sit at the butt of the tree line. This time he likes best. Me too, Squint, I say. Our meetings now have become a regular thing. As always, I do the talking. I wait for the day he will sing again. Or even scream again. Though sometimes, out of the blue, he'll start shaking, reminds me of nothing but the vibrations of a wasp's wing. First time it happened I got an awful fright. Other than that, I like to believe he's doing well. Out over the valley that splits the Slive Felim mountains we look.

Things have been quiet now for a while, haven't they, I say.

Not a good sign.

Indeed.

Squint lights up. Gone, the hollows of his face, replaced by pudgy ridges, giving him the look of an almost different person. Some might even say he looks better. More peaceful for sure. I look at Squint. At least I've known the love of a woman. You never will and you know it. That's why you come here.

All around us silence.

Stone. Grass. Wind.

Silent all.

Did you hear the Serge is not well. Few months at most. Time passes quickly. Time passes slowly.

It passes. That it does.

He's doing well I hear. Danny. Dry. Off the Drink. Not a drop they say. According to some. Not that you'd care. Hardly close. Nesbit must be only bones now.

And bits of hair. Any more insights into your past?

No. Dried up. Not a drop. For the best I suppose. Squint, my past is in Spit. My future is in Spit and my now is in Spit. Tell you the truth I've stopped looking. Stopped writing too. Oh yes, I used to write down all the details of what happened round here.

I thought I had to, I fully believed somebody was reading them, it gave me a feeling of purpose. But seems it was all in my mind. Since I've stopped nothing's changed.

I thought you said you were once a great bard?

Well, I'm not sure, memory is a tricky thing. See Squint, it might be the product of too much time and loneliness. We have to make up stories, to believe them, to live them even.

Takes what it takes, I suppose.

Squint, we are little different. Both nobodies. You know you've become a friend to me. Have we not drove spears into the flesh and pawed through the guts looking for the gold. Us Squint. Just you and me now. For a while at least. For a decade. An eternity for me. Pair of alchemists that's what we are. Spits alchemists. We take the shit, recycle it into rainbows, little gusts of wind, photons of emotion, darts of inspiration, shivery things running down their backs to remind them there's much more going on than they understand.

And her, Little Snow?

Well, I do my best not to remember, I say in a low voice.

What's was and always will be.

Indeed. Look around you Squint, if this place could speak to you, if the spirits of the air could converse with you, it would be the very words coming out my mouth. I am it and it is I and what it wills I do and what it says I speak.

You're nothing at all, isn't that what you're trying to say?

Vapour. Mist. A cloud throwing its shadow over the rushes. Here one second, gone the next. That's me. But do not misunderstand. I am not immaterial. Of the black earth I am the faithful son. And someday I will return. Know me well before you disbelieve me.

He lights up another fag.

All around us silence.
Stone. Grass. Wind.
Flesh. Bone.
Silent all.

ACKNOWLEDGEMENTS

From August 2022 to August 2023 I spent a year working in Hirakata, a small city right between Osaka and Kyoto. Spit was written here. Written in one-hour spurts, in the mornings before work and in the nights after work in the big Starbucks at T-Site. Big thanks to the staff there who saw me as soon as the doors opened every morning at seven. I returned to China in August 2023 and worked on a second draft, again mostly at a Starbucks in Suzhou, which has been a regular haunt for many years. A big thanks to all the staff there who see me early most mornings and late most nights. A simple smile, a word of kindness can mean a lot when we are in a difficult place. And Spit was born out of a difficult time, a period of turmoil, a period of mourning for the loss of someone precious. Perhaps this lonely, slightly haunting wind, blows through its pages.

Of course, there were many others I met in these places, strangers who became companions on the road for a while, some who became more, and some who were brief but beautiful illuminations that crossed the night. They shall remain nameless but their names will not be forgotten, nor will they.

My students always teach me more than I teach them, so I must mention them, with a particular thanks for their energy and freshness that helps me from being as old as I am.

To Sinead Brennan for the original artwork on the cover. The scene perfectly captures the landscape of Spit.

To Sean and all the team at époque press for pushing me to dig deeper. The work they are doing to champion literary fiction is not just daring, it's profoundly important, especially in these current times when reading and all things books are already in precarious waters. But I guess stories will always have a place. And people will always have a place. And the people we meet everyday – the good, the bad, the ugly – are the people who change, shape and inspire us.

As always, I must mention my parents Breda and Joe, everyday people, who are extraordinary in too many ways to mention.